THE PERFECT OUTCAST

MELISSA HANSEN

Immortal Works LLC
1505 Glenrose Drive
Salt Lake City, Utah 84104
Tel: (385) 202-0116

© 2020 Melissa Hansen
https://www.melissaohansen.com/

Cover Art by Ashley Literski
http://strangedevotion.wixsite.com/strangedesigns

ISBN 978-1-953491-98-5 (Paperback)
ASIN B08FGGSC39 (Kindle Edition)

For Derek, who believed first

CHAPTER 1

Alina took her seat in biology class and clicked on her panel, hiding behind the screen. When she'd looked in the mirror that morning, she had despaired to see the trail of bumps on her face had erupted into flaming red peaks. She begged Jade to let her stay home, but it was no use—her absence would only get her in trouble. For almost an hour, Alina worked with her makeup to conceal the blemishes. Despite Jade's assurances no one would notice, Alina felt them protruding like mountains—so enormous she could see them from the corner of her eyes.

Over the past three years, the other girls in Pria matured in ways Alina did not. Their bodies slimmed and lengthened, their figures blossomed, and cheekbones sharpened under thick eyelashes. They were each beautiful, but unique, and flaunted any feature that stood out. Now, at seventeen, Alina stood out in ways she didn't like. Instead of growing slender, her skin puckered around her waist and thighs. Her caramel-colored hair looked limp and wiry even after she brushed it, and her teeth were crooked compared to the clean smiles around her. In the rare event she *did* smile, she kept her lips closed.

Three girls entered the classroom and as Alina glanced up, she met eyes with Flora, who gave her a haughty sneer. Gwen and Zelma batted their eyelashes at two passing boys and after flirting outrageously for a minute, huddled near Alina to complain about them.

"I can't wait to be done with young boys," Gwen sighed. She opened a compact mirror and held it close to her face, puckering her lips.

"I *am* done with them," Flora replied. "You won't believe who came to see me last night." She paused, waiting for their response.

"Who?" both girls said at once, a hint of jealousy in their voices.

Flora leaned in. "Rufus. Do you know him? He's *so hot*, and he's, like, two hundred years old! Pearle was ticked off when he came. I think she was jealous. You should've seen her—trying to flirt with him when he came to see me! Can you believe it? My *caretaker* trying to steal a guy from *me*? But he totally ignored her. We were alone in the front room and he told me—"

Flora dropped her voice, but Alina heard every word and cringed behind her panel. She understood why Jade never dated. The way older men flirted with young girls made her shudder, despite Flora's exaggerations.

Miss Rhonda stood up and addressed the class, and Alina shut off her panel, knowing it would draw attention from her teacher. Miss Rhonda's glossy curls bounced as she shimmied between their desks in tight jeans and stiletto heels. She seemed proud of her large teeth because she smiled at every turn, except when her eye fell on Alina. Then she visibly twitched.

Alina was used to this reaction; in all her years of school only one teacher, Miss Vivian, had positively acknowledged her. Miss Vivian praised Alina in front of the class and didn't scold her when she daydreamed. She was almost like a friend.

Once, after a boy called Alina ugly, Miss Vivian slipped her a note telling her she understood what it felt like to be different. Alina found that strange since Miss Vivian was beautiful like everyone else, but the words comforted her anyway. She still had the note in a jewelry box on her dresser.

But now Miss Vivian was gone.

Tears sprang to Alina's eyes and she blinked them back. She hadn't cried over her former teacher in years.

"Alina, will you please join the class?" Miss Rhonda barked. "Everyone is on page ten except for you."

Alina reddened as she switched on her panel and found the

biology tab, then swiped to page ten. Miss Rhonda glared for another moment, then turned back to the class.

"Today we'll discuss the process of creating life in the Gordian laboratories. Take a look at the magnificent illustration before you," she raved.

Page ten displayed a diagram of a child's growth, from a small drop of ageless serum, to a perfect Prian baby.

"Now, as you remember from our lesson last week on reproduction," Miss Rhonda began, while a few snickers broke out across the class, "the mortal world of Carthem is a place where babies grow inside women. For nine months the baby develops, and this is very unpleasant—what's so funny?" Miss Rhonda glared with a hand on her hip.

A boy, with tears of laughter in his eyes, raised his hand. "We can't see how a baby could grow *inside* somebody. Wouldn't the woman get really big?"

"Of course," snapped Miss Rhonda. "Why do you think pregnancy was so uncomfortable? Not that any of *you* understand what that means. No one in Pria has ever been uncomfortable. So, try to imagine. But pregnancy wasn't the worst part! Think of a baby being forced out the woman's body! The pain was excruciating, and many women and babies died in the process." Alina glanced around the room. The students looked both fascinated and disgusted.

"Babies *died*?" Zelma asked, puzzled. "Did they keep growing, you know, into dead adults?"

Miss Rhonda shook her head. "No. Death means they no longer exist."

"But what happens to the bodies?"

Miss Rhonda seemed surprised at the question, as if she'd never thought of it before. "Well they—" she broke off, frowning. "The dead bodies are—"

She stood still for a moment, eyebrows knitted, then flashed a smile. "Moving right along," she dodged, ignoring their confused faces. "Father Sampson, as we know, wanted his world to be free of pain, and this he achieved. Immortality makes conception between men and women impossible but also unnecessary, as he forms life from his ageless serum. As a result, we enjoy the pleasures of intimacy without the inconvenience of pregnancy and childbirth." The class burst into giggles again.

Miss Rhonda rolled her eyes and went on. "Now, Father Sampson is aware endless life can get dull without variety, so he enjoys being creative with the lives he forms."

Zelma snorted and whispered, "Especially his women. He molds them twenty years in advance." The girls around her stifled their laughter.

Miss Rhonda's eyes snapped to Zelma. "What did you say?"

A long, frigid pause followed, and Alina held her breath. Zelma dropped her eyes.

Miss Rhonda flounced over to Zelma and hovered above her. "Did I hear you say something disrespectful about Father Sampson?" Miss Rhonda's lips turned white, her willowy figure taut and forbidding.

The cold silence lingered. "Um, no," Zelma panted, her voice barely audible.

Miss Rhonda circled the desk, her face hard as stone. "Perhaps you'd like to stand and repeat your little joke so the proper punishment can be administered."

Zelma flushed and shook her head. "I'm sorry. I didn't mean to. Forgive me."

Miss Rhonda's bangles tinkled as she rested her hands on Zelma's desk. "Mocking Father Sampson is unforgivable," she hissed. "Say something like that again, and I'll make certain he hears of it. Maybe that will teach you to watch your words."

Zelma nodded, her pretty cheeks a bright shade of pink. Miss Rhonda glowered a moment longer, then turned to the class and continued as if no interruption had occurred.

"Look around our room, for example," she said, waving her hand over the class. "You'll notice none of us is alike. Skin, hair, and eye color differ. We have tall and short, black and white, blond and brown. Father Sampson is creative with hair color, so occasionally you'll see a redhead. However, he doesn't use the same creativity in people as he does in animals. He likes his people to resemble the humans of Carthem, but perfected and beautified."

Flora's hand shot up in the air. She spoke before Miss Rhonda could call on her.

"Why doesn't Father Sampson experiment more with people? I have lots of friends who want a different hair color, like blue or pink. I've heard caretakers can give requests for their wards. What if I request one with purple hair?"

The class giggled, but Flora didn't flinch, showing absolute sincerity. Alina's face grew warm. She didn't know caretakers could request how their wards looked.

"First of all," Miss Rhonda stressed, "it's unlikely any of you will raise a child. There are thousands of applicants each year, and only a handful are approved. But as a matter of fact, Father Sampson *has* experimented with people and that's why he now chooses not to. This happens to be what our lesson is on today. Swipe to page sixteen."

Panels clicked throughout the room, and Alina grabbed hers with wet palms. She didn't like the direction of this lesson.

"Around the time each of you were being formed," Miss Rhonda explained, "Father Sampson was under enormous pressure to produce more variety in babies. So, he decided to experiment. Unfortunately, his first batch went drastically wrong. He repaired the damage as best he could, but one case was severely affected."

Miss Rhonda glanced at Alina before continuing. "He was unable to alter the serum cells without disfiguring the child, who continues to grow abnormally to this day. He learned a hard lesson and now wishes the case to be known—a reminder of what can go wrong when we desire too much."

Miss Rhonda didn't need to say more. She fixed a sharp glare on

Alina, and every eye in the classroom followed. Alina went crimson and felt the dreaded lump form in her throat.

This information didn't surprise her. She suspected something had gone amiss during her commencement. But she'd always hoped to be wrong.

Now everyone in Pria would know. She'd be labeled as Father Sampson's biggest—and only—error. The heavy disappointment threatened to choke her.

CHAPTER 2

Alina stared at her panel and blinked her eyes. *No tears. Not one. If one slips out, the rest will follow.*

After biology was history. Could she endure another class? She couldn't risk stopping at the bathroom—the tears would surely come. If only she could sneak through the back door of the school and run to Jade's work, into the comfort of her arms.

No, not to Jade. Not about this.

Alina stared blankly at the screen until class ended, then kept her eyes on the ground and fidgeted with her necklace as she walked to history class. She'd walked those hallways enough to know what occupied them: a kaleidoscope of bright fabrics, red lipstick, and designer jeans hugging slim legs and backsides. Musical laughter rang through her ears and voices spoke over each other, trying to be heard. The chatter abated when Alina walked by. Even the smacking of couples kissing ceased as they watched her under plumes of lashes. A few noses wrinkled as if ugliness smelled bad. As if, drenched in their zesty perfumes, they even knew what a bad smell was.

She ducked into the classroom and found her seat, hiding her face as she clicked on her panel. History was her least favorite subject, and as she struggled to focus, she made the mistake of glancing around the room.

She met eyes with Eris, the red-haired beauty Alina once asked to play with, and who hadn't stopped tormenting her since. At only eight years old, Eris discovered the exhilarating—if temporary—buoyancy that came from sinking another.

The encounter happened on the annual Day of Genesis, back

when Alina found the celebration enchanting. She awoke excited to wear her new blue dress and shiny white shoes. Jade curled Alina's hair and laced the ringlets with ribbons, and Alina felt almost pretty —like the other girls.

They were walking to the outer gardens when she first saw Eris, clasping hands with her friends and running to the park. Alina twisted her waist until her dress swayed, her feet aching to run with them. They had flowers in their hair instead of ribbons, but her dress looked like their dresses. If she could catch them, she might blend in.

"May I play with the girls at the park?" she asked Jade.

Jade hesitated; her jet-black eyebrows pinned together over her dark eyes. She started to shake her head, then noticed Alina's face and sighed. "All right. I will be at our usual spot, near the fountain, when you want to find me."

Alina grinned and took off skipping, but as she approached the girls a knot formed in her stomach. She feared them almost as much as she longed to giggle and run with them.

She chewed on her lip, hoping they would see her and invite her in. Eris was the prettiest, with her long, flowing red hair, but her friend with the ebony skin had the prettiest dress. Alina waited on the edge of the park until one of them noticed her.

"Hey!" the girl called out. "Do you want to play?"

Alina beamed and started towards them. The others stopped to watch.

"Hi," she said as she joined them. The girls stared for a moment, frowning. They glanced at each other.

"I'm Alina," she said, to fill up the silence.

"We know who you are," said the girl who called her. "I thought you were someone else."

Alina swallowed. "Can I play?"

Eris narrowed her eyes. "Isn't Jade your caretaker?"

"Yes," said Alina, with more confidence.

Eris put her hands on her hips. "My caretaker told me Jade used to be the most popular lady in Pria until she got you. Now she's boring and doesn't have any friends. I know why. Who would be happy with someone who looked like you?" She smiled as the girls around her burst into giggles.

Alina shifted her feet. A tight lump formed in her throat, and she knew what that meant. She clenched her hands, digging her fingernails into her palms. She would *not* cry.

"Jade *is* happy with me," she gulped. "She says—"

"*Sorry,*" Eris cut in. "Only pretty girls are allowed to play with us." She whirled around, clasped hands with the others and they skipped away, giggling.

Alina put her face in her hands. She could hide in the trees and cry, then go back to Jade and maybe she wouldn't notice. Alina didn't want anyone to know what happened. But when she looked behind her, Jade was kneeling with outstretched arms.

She had seen the whole thing.

Alina clung to Jade's arms as they surrounded her, releasing her tears into the soft velvet of her dress. Jade didn't care for those fancy dresses anyway.

Alina adjusted her seat and tried to focus on her history lesson. She shouldn't have reflected on that memory, with tears already at the surface and Eris's teal-blue eyes staring at her from across the room. Alina slouched as Eris walked toward her.

She loomed above Alina for a moment, peering over her shoulder. Alina rubbed her forehead to hide her face, but Eris had seen enough. She scrunched up her nose in disgust.

"Ugh, Alina, what's that all over your face?"

Her voice cut through the room, and the class flocked over. She moved out of the way to provide an unobstructed view. Alina's peers often examined her with curiosity and repugnance, as if she were a specimen in science class. No one looked her in the eye.

After they'd inspected and recoiled enough, Eris stepped in the circle to reclaim the attention. "Really, Alina, you should find out what went wrong when you were formed. Maybe one of your friends can help—oh wait, you don't have any friends. Well then, why don't you talk to Jade about it? Oh wait!" she exclaimed to the giggling crowd. "She doesn't talk to you. In fact, I believe she hasn't said much at all since you came along. Looking at *you* every day, I can see why."

Alina shot to her feet and balled her fists, her face flushed with anger. Her mind searched for a retort, but after a tense moment, she snatched her panel, shoved it in her bag and ran to the door. Eris's laughter rang out behind her.

Before she slipped out the door, Alina lifted her hot face and caught a boy's eye from the corner of the room. Zaiden. The only one who hadn't left his seat.

He looked upset, or embarrassed for her. She bit her lip. Pity humiliated her more than outright insults.

Tears stung her eyes as she darted through the hallway and ducked into the small corridor to her bathroom. She called it *her* bathroom, because as far as she could tell, no one else used it. Today, she was grateful.

She burst into the room and slammed the door behind her, then covered her mouth with her hand. She hated crying but couldn't stop the tears this time.

Most people in Pria loved to cry. Tears deepened their eye color and gave their cheeks a fresh glow. Some women even forced a good cry any time they wished to look more attractive. But when Alina cried, her eyes puffed up and her face looked splotchy for hours. She decided to spend the rest of school in the bathroom and wished she had skipped history altogether. She no longer cared about getting in trouble.

The hot tears fell for a long time, and the release soothed her. Jade told her tears must have a place to go, and the longer they collected, the greater the flood when they broke through. This confused Alina because no one else seemed to have a problem controlling feelings. She'd never seen Jade cry—except once.

She didn't actually *see* her. But those tears forever changed Alina's perception of Jade, who went from infallible one night, to fragile, weak, and defenseless the next.

After the Day of Genesis celebration, the same day Eris snubbed her, Alina lay awake in bed. She never rested well the night after the Sleep, and knew Jade didn't either, as she was often reading her panel or watching the monitor when Alina tiptoed out of bed.

Despite her restless eyes, Alina had stayed in bed, thinking about the people Jade knew. Several greeted her at the celebration, but she didn't talk with them long—except for Ellyn and Sasha, who joined them at the feast.

Alina smiled as she remembered how pretty Sasha was. They were all pretty, but the kind ones more so. Sasha called Alina's dress lovely and gave her a small chocolate from the youths' table.

Alina swallowed in the darkness of her room. Ellyn and Jade had whispered and laughed for a long time, and Sasha meant to be kind when she mentioned how much Ellyn loved Jade and how much she missed her—how much she missed the old Jade.

Who *was* the old Jade?

Alina once asked Jade about her age, and the answer surprised her—one hundred and six. Jade lived ninety-eight years before Alina came along, plenty of time to have a career, go to parties, and date, like the other women. But Jade didn't do any of those things. Did the red-haired girl speak the truth? Did Jade no longer have friends because of her? Alina had tried to make friends her whole life. It made sense Jade didn't have any either because of her.

Alina kicked off the blankets and crept into the hallway, her bare feet padding along the polished floor. She *must* find out. The question would make Jade uncomfortable, and Alina feared the answer, but she had to know.

She caught a faint sound as she approached Jade's room, and putting her ear to the door, realized Jade was crying. Her sobs were intense but muffled, as if buried in a pillow. Alina grasped the doorknob to burst in and run to her, then stopped and bit her lip.

Jade wept because of the curse an ugly child had brought her. When she requested a ward, she expected a beautiful one like everyone else but received Alina instead. Alina saw the way Father

Sampson glared at them during the Day of Genesis celebration. He didn't like Jade, so he gave her Alina, a mistake of his own creation—perhaps an intentional mistake made specially to insult her.

Alina had slipped back to her room with tears dripping off her chin. For the first time, Jade wasn't there to wipe them away, which brought the greatest sting to her heart.

And now, huddled on the floor of her school bathroom, was the second time.

The pain felt different from when she was eight. She'd longed for words then, for the gentle assurance of Jade's love no matter how she looked or what regret she may have caused. But that pain eased over time as Jade's constancy never wavered, as Alina felt certain of her caretaker's love.

Now Alina knew the truth, and any words from Jade would confirm it. Those words would be the most unbearable pain of all.

She closed her eyes and took a deep breath, trying to stall the fresh tears pooling under her eyelids. She knew disappointment well; she anticipated and expected some letdown each day, the same way she expected the sun to darken each night. But she'd never known disappointment like this.

She blew her nose and stood up to confront the mirror. Her tears had washed the makeup from her face and the blemishes glared back at her. She touched them, feeling their rough texture against her fingertips. What a strange thing to have on a face. How much *had* Father Sampson experiment when he formed her?

The bell rang, jarring through her body, and she panicked. Her choice to skip class had been rash, and now Jade would suffer for it. She snatched her bag and fled the bathroom, ducking her head to hide her face.

Students poured into the hallway. Alina dashed around the corner and slammed into a tall, solid figure. She lost her balance and started to fall, then felt strong fingers wrap around her forearm, steadying her. She recognized the faded blue t-shirt she'd seen earlier. Zaiden.

Her skin felt warm under his touch, and she cringed as he viewed her swollen eyes and red cheeks. "Thanks," she mumbled, avoiding his eyes.

His grip around her arm tightened. She glanced up and found him staring at her.

"I've been looking for you, Alina. I'm sorry about what happened —I should have said something to them. It must be hard for you to be so different from everyone else." His hand trembled, and with a small shake of the head, he looked away. Alina's heart picked up in her chest. What made him so nervous?

He lifted his head and held her gaze, his brown eyes intense and anxious. He didn't look at the blemishes on her face, but deep into her eyes. Then he released her arm, swung his pack over his shoulder and turned to go.

"Zaiden," she rushed. He looked back at her.

"Thank you." She paused. "It must be hard for you as well."

"For me?"

Smiling, she said, "To also be different from everyone else."

He stared at her for a moment before returning her smile—gentle and knowing. As he walked away, she hid her crimson face.

Something in his smile inflamed her, stirring her disappointment into hope. He seemed to be searching, even longing, for meaning behind her words.

CHAPTER 3

Why haven't I noticed him before?

Alina reflected on this as she walked home, though she knew the answer. Prian boys blurred together in her mind, with their tall, muscular bodies and chiseled features. Tan, fair, or dark-skinned, it didn't matter—they were all bullies she feared and avoided. Girls were cruel, but nothing like the boys. Girls insulted each other because of competition, which meant their words could be false. Boys' insults were always true.

For this reason, she took the long way home. She'd arrive fifteen minutes sooner if she walked on Emrys Street, but that meant passing the thrill park occupied by loud, lecherous boys who believed a girl's worst crime was to be unattractive. Emrys also crossed an upscale section of Pria with homes four times the size of Alina's. Swimmers in bikinis on every deck made her feel two feet shorter and wider.

She preferred the back trail that twisted through rows of symmetrical, six-petaled flowers. No flower had the same color or pattern, and they extended for miles over the green hills in the distance.

When she reached the homes on her street she often saw Cecilia, an aspiring aerial dancer, practicing a routine between her front trees. Three doors down lived Roger, who switched careers so many times over the decades he finally gave up and spent his afternoons drinking on his front porch. He wasn't friendly, but occasionally nodded at Alina and sent Jade his regards. Otherwise, the street was empty. Most people who lived on Evergreen Loop stayed hidden.

But today, Alina didn't notice the flowers, Cecilia, Roger, or the pink fleecy kitten that followed her, purring for attention. Her thoughts were fixed on Zaiden.

He'd been in her history class all year, but he sat in the back—perhaps this was why she overlooked him. Who were his friends? She couldn't recall seeing him with anyone. He'd never been rude to her—she knew that much. Maybe he was a transfer student from the opposite side of town. A dip in social status sometimes drove people to the outskirts of Pria, and a change in schools concealed this downgrade at least for a while. But he didn't seem like the type who'd care about that.

Their history teacher called on him often in class, and he knew the answers as if he'd memorized every historical fact about Pria. Alina paused her steps. She *had* noticed him before. He sat on a bench in front of the school each morning, reading his panel. She entered through the front door on occasion, and once he glanced up when she passed. Their eyes had met. But they hadn't spoken until today.

She smiled as she skipped up the steps to her door, until the memory of Miss Rhonda's lesson washed over her like a cold shower. Her hands shook as she tapped the code on the lock-screen and slipped inside. Jade had surely been notified she'd skipped class. Alina hoped the repercussions wouldn't be too severe, for either of them.

The house was empty, so Alina made a sandwich, sank into the couch, and clicked on the monitor. Jade didn't let her watch until she completed her homework, but she didn't care. *I'm in enough trouble already. I may as well live it up.*

She clicked aimlessly through the streams and stopped when a man, dressed in black, peered through a window at a girl lying in bed. A long knife glistened in his hand.

Jade once told her that because no one understood death, they had an extreme fascination with it. The obsession seemed silly to Alina, but now she found herself unable to pull her eyes from the screen.

The man opened the window, crept into the room, and peered down at the girl. Her blonde hair flowed over her pillow in the moonlight. He flashed a cold smile, then lifted the knife and plunged the edge into her throat. Alina screamed and covered her eyes, fumbling with the controls until the screen went black.

She curled up on the couch and squeezed her eyes shut. The sandwich churned in her stomach. *Think of something else, anything else. No, not Miss Rhonda's lesson, something happy. Jade. No, she's angry with me. Something nice. Zaiden.*

She took a deep breath and released it with a shudder. No boy had looked at her that way before—past her blemishes as if he didn't see them. He didn't care if anyone saw them together—in fact, he seemed to like it. For the first time in years, she felt someone wanted to be her friend.

She had a friend once—Pierce. He'd lived next door and didn't mind that she looked different. They scaled trees together and threw the squishy fruit at the ground critters, where the flesh bounced off their fur and hit the ground with a splat.

With Pierce, Alina first noticed she couldn't run fast or do tricks. Once, after climbing the glossy trunk of a rainbow tree, Pierce leaped from a top branch and did two flips before landing on his feet.

"Try it!" he called to her. "You think you can't, but that's only 'cause you haven't tried! It works for everyone, I promise."

Alina shuddered as she reached the top branch, her body crying a warning to her.

"Do it!" he called again. "I didn't know how it was going to happen either, but it just does!"

She swallowed, bent her knees to push off, closed her eyes and then—

"Alina, no!" a frantic voice called.

Jade's panicked face appeared above the fence of their yard. Alina cowered and climbed down, muttering goodbye to Pierce as she ran home.

He and his caretaker moved the following day. He lived

somewhere in Pria, but she never saw him. She might not recognize him if she did. They had grown up.

But she had a friend once; that's what mattered. And now, perhaps, she had one in Zaiden. She stretched her arms above her head and smiled, then masked a lengthy yawn with her hand. The emotions of the day had drained her, and she closed her eyes. Sleep came as a welcome relief.

ALINA AWOKE to a crystal bird twittering outside her window. She parted the blinds and found its clear feathers among the satin leaves of the rainbow tree. The crystal bird differed from the other flashy birds, and its translucence brought rest to her overstimulated eyes.

Outside, the street swarmed with people, though the sun barely peeked on the horizon, and Alina fell back on her bed and groaned. She despised large crowds. Jade hated the Day of Genesis too, but attendance was required for all citizens. Each year was the same: the dancing, the eating and drinking, the long, emotional speech by Father Sampson, and the Sleep. Children snuggled with their fluffy pets, grown-ups dressed in their finest nightclothes and clasped their lovers, if they had one—and everyone fell asleep for a night and a day. Big deal.

The Sleep *was* a big deal. Alina didn't understand why everyone loved sleeping under those blinding stars. She suspected some didn't sleep but did something exciting instead, and only those who stayed awake knew about it. Each year she vowed to stay up no matter how tired she got, but she never kept that promise. She admitted she dreamed her best dreams on the night of Genesis, but still, why did everyone make such a fuss over sleeping?

She heard Jade in the kitchen, singing softly, opening and closing the cupboards. Alina left her room in her nightgown. She didn't care to get ready for the day.

Jade wore stretch pants and a slim top and kept her raven hair swept back in a messy bun. She looked up from the fruit she was slicing and smiled.

"You're not excited for today, either," she noted, handing Alina a plate of fruit. "You won't have to eat much this morning. You know how much food there is at the feast."

"Thanks."

They said nothing else through breakfast, but it was more words than usual. Alina had long given up asking questions, as they caused Jade to drop her heavy eyelashes, run her fingers through her hair, and pretend she hadn't heard. If she answered at all, she said the same thing each time:

"Don't tell anyone these things, or they might be mean to you. It's best to keep them secret."

"They're already mean to me."

"I know, and I don't want it to get worse."

Then Jade pressed her lips and furrowed her brow, a look Alina had seen many times before. For some reason, these questions troubled Jade. But in spite of how little they spoke, Jade seemed to sense Alina's emptiness and wrapped her arms around her or rubbed her back when they were together. Her strong palms were a salve to Alina's aching heart.

They ate slowly, trying to delay when they would have to join the masses outside. When the excitement grew so loud they could hear it through the closed windows, Jade met Alina's eyes and gave a small sigh.

They slipped into their dresses and fixed their hair, then walked across the manicured lawn to the bustling street. Pria was a perfect circle of continuous round streets, smaller circles set inside larger ones, connected by long, intersecting avenues. Gordian Palace, Father Sampson's home, sprawled over a high hill in the center. The bull's-eye.

Jade and Alina lived on Evergreen Loop, the outer ring, where the small houses all looked the same except for their crisp, candy-colored exteriors. The kids at school teased her for living on

Evergreen, so she avoided speaking of it. Sometimes she overheard the neighbors gossiping, discussing who had moved to a 'better' street. There was always something better out there. No one on Evergreen stayed for long, if they could help it. But Alina had known no other home.

The important people lived on Infinite Way, near Gordian Palace, in sprawling estates with massive grounds. Alina used to love the turrets and balconies that glittered like fairy castles, even in daylight—but she hated them now. They reminded her of what she and Jade couldn't have.

This was her twelfth Day of Genesis, and the celebration had long lost its appeal. She watched with glassy eyes as children tapped their feet in unison for the *Forever Pria* performance and throughout the Last Great War reenactment. She didn't scream with the crowd when Father Sampson stood and waved from the stage with his sumptuous girlfriend at his side. In the evening, after a brief adjournment to change into their sleep clothes, the people gathered in the outer gardens for Father Sampson's speech. Jade and Alina always sat on the edge of the gardens during the speech, isolated from the congregation. Jade spread a soft blanket under them and brushed and braided Alina's hair, whose eyes grew heavy at the gentle tugging of her hands.

Applause broke out, signaling the beginning of the speech. Father Sampson ascended into the air where his voice carried to all twenty thousand citizens of Pria. Alina knew a pedestal raised him, but he appeared to be standing above the ground as if by magic. Large screens transmitted his face up close for all to admire. He bowed and blew kisses for a long time, basking in the flattery. Women screamed with their hands outstretched, tears rolling down their cheeks, and men stood upright in a stiff salute. One man rolled his eyes back into his head and bellowed Father Sampson's name in a loud, rhythmic chant. His expression frightened Alina until she caught Jade covering her mouth and shaking with silent laughter.

"Dear citizens of Pria," Father Sampson's voice boomed. "Welcome to the annual celebration of our Genesis!"

The audience cheered, then broke into Pria's anthem, "O Hail, Fair Pria." Alina's voice embarrassed her, so she didn't sing. Jade never sang the anthem either, though she sang and hummed plenty at home. By the eighth verse, she fidgeted and rolled her eyes.

When the song finally ended, Father Sampson nodded and continued. "As you all know, today we celebrate the establishment of our world. Many hundreds of years ago, before Pria existed, I was born in Carthem and grew to adulthood in its savage environment."

Father Sampson paused, his broad chest heaving with emotion. "In Carthem, violence overshadowed peace, hatred destroyed love. Wars were fought in succession, the intensity increasing with each one. In its final, bloodiest war, of which I fought many battles, nearly all inhabitants were destroyed. Friends turned against friends, lovers against lovers. Men betrayed their own kin. Women were ravished and slaughtered. Orphaned children cried from their demolished homes and blood flowed through the streets, carrying the rancid smell of death."

Alina rarely paid attention to Father Sampson's words, but this time they interested her. She tilted her head to Jade and asked, "What is blood? And what is death?"

Jade corrected Alina's head and continued to braid, then answered in a fixed tone. "Blood is what flows through the bodies of mortals, and death is what happens to all of them. Their bodies stop working, their brains stop thinking, and they fall to the earth, never to rise again."

The finality in those words stunned Alina. "Never? Will death happen to me? Or you?"

Jade's hands paused. "No. Because of Father Sampson, all of us will live forever. No one in Pria can die."

Alina felt relieved, not for herself, but for Jade. Nothing terrified her more than losing her caretaker. Perhaps Father Sampson deserved the praise he received. If no one in Pria could die, then she and Jade would always be together.

She listened with new ears as he spoke of the Last Great War and how he'd watched his loved ones die, including his beloved lover and their only child. The audience shed tears and Father Sampson choked on his words, allowing the despair to thicken the air.

Then he squared his shoulders and raised a clenched fist.

"I decided in that moment of ultimate suffering, I wouldn't rest until I found the cure for death, and once found, I'd create a world where no one would *ever*" —his voice swelled— "know the meaning of pain, war, or death again!"

The audience leaped to their feet, clapping and crying, and Jade laced Alina's hair so fiercely, her head jerked with each pull.

Father Sampson bowed his head, and as the applause faded, he paused for several moments before speaking again.

"It's difficult to reflect on these things," he said, as one long finger brushed a tear from his cheek. "But I know I must share my story. No one here has experienced such pain, such terror. For that I am glad. But there is a risk of forgetting how blessed we are because we have no painful memories to remind us. Our world is fragile. We cannot allow divisions of any kind to exist, or *Pria will fall*. We must all be vigilant in our loyalty to Pria, to *me*, if we are to avoid the fate of Carthem. We must pledge *ourselves* to preserve our peace."

At these words every person stood up. Jade and Alina followed. They crossed their hands over their mouths, moved them to the heart, and directed one open palm toward Father Sampson. Alina heard the echoes of thousands reciting the Prian pledge: some shouting the words, others whispering through their tears. They swore fidelity to Pria and Father Sampson, their Creator, or be cast into Carthem to die.

Alina glanced at Jade, who went through the motions with a face of stone. Just as Jade didn't sing the anthem, she never recited the pledge. But the last few years Alina noticed something she found the most peculiar of all. She waited to see if it happened again.

As the citizens chanted, Father Sampson turned his eyes to where Alina and Jade stood, by themselves, on the outskirts of the crowd. He never took notice of them at any other time, but on the Day of Genesis, and always during the pledge, he glared as if they were the only ones he could see.

Jade returned his glare with icy contempt in her eyes.

When they sat down, Alina leaned over to Jade. "Why does Father Sampson look at you like that? Have you offended him?"

Jade's eyes widened for a moment. "He wasn't looking at me."

"I saw him," Alina insisted. "Every year, he stares at you during the pledge and he seems angry."

Father Sampson blew kisses from his pedestal and extended his arms as he descended, dismissing everyone for the Sleep. People began to stand, gathering their things.

Jade shot to her feet. "I haven't noticed." She bent over and picked up her bag. "Hurry, let's go claim our spot for the Sleep."

"But—" Alina started, then sighed. When Jade closed down, there was no way to press answers from her.

Alina stood up, and as she gathered the blanket, a spot of red caught her eye. She stretched out the heavy cloth. "Jade, look! Where's it coming from this time?"

Jade looked at the blanket and gasped. "Are you—" She grabbed Alina's shoulder and whipped her around. When Alina looked back, Jade's face was white.

"What is it?" Alina's heart sank. "Is it on my new nightgown?"

Jade tried to smile. "Don't worry, it's perfectly normal. Good news—now we can enjoy the Sleep at home!"

"What? But I thought no one was allowed to spend the Sleep at home."

"We are," Jade rushed. "Father Sampson permits it for special circumstances, and this is one of them."

"But I thought you said it was normal," Alina puzzled.

"Don't you want to go home?"

"Yes, of course," Alina replied.

"Then I'll explain later. Hurry, or we'll fall asleep on the way."

Alina grabbed the blanket and followed Jade to the street, clasping her nightgown behind her to hide the stain. They darted between men in silk pajamas, partially buttoned to flaunt their pectoral muscles, and women in frilly robes with long trains trailing behind. Children danced around in their slippers, giggling as their caretakers set up sleep stations with mounds of blankets, deep pillows, and furry pets.

Father Sampson shut off the sky and lit the stars, and everyone stopped to look up, a chorus of oohs echoing around them. Jade quickened her steps.

"That was fast," she murmured. "I hope we make it in time."

"Are you sure we won't get in trouble?" Alina fretted as she skipped to keep up with her.

"I'm sure," Jade answered, and her confidence put Alina's mind at ease. Jade seemed to relax as they distanced themselves from the crowd.

"So why am I leaking? I didn't fall down or touch anything sharp," Alina whispered.

"Sometimes it's just the way our bodies work. Like when your teeth came out and you grew new ones."

Alina cringed. She never understood that about her teeth. They took so long to grow back, while everyone else seemed to get theirs immediately. But she learned long ago her body didn't work like theirs.

"Why do we need to go home?"

"You need something to absorb it, so you don't feel embarrassed."

"I see." Alina's face softened. "People are good at hiding when they leak. It's not something we show in public."

Jade nodded. "Exactly. I should've been better prepared for you. I'm sorry."

"It's okay. No one saw." Alina smiled at her. "I'm glad, because now we get to sleep at home in our beds."

Jade grinned back. "Yes, if we make it that far. But tell me—are you feeling okay?"

"What do you mean?"

"You don't feel strange? Like the time you rode the air coaster at the park?"

"No. I feel fine."

Jade sighed and squeezed Alina's hand. "Good. Let me know if you start feeling different, okay?"

"Okay." Alina scratched her chin. She had leaked many times before, but never like this. And Jade seemed more worried this time. *What could it be?*

A block from home, the Sleep overcame them. With blurry eyes and sluggish legs, Jade threw their pillows on the lawn of an empty house as they collapsed. As Alina's eyelids closed, her last aching thought was how they didn't make it home in time, and her nightgown—the only beautiful thing about her—was likely ruined.

CHAPTER 4

"Alina."

She heard the muffled voice again, and her eyes popped open. Jade stood above the couch, her dark eyes narrowed with concern.

"Are you okay?" she asked.

Alina rubbed the bridge of her nose. "Yes, I'm fine. I just saw something gory on the monitor."

Jade dropped her shopping bags to the floor. Alina peeked at her and was surprised to see a tiny smile on her face.

"Well, I hope you learned your lesson. Don't say I didn't warn you."

"Do people really die that way?"

"What way?"

"This girl in the movie—some psycho stabbed her in the throat, then her eyeballs turned black and her skin melted off. She dripped and oozed this bubbly red stuff."

"What on earth were you watching?" Jade put a hand on her hip.

"Sorry," Alina mumbled. "I had a bad day."

Jade sighed and sat down next to her. "Remember how I told you how obsessed people are with death? They seem to think it's always morbid and traumatic, and movie makers go overboard in depicting it. As for myself, I believe some mortals die peacefully, like in their sleep. I've always been an optimist, though." She smiled, but it faded as she cleared her throat. "Now about this bad day you had—"

Alina groaned and covered her face with her hand. "I know, I know. You don't have to lecture me. I should've ignored Eris and stayed in class."

Jade's eyes widened. "What—you didn't stay in class?"

Alina cringed. "I thought you'd heard."

Jade shot to her feet and paced the room, rubbing her forehead. "Alina, you *can't* skip school! You know that!"

"I'm sorry! But you were wrong about no one noticing these bumps on my face! Thanks to Eris—she announced it to the whole class, and of course they all came over to look. And then she started teasing me about the friends I don't have and how you and I never talk—" Alina broke off. She hadn't meant to say that part.

Jade spun around, her face full of hurt. "What?"

Alina regretted the slip. She didn't like to hurt Jade, but she couldn't take the words back—they had too much truth in them. So, she became defensive instead.

"Why are you so surprised? We *don't* talk! You never say anything to me—nothing worth talking about anyway—and you don't answer me when I ask questions about myself. You know what? I found out today why I'm different. I found out the same time everyone in my class found out." Alina's voice grew louder. "And it hurt that I found out from a teacher, and not from you. Why didn't you tell me?"

"What did your teacher say?" Jade whispered hoarsely.

Her soft tone set Alina off. "AS IF YOU DON'T KNOW! I'M A FREAK! A MISTAKE! FATHER SAMPSON'S WORST EXPERIMENT GONE WRONG!" Alina screamed.

Jade's face lost all of its color. She opened her mouth, but nothing came out.

"It's true then! Even you can't deny it—thanks for not telling me!"

"Alina," Jade begged, reaching out to her. "Listen to me, please. I never told you that because it's *not* true." Jade bit her lip, as if she said something she shouldn't have. But the sincerity in her voice gave Alina a spark of hope.

"What do you mean? Why am I so different then?"

Jade hesitated, then shook her head. "It's—I can't—I don't know."

Alina's nostrils flared. "See, there you go again—avoiding my questions! I'm not stupid, you know! If I'm not a failed experiment, then what am I? Because I'm certainly not like the other girls at school, and YOU KNOW WHY!"

Jade's eyes faltered.

"You know why. Don't you," Alina repeated, this time in a whisper.

Jade was near tears. Alina glared at her, and when she said nothing, Alina put her face in her hands and screamed. She bolted for the door.

Jade stepped in front of her. "Stop, please. Don't go anywhere—I know you're upset, but let me explain. Oh! You're—" Jade hesitated, staring at Alina's face. "Let me get you something for that." She dashed into the kitchen.

"What?" Alina asked, turning to the mirror by the door. A red stream trickled from the cluster of blemishes on her forehead. She was leaking.

"Here you go," Jade said, placing a wet cloth on Alina's brow. Alina's eyes were glued to the mirror. She narrowed them as the stream oozed between her eyebrows.

"Jade, what is this?"

Jade averted her eyes. "Um—"

"You told me everyone leaks, but that's not true, is it?" She met Jade's eyes through the mirror. "I've never seen it on you before."

Jade's face was calm, but Alina could see the panic in her eyes.

"Tell me what this is, or I'll never speak to you again," Alina ordered.

"It's bl—," Jade cut off, catching herself.

"Blood?" Alina finished. She knew that word. Where had she heard it?

Blood flowed through the streets...

Blood is what runs in the bodies of the mortals...

Alina whirled around, her eyes wide.

"I'm mortal, aren't I?" she whispered.

Jade didn't answer.

"That's why I'm different." Alina stared at her. "Father Sampson messed me up so completely, I became mortal. That's why he's ashamed of me. He wants everyone to hate me because of it. Jade," she demanded, her voice rising, "how long have you known?"

Jade shook her head. "Lina, I don't know what you're talking about. You're not mortal. You're upset because of what happened today, so you're jumping to conclusions—"

"You're lying!"

Jade pursed her lips together. "It's not what you think—"

"WHY DO YOU LIE TO ME?"

Alina burst into tears and lunged for the door. Once again, Jade slipped in front of her. With a hint of pleading in her voice, she said, "Go for a walk down Infinite Way. I hear Rex is putting up decorations for the Harvest Feast. You could watch—or talk with him to help you feel better."

Alina stormed past Jade and slammed the door as she left. She bolted across the lawn, pounding her feet on the pavement as she walked. Why was Jade such a fraud? Like everyone in Pria, she pretended life was perfect and sweet when it obviously wasn't.

But through her anger, Alina's heart felt lighter.

I'm mortal.

I will die someday.

The thought of death, so mysterious and terrifying to others, comforted her. There was an end. She wouldn't live forever as an outcast in a perfect world. Tears came to her eyes and she lifted her head, expressing gratitude, though she wasn't sure to whom. Father Sampson? If his mistake made her mortal, she'd have to thank him one day.

Even Carthem didn't frighten her anymore. Though a miserable place, her life couldn't be any worse there. She took a deep breath, filling her lungs with this new freedom.

She had no place in mind to go and hesitated when she reached the crossroads to Infinite Way. How strange for Jade to suggest she go see Rex. Alina had never spoken to him before and felt certain he didn't know she existed. Did Jade know him? They didn't speak to each other. She must have mentioned him for a reason, because as much as Jade concealed her feelings, Alina knew their quarrel had distressed her.

Curious, she turned down Aiona Avenue toward Infinite Way. She rarely, if ever, walked this road. It ran the length of Pria, intersecting the circular streets. The neighborhoods near Evergreen Loop were modest enough, but the closer she got to the center of Pria, the more lavish the homes became. Most of the popular kids, including Eris, lived on Aiona, but Alina had no idea which home was hers.

Today, she didn't care. She half hoped to run into Eris because, armed with new knowledge about herself, she was ready for a fight and indifferent to the consequences. Nothing Eris said or did would hurt her now.

She stormed down the street, glaring at the homes as they became larger and flashier. She stared into each sprawling window without caring how rude it looked. These garish homes exceeded the ones on Emrys Street, which she sometimes passed on the way home from school. Instead of mid-sized swimming pools on front decks, these mansions concealed their infinity pools on rooftops and backyards, complete with waterfalls and elaborate balconies for diving. Pristine flower gardens adorned the front grounds, paved with sleek stones in every color—browns, greens, blues, and even pinks. The homes matched the yards in extravagance and luxury, each one competing to be more awe-inspiring than the next. They were nothing compared to the estates she'd soon see on Rex's street, but she hated them just as much. In Pria, the value of a person mirrored the value of the home in which they lived.

A few people lounged outside, stretched out on chaises with panels in hand, eyes never moving from their screens as they sipped from crystal goblets. One woman on her balcony spoke so loudly into her panel, Alina overheard every word as she passed.

"I won't forgive him this time. I've caught him with other women too many times. I'm going to tell him at the feast tomorrow that it's over. He'll come crawling back because he knows I can turn people against him. Anyone worth associating with, that is."

Alina stared up at the woman in disgust. She didn't notice Alina but leaned against the decorative railing of her balcony and scrunched her glossy ringlets. She placed a hand on her hip under a silk robe, her painted fingernails matching the hot pink of her negligee. Music blared from an open window below her, and as Alina glanced at the lower room, she did a double take. She'd found Eris's home.

Eris stood before an enormous three-sided mirror, sweeping her flaming red hair into different styles and admiring herself. After each pose, she broke into a smile and giggled, then said something to the mirror. She shook her curly mane around her shoulders and turned up her nose, puckering her lips with air kisses. Alina watched, amused, then planted her feet directly where Eris would see her when she looked out the window.

"Girl!" a high-pitched voice squeaked out. "Why are you laughing and staring at my house?" Alina glanced up at the woman on the balcony. She crossed her arms over her pink negligee. "Why are you on this street, anyway? You don't belong here. Off you go, or I'll call Social Enforcement."

Alina ignored the woman and glanced back at the window, hoping Eris would look. But she was busy dancing to the music, whipping her red curls from side to side as she tossed her head.

"Shoo!" The woman called again, flapping a hand at her. Alina released a disappointed sigh and turned to go, just as Eris flipped back her hair and swayed toward the window. She stopped shimmying when she caught Alina laughing at her.

"Hey!" Eris hollered and bolted to the window, her eyebrows pinched together.

Alina continued walking but kept glancing back so Eris would see her laughing. Eris swelled with fury and stuck her head out the window, screaming after her, but Alina didn't catch the words. Eris would make her pay for this later, but for now, she enjoyed herself. Alina spotted Rex's estate the moment she turned on Infinite Way—the largest home on the street, surrounded by acres of flowery grounds and illuminated trees. Alina shielded her eyes as she approached. People couldn't get enough of shimmery things, it seemed. Even the sun couldn't compete with Pria's celebrations.

On the highest balcony, she spied a man hanging a banner from the twisted steel beams. Rex was head of the Celebrations Committee—a prestigious and busy job, as parties constantly filled the venues and streets of Pria—especially on Infinite Way. Jade said people were always looking for a reason to dress up and find love, or at least something to mimic it. If a party didn't produce what they hoped for, they could always find love in a drink. From what Alina could see, this was the usual outcome.

Rex acted peculiar at the celebrations he planned. He was the one who praised Father Sampson with deep, bellowing chants that put Jade in fits of laughter. Alina stopped walking when she thought of this. She had no desire to see Rex. But the memory of Jade's pleading voice held her interest, so she continued her steps. Perhaps she would walk past and return home.

Rex climbed his balcony, spread out his arms and leaped into a perfect dive, somersaulting when he touched the ground. He shuffled backward into the street to gain a full view of his mansion and seemed so immersed, he surprised Alina when he turned to greet her.

"Alina! How are you?" he called.

She blinked, astonished he knew her name.

He walked toward her. "Please give me your honest opinion about the lights. Will they do for the feast tomorrow?"

She shaded her eyes with her hand as she viewed his grounds. "I hate them."

He didn't seem ruffled by her blunt answer but nodded his head.

"Yes, I think they're a bit outrageous myself. It's what I hate most about my job. I have to do what everyone else wants, no matter how excessive it gets."

"You hate your job?"

Rex glanced around then dropped his voice. "Between you and me—yes. There, I said it. Out in the open too. I must be getting careless." He smiled. "Anyway, are you just going for a stroll, or is there something I can help you with?" He gave her a searching glance.

"Jade said you were putting up decorations and thought it would help me feel better to see them. I had a bit of a rough day."

He threw back his head and laughed. "But you hate my decorations! So much for helping you feel better. Well, come inside— I bet sampling the food will cheer you up. I need feedback, and your honesty is refreshing. Everyone's so fake around here, I don't know what they really think."

Alina raised an eyebrow and decided to follow him inside. Maybe she'd misjudged him. She'd dreamed of entering the mansions on Infinite Way and held her breath as she stepped inside. A grand staircase with no railing overlooked the foyer, and a brilliant chandelier refracted the late afternoon sun into countless tiny rainbows on the floor. White couches with square corners and bright decorative pillows sunk into the lush carpet of his living room, facing the largest monitor Alina had ever seen. The screen stretched from the carpet to the vaulted ceiling of the second floor. Rex dashed inside and pulled curtains over the front glass wall. Alina tilted her head as she watched him.

Though she knew little of him, she was aware his job made him popular with the ladies. Every woman in Pria coveted the position of hostess to Rex's lavish celebrations, except perhaps Jade. He was exceptionally handsome, with sandy blond hair and green eyes as bright as the grass. She found it strange he lived alone in such a large place, yet as he shuffled about the room, he did seem rather eccentric.

He peeked through the curtains, then turned to her and clapped his hands together. "Have a seat!"

She sank into the plush cushions. He disappeared through a swinging door, where she caught a glimpse of a black and white checkered kitchen. He returned with a tray of plump fruits and pastries, dark chocolate, spotted cheese, and a round, soft bread Alina hadn't seen before.

She dug in and ate half the tray before remembering she should only be sampling the food. But Rex didn't mind. He encouraged her when she slowed, complaining he ate leftovers for days after each event.

"Rex," she said, pausing after a swallow, "have you ever had a strange feeling in your belly that doesn't go away until you eat?"

He stared at her. She waited for him to say she was delusional.

"I've heard of it," he answered.

"Really?"

"It's called hunger." He stood with his arms crossed, watching her. Then he spoke in a stern whisper, "I'm assuming you're here because you've learned something about yourself."

Alina's heart skipped a beat. She nodded, and Rex took a seat beside her on the couch.

"What do you know?"

She whispered, "I'm mortal."

He paused, and a tiny smile came to his lips. "Jade has sent you to me for a reason. You have much to learn, but you can't hear it all now. You must leave before long and promise not to repeat what you hear to *anyone*." He kept his eyes locked with hers. "When you leave my home, you must act convinced of your immortality to all you speak to, *especially* Jade."

Alina's mouth dropped. He spoke too severely for her to disobey. "Okay," she stammered, "but why?"

"Because Jade is under surveillance."

"What?"

"When Jade became your caretaker, Sampson implanted a device in her brain so he could watch her. He monitors her life as if looking through her eyes. He sees what she sees and hears what she hears."

"But why does he care about her so much?"

"He cares what she says to *you*."

Alina blinked her eyes. "I don't understand."

Rex got up and peeked through the curtains again. He rubbed the back of his neck as he turned to Alina and spoke in a harsh, urgent whisper. "You are the biggest threat Sampson has ever known. You pose such a danger to his 'perfect' world, that for seventeen years he has made your case top priority in his laboratories. Surveillance was the only way to keep Jade silent."

"*What?*" Alina exclaimed. "I'm a *threat?*"

"More than you realize."

Alina stared at him. "And Jade knows all this?"

"Everything. Sampson doesn't want her revealing it."

"That explains why she doesn't talk to me," Alina whispered.

Rex's face softened. "I can't imagine how difficult it's been for her. I don't talk to her, either, but I see the pain in her eyes. She's not naturally aloof, you know. She has a gift with people. I know she wants to be close to you."

Alina bit her lip. "Did she ask to be my caretaker?"

"Sampson wanted to keep you at Gordian but didn't know how to care for you. Jade knew about you, which should have sent her straight to Carthem, but she made herself useful by volunteering to be your caretaker. She had other reasons for raising you though, not just to avoid banishment. In fact, she would've preferred Carthem, had her desire to protect you not been stronger."

Tears came to Alina's eyes. She wasn't a punishment, or an insult. Jade wanted her.

Rex started pacing the room. "Sampson agreed to let Jade raise you only because there was no other option at the time. He made one condition: she be put under surveillance to keep her in check. The device is very effective—it does everything short of reading her thoughts, so her words must always be convincing. There's no better actress in all of Pria because she knows the more proficient she plays her part, the longer you stay out of Sampson's laboratories."

"His laboratories!" exclaimed Alina. "But—what can he do to me there? I've been to those laboratories and there's not much to them—"

"Oh, honey," Rex cut in, shaking his head sadly. "There's so much of Gordian Palace you don't see on school field trips."

"So, why doesn't he put something in *my* brain, if he's so concerned about what I think?"

Rex held up his hand. "Take a breath. This is a lot of information to soak in. The perfect world you've known your whole life has just turned upside down."

"Oh, believe me, I haven't thought too highly of Pria lately."

"Yes, well, it's worse than you think." He sat down next to her and tapped his fingers on the arm of the sofa. "To answer your questions, not many people have the device—very few, in fact. It's difficult to make, and implant, so Sampson uses other means to monitor people. If someone is chosen for surveillance, it's because they're of great interest to him—usually an enemy or threat. It keeps them in line, you see. Surveillance wasn't an option for you because the procedure would kill you, and your death would ruin him. So, he's searching for a way to keep you alive indefinitely, in some kind of comatose state."

"What's that?"

"Permanent sleep. Forever."

Alina gasped. "But—but why does it matter if I die?"

Rex put his hands on her shoulders, his eyes twinkling. "Alina, you don't have the slightest clue who you are! Your existence has penetrated the immortal spell of Pria. If you die, all of Pria will collapse, and Sampson with it. Everyone will be subjected to mortality if you succumb to it."

Alina couldn't believe his words. "But—why?"

"Let's just say there are many things about Pria you don't learn in school. Pria is beautiful on the surface; underneath, it's ugly and corrupt. Sampson is not as dear to his people as you think. There's been a secret resistance growing for over two hundred years. My caretaker, Camden, helped organize it."

"A secret resistance! Does Father Sampson know about it?"

"Oh, he knows it exists, but so far we've been pretty good at keeping our identities hidden. Occasionally he discovers a participant, who is then banished. Fortunately, because no one feels pain, there is little he can do to force information. Torture wouldn't work anyway—we're too strong. Strong enough to pull off the biggest conspiracy Pria has ever known." He looked straight into her eyes. "You."

Alina stared at him. "*Me?*"

Rex nodded, and grinned.

"But—"

"Try not to feel overwhelmed, or frightened. There are many powerful people protecting you."

"You speak as if you're part of this secret resistance," she noted.

He winked.

"But wouldn't Father Sampson suspect you, being raised by a traitor? Why did Jade send me to you? Won't he suspect—well, the truth?" Alina asked.

"Don't worry, I have fooled him," Rex said with a sly smile.

"How?"

"I underwent his indoctrination process when I was thirteen, after he sent Camden away. It's how he handles these special cases—when a young one is exposed to dissent. Sampson has a law, which he more or less follows, that children and youth can't be sent to Carthem. He'd become unpopular very fast. Children can't be expected to always behave themselves. Learning to control one's temper is a process, so the young are allowed to make mistakes. With adults he plays his cards carefully, using banishment to create a margin of fear, but not to cause unrest. If he must expel more, he does so secretly. Camden was a tricky case for him. As one of the original founders of Pria, everyone knew and revered him, so Sampson couldn't secretly dispose of him."

"What did he do, then?'

"He exposed Camden as a law breaker, and with enough evidence, it worked. Of course, he twisted things to make Camden appear power hungry and selfish. People respected Sampson all the more when he, so reluctantly, sent an old friend and usurping traitor into Carthem to die," Rex said bitterly. "For the indoctrination process he brainwashes those who might be influenced by the traitor, especially if it's a child. Sampson believes this process is infallible—it almost is. I was raised by probably the only man who discovered its weakness. Camden fooled Sampson for a long time and taught me how to resist the indoctrination so I could do the same."

"Father Sampson believes you have forgotten everything?"

"Yes, but more importantly, I'm ingrained with his propaganda. When I hear negative comments about Sampson or Pria, I immediately refute it. I've kept up my act perfectly since I was thirteen. Have you seen me at the Day of Genesis?"

Alina couldn't help laughing. "Yes, and you're a little over the top. Father Sampson might still suspect you."

"Nah, he has no reason not to trust me. I obey, I perform, and he gets the results he wants from me. That's why sending you to me was the best plan Jade and I made. We arranged it before she was put under surveillance. It's also why you must act fully convinced of your immortality and loyalty to Sampson. If he buys it, we keep you out of Gordian longer—and we need more time. We've been working on a plan for years, but it's too risky to execute right now."

Alina's eyes grew wide. "You have a plan? What is it?"

Rex sealed his lips and shook his head.

Alina sighed and thought for a moment. "So, if I'm mortal, I'm not a bad experiment after all?"

"Huh?"

She explained Miss Rhonda's lecture. Rex shook his head and laughed bitterly. "So good ol' Samps saw people noticing you and decided to make up a cruel explanation for your differences." He gritted his teeth. "How I *hate* that man."

Alina inhaled as tears sprang to her eyes. Miss Rhonda was wrong! She hid her face in her hands.

Rex scooted near her on the couch and put his hand on her back. "Why don't you go home and put Jade's mind at ease. I'm sure she's beside herself. We can meet again another day and I will explain more."

Alina lifted her head. "I'm okay, I want to hear more right now."

"No, you've stayed long enough. You must be careful on the way home. It's likely you've been followed." Rex stood up and peeked through the blinds again. "I don't see anyone, but I know they're close by."

"Who, exactly?"

"Sampson's officials. Don't be afraid," he rushed. "Fear will give you away. They may approach and ask a few questions. Tell them in your most convincing voice you know you're immortal and express your loyalty to Pria. Go home and tell Jade, too. She'll know we had a good discussion."

Rex noticed the apprehension on her face. "Don't worry! They won't want to make a scene, either." He led her to the door, put his hand on the doorknob and paused. "One more thing. When you talk to Jade, don't be emotional about this. Today you've learned a lot about her and what she's done for you. But remember, Sampson doesn't want you to bond with her. If you grow closer because of this, he'll notice right away." Alina chewed her lip and nodded, and Rex swung open the door.

"Thanks for the visit, Alina," he projected as she stepped onto the porch. "Promise me, you'll come to the feast tomorrow and bring Jade. I've always wanted to get to know her better. You'll persuade her to come, right?"

"I will. Thank you," she said, surprised at the calm in her voice.

"Goodbye, sweetheart," he said in a sugary tone.

"Goodbye, Rex."

His mouth stretched into a dazzling smile as he waved and shut the door. His pretense was solid and convincing. She pictured him now behind his door, darting anxiously to the window to watch her leave.

She slowed her steps and lifted her chin to mask the worry in her eyes. If confronted now, would she hide her emotions well? Too many thoughts swirled in her brain, but a clear picture began to form —the product of many pieces falling into place.

There was Jade and her distance; Pierce moving abruptly after the tree climbing incident; Miss Rhonda's unusual biology lesson, and the bathroom at school no one else used. There was Father Sampson glaring at her and Jade at the Day of Genesis celebration. Was he always watching?

Before long, she spotted them—two men behind her, dressed in casual clothes. Though absorbed in their own conversation, they quickened their pace to overtake her. She fought a sudden urge to run, and her muscles tightened in preparation. She closed her eyes and took a deep breath. If she appeared happy about her visit with Rex, maybe they would leave her alone. Slowing her steps, she started humming Pria's anthem, but the notes didn't sound right. She could never carry a tune.

She turned the corner to Aiona Avenue and released a long breath. The men were out of sight, for now. She would soon be home.

She risked a glance behind her, and the two men came into view. *Don't appear anxious.* Pausing her steps, she bent over to examine the flower garden of a large mansion, when someone called her name.

Her heart stopped when she looked up. Zaiden stood in the garden not far from her.

The men came closer. A few more steps and they would be within hearing distance.

Alina fluttered her eyelashes. "How are you, Zaiden? I want to thank you for helping me feel better today. I had a beastly day, but I'm much better now." She giggled, then held her eyes closed for a moment. She sounded like the flighty girls from school. *Of course. That's the point.*

He hesitated before speaking. "Oh, good, I'm glad. I've been thinking about you today and about what happened—" his eyes glanced down the road and narrowed. The men nodded a stiff hello as they passed and continued talking between themselves.

Alina no longer cared about the men. Zaiden had been thinking about her! She dropped her eyes; afraid he might see her blush. She prayed the men would keep walking so she could be herself. She could tell Zaiden didn't appreciate her act, and she liked him more for it.

Her heart sank when the men stopped, as if engrossed in their conversation; they couldn't move on. They must have been instructed not to let her out of their hearing. After all, she could do a lot of damage if she believed herself mortal.

Alina pressed her lips together. She hated herself for it, but what choice did she have?

She gave a high, musical laugh. "Oh, Zaiden!" She slapped his arm. "You're sweet to worry for me, but there's no need. I was out of my mind today. I talked to Rex, and he reminded me that while I look different now, the serum runs through my veins, so with time I'll look like the other girls. He even said my appearance could help me go far, like make me famous!" She almost grimaced and gave herself away. She was taking this too far. "Pria is so full of opportunities, and—well, um, I just love it here!" she finished, not knowing what else to say. She hoped the men were convinced, because Zaiden's expression was killing her.

"Are you okay?" he asked. His eyes flickered to the men nearby.

"Of course!" Alina exclaimed. "Why do you ask?"

"You're" —he cleared his throat— "acting a little strange."

"I'm a new person since I talked to Rex."

He stared at her for a moment, then nodded. "Yes, well, it seems you're right." He looked away. "You *are* like all the other girls."

Alina's heart plunged. She opened her mouth to confess everything but stopped and bit her lip.

Zaiden glanced once more at the men as he turned back to his house. "I'll see you later, Alina." He ran his fingers through his hair as he walked away.

The two men looked at her, and she flashed them a smile. This seemed to satisfy them; they turned and continued on their way, leaving her alone in the street.

She wanted to rush after Zaiden, grab his arm, and explain everything. But she'd promised to tell no one, and she knew so little about him. Someday, she hoped, they would be close friends and he could learn the truth about her.

As she started toward home, a warm rain began to fall, something Father Sampson gave sparingly. Appearances meant everything to him, including the weather. But at times, his moods crept in, disrupting the constant sunshine.

This storm fit Alina's mood perfectly. Invigorating, brisk, and cleansing, the rain poured over her like her feelings for Zaiden—fresh, unsteady, and exhilarating. The ground seemed to shake beneath her feet as the rain dripped through her clothes and tickled her back. When she reached the end of the block, she paused and glanced back toward Zaiden's home.

She blinked her eyes. *Am I dreaming?*

It wasn't a dream. He was watching her through the rain, his bronze hair slicked back and his wet shirt clinging to his shoulders. At her distance, Alina couldn't tell if he was relieved, or sorry, to see her go.

ALINA WALKED INTO HER HOME, drenched, and Jade sprang from the couch to retrieve a towel from the closet. She ran to Alina, searching her face as she wrapped the towel around her.

Alina beamed. "Don't worry, Jade. Rex explained everything to me. I can't believe I thought I was mortal! In Pria? That's impossible!" She squeezed out a giggle as she ran the towel over her face and hair. "He said my beauty will come, and I'm sure it will. I'm already improving—look, the red bumps are gone!" She framed her face with her hands. Of course, the blemishes were still there, but she hoped this might prove her conversion.

Jade smiled knowingly. "Yes—I knew Rex could explain things better than I could. He has a way with people. What do you think, should we go to the feast tomorrow?"

Alina knew Jade had no desire to go. The feast was an excuse for people to dress in fancy clothes, overeat, and over-drink, to celebrate the harvest they didn't need. Father Sampson would speak about the hard work mortals must do to obtain food, and how Pria had such plenty—for their enjoyment, and not because they needed it.

But Pria was different to Alina now, and she and Jade could no longer hide in the background. The more involved they were, the more convincing her indoctrination would be. Now she understood why she didn't have friends growing up. Father Sampson isolated her because any close friend might come to learn her secret. This no longer mattered; she didn't care to be friends with the superficial people of Pria. But perhaps Jade could renew friendships with those she loved.

"Yes, we have to go. I promised Rex. I think he likes you! You should give him a chance. Every woman in Pria would envy you."

"Oh, I have no interest in Rex," Jade replied, but Alina caught a blush. "On second thought, maybe we shouldn't go tomorrow."

Alina almost agreed; she didn't want to go, either. But she had an act to keep up.

"Let's go, please? I promise I won't mention anything about Rex. But I want to talk with him again. He helped me feel so much better today." She searched Jade's eyes for understanding.

Jade nodded. "Sure, we can go. But remember how busy Rex will be. He probably won't have time to talk with all those people around."

Alina hadn't thought of that. Disappointed, she put on her best smile. "Okay. We'll have fun anyway." She yawned. "Well, I'm tired, I think I'll go to bed."

Now she realized why Jade told her to keep her nightly routine a secret. All of Pria would envy her if they knew she slept each night. Jade concealed the truth because the longer the pretense held up, the longer they could be together, and Alina would be safe.

Tears came to Alina's eyes, and she reached out to Jade, pulling her into her arms. "Thank you," she whispered.

This wasn't good. Rex told her not to be emotional.

Jade's expression remained steady, but Alina felt her shaking through the embrace. For the first time in seventeen years, she understood her caretaker. Their connection went beyond their clasped arms, and Alina held on much longer than she should.

CHAPTER
5

The next evening, Jade and Alina walked to Rex's home as the leaves transformed from emerald green to golden yellow, orange, and crimson. The Harvest Feast launched summer into autumn, patterned after one of Carthem's few beauties. Immortals craved variety, so Pria revolved through the seasons with leaves changing in autumn, snowflakes falling in winter, bright blossoms in spring, and countless flowers in summer. Outdoor recreation rotated through the seasons, the years, and decades. Sometimes Sampson constructed mountains with sheer cliffs and powdered slopes for skiing or blue-green lakes for boating and deep swimming. People climbed those same cliffs to leap from their heights and explore the valleys—always searching for bigger thrills and prettier flowers. Sampson had a demanding job, trying to keep his subjects entertained.

Yet nothing enthralled Alina. The snow drifted, new flowers bloomed, fresh fruit grew—but underneath it all, Pria remained the same.

Alina smoothed the curls in her hair and fidgeted with the bodice of her scarlet gown, which was too low-cut for her liking. She and Jade shopped for hours but found nothing that flattered her body. Most women loved to flaunt their perfect figures, but Alina knew the more she covered, the better she looked.

Lights pulsed on Infinite Way, flashing over the writhing dancers who crowded the street. Occasionally someone sprinted across the roof of Rex's estate and hurled himself into the air, landing in the center of the dancers. Long tables filled with wine bottles, crystal goblets, and trays of food lined the road. Swarms of people hovered nearby, laughing, kissing, or nuzzling with each other. The music throbbed through the ground up into Alina's bones, and her teeth chattered nervously. She wiped her clammy palms on her dress. Her task overwhelmed her. Could she pretend to love Pria when she despised everything about it? She might do well tonight, but what about the next celebration? Or school next week? Jade flashed Alina a sly smile, then spun on her heels and strode toward a man and woman conversing nearby, holding glasses of blood red wine.

"Donovan! Selena!" Jade's voice rang out.

The couple shared a surprised glance as Jade walked toward them, her sapphire gown clinging to her long legs. "I haven't seen you in so long! Isn't the wine *divine* tonight?" She gave an exaggerated but plausible giggle. Alina looked down and smiled. Jade hadn't tried the wine. Rex spoke the truth—she was a good actress.

She's showing me how it's done.

Alina squared her shoulders and followed Jade, wobbling in her jeweled heels. Jade's body swayed as she prattled and flirted, and before long a small crowd gathered around her. Alina joined in and forced laughter until her eyes bulged. She could never hold a group's attention like that. Too bad she wasn't more like Jade—she'd have no problem convincing Sampson she loved Pria. But she couldn't feign interest in their shallow words. Bored, she turned her head and scanned the crowd for the person she most wanted to see.

She found Zaiden a short distance away, standing with his caretaker and a woman who looked vaguely familiar. Maybe his caretaker had a partner, and they raised him together. This was rare, but not unheard of. Alina smiled as she watched him, hoping he would turn and look at her. He looked perfect in his tailored suit and white collared shirt, his hair slicked back, his square jaw shadowed with facial hair.

Her smile faded as a girl approached him and placed a manicured hand on his shoulder. Her flaming red hair swirled past her shoulders and her silver gown shimmered as she slunk around him. She was so stunning, all the women around her seemed plain.

Alina's face burned as Eris batted her eyelashes and stroked Zaiden's arm. She tossed her hair and leaned in toward him, but he stepped away.

Alina bit her lip to suppress a laugh just as Eris looked over Zaiden's shoulder and met her eyes. Eris flared her nostrils, dropped her hand from his arm, and started toward Alina.

She turned to Jade for help, but Jade was deep in conversation with a man Alina didn't know. She glanced back at Eris and caught Zaiden's eye instead, who had turned to see what captured Eris's attention.

His eyes lit up and he smiled at her. She started to return his smile, but Eris's sour, puckered face interrupted them.

"Alina, darling! You look almost decent tonight. How much makeup did it take?"

Alina rolled her eyes. This time she wouldn't give Eris the pleasure of a dramatic reaction. She smiled sweetly. "At least makeup can make me look better. No amount can hide a sneer, but you did your best."

Eris glowered at her. A sneer made a woman wholly unattractive, and to point one out was a terrible insult. Zaiden kept glancing at them, and without meaning to, Alina's eyes flickered in his direction.

Eris turned and caught Zaiden as he looked away, then let out a high laugh. "So, you have your eye on Zaiden! How perfect. Did you know my caretaker is dating his? I'm seeing him a lot these days, and he likes that. It was a game for me, but now that I know it'll break your heart, I think I'll get more into it." She pivoted in her stiletto heels and pranced back toward him, her curls bouncing against her bare back.

Zaiden watched her as she approached, his face a mix of suspicion and interest, and he shot Alina a careful glance as Eris slid her arm through his. Alina's heart dropped. She had no hope of getting to know him with Eris hanging around, and now she couldn't convince anyone she was having a good time—especially Sampson. She scanned the street for Jade. Perhaps they could leave. But Jade was nowhere to be seen.

The situation was familiar to Alina: complete isolation though thousands surrounded her, never a friend to rescue her from the awkwardness. She ducked into the crowd, her eyes picking out and examining every blue dress. *Jade, where are you?*

Maybe she could find Rex. He might not know where Jade was, but the idea of talking to him comforted her. She crossed the street to his estate, slipping through the tangled lovers on his lawn to the front door. More couples filled the corners of his foyer and front room, and she felt their heavy eyes on her. Rex wasn't there.

She stepped back onto the porch and her heart rose to her throat. In the front yard she saw Eris and Zaiden, fused together, her white-tipped fingers running through his hair. Alina clutched the pearls around her neck and swallowed. Eris met her eyes and smirked, then locked her lips with his in a tight kiss.

Alina lifted her gown and ran into the street, her eyes blurred with tears. She ran to where she last saw Jade, then stopped. She couldn't face Jade like this. Sampson would see her upset when she should be happy. She'd have to go alone and invent an excuse for leaving early. She spun around and started toward home, but after a few steps, a hand seized her arm.

"Come with me, Alina," a low voice commanded. The grip tightened, as if he expected her to run away. She wiped her tears with her free hand before turning to face him. She recognized him as one of the men who followed her from Rex's the night before.

She forced a smile. "Where are we going?"

He didn't smile back. "You'll see when we get there." She didn't resist as he led her, but her eyes scoured the crowd. It was unlike Jade to leave her.

They reached the end of Infinite Way the same moment a sleek, black aircar pulled up. Only Sampson's top officials owned aircars. Her heart raced in her chest. This was it, her final moments before she vanished forever. Sampson had planned her capture perfectly. By ensuring she had no friends, only Jade and Rex would know if she disappeared. Even Zaiden would forget her, if he hadn't already.

The man opened the door for her, and she gave one final, desperate glance down the street. No one noticed her; their wine and dance partners consumed them. Alina ducked into the aircar, slid across the smooth seat, and gasped.

Father Sampson was sitting beside her.

CHAPTER 6

"Hello, Alina," he said in his deep, oily voice. The aircar began to move. "How nice to see you again." She could see one side of his face where the party lights illuminated his perfect features. He was the handsomest man she'd ever seen, but his was a dark, threatening beauty.

"I d–don't remember meeting before," she stammered.

He chuckled. "Oh, you wouldn't remember, I suppose." He spoke as if he knew her intimately. Her pretense had failed.

What about Rex? Sampson must never find out what he'd told her. The game had to go on.

"I'm sorry not to be more presentable," she said, smoothing her hair. "You caught me at a bad moment—a girl was rude, and I was upset. Please don't be angry. I love Pria so much, I don't want to be sent away."

Sampson's hard eyes unnerved her. She kept talking.

"I think Rex can help me feel better; he did yesterday. Can I see him now?" It was a daring move. She wrinkled her brow innocently.

Sampson continued to glare. "Don't worry. You must know I can give you more than Rex ever could. I will be far more helpful in soothing you." His chilling tone made one thing clear: he didn't trust Rex.

"Oh—yes, of course." She cleared her throat and looked out the window at the passing lights, crossing her arms to hide her tremors. "Where are we going?"

"You are my special guest tonight," he said. "How would you like to see Gordian Palace? Have you been there before?"

"Um, once, on a school trip."

"Ah, yes. Then you haven't seen what I will show you tonight." He stared as if he saw right through her, down to her naked skin.

She straightened her back and tried to appear calm. What could he do to her? Put her in a comatose state or torture her to speak? She shivered. Could he trick her into exposing Rex or Jade? She was grateful Rex hadn't told her any of his plans. She didn't trust herself to keep them safe now. She forced a smile. "I'm interested to see it."

He smiled back, showing white, even teeth. *He must be the handsomest man in Pria. He makes sure of it.* His silver hair fell behind his ears, bright against his olive complexion. His eyes were dark and captivating, his shoulders wide and solid. Any girl would covet her place. Everyone knew he had a way with women. But she felt only repugnance as he stared at her.

"Can I ask you something?" Alina said.

"Of course."

"Why are you taking me now, during the feast? I was having a great time—well, except for that rude girl—but I'm sure you don't want to miss the party either—"

"Quit the charade, Alina," he ordered. She froze in her seat.

He leaned in, his face inches from hers. "Do you think you can fool me? Do you think I don't see right through this pathetic act?" He straightened in his seat, his black eyes flashing. "I know more than you realize, and what I don't, I soon will. Ah! Here we are."

An iron gate opened, and the majesty of Gordian Palace stretched before them. The innumerable gold turrets looked sharp and threatening, as if piercing the sky.

Alina's mind raced. If he knew the truth, then he knew about Rex. Was Jade safe? She had no time to think of a plan.

"Thank you, Leonard," Sampson called to the driver. "I'll take it from here." The aircar slowed to a stop and Sampson jumped out, then walked around to Alina's door and opened it. He didn't look at her as he held out his hand to assist her.

She took a deep breath. He was about to find out how difficult she could be when she didn't have to pretend.

Alina ignored his hand as she stepped out. Without waiting for him, she squared her shoulders and strode toward the front steps of the palace. She released a faint cry as his fingers enclosed her throat, holding her in place.

"No one goes before me," he growled in her ear, "especially in my own home." He tightened for a moment before releasing her, and she clasped her neck and let out a wheezy cough. Sampson marched ahead of her toward the stairs. Alina followed.

The porch steps seemed endless. He waited patiently for her at the top, then led her through the towering front doors into the foyer of Gordian Palace. A giant chandelier sparkled in Sampson's eyes as they walked under the staircase and toward a hallway with thick, velvet carpet. Memories of her field trip came rushing back to her. School kids were allowed to visit Gordian Palace just once during their educational years, at the age of ten.

Gordian officials were too busy to devote much time to palace tours, so every child looked forward to this special occasion. Father Sampson himself greeted the children at the end, answering their questions and shaking each hand. Alina still remembered his coldness when he shook her hand. She didn't dare look up but sensed him frowning at her. She'd always believed her looks disappointed him back then. Now she knew the real reason.

The grand hallway held the sculpture exhibition she remembered most about her visit years ago, named *The Noble and Everlasting Life of Victor Sampson*. The first bronze statue displayed him in tattered clothes, kneeling over the lifeless bodies of a woman and child in a pile of rubble. Clenched hands cradled his head. Her teacher told the children to squat down so they could see his face contorted with grief and tears. The name plate in front read *The Last Great War of Carthem*.

The second sculpture was simply named *Hope*. Sampson stood

in a shabby laboratory uniform with a vial in each hand. He held one up, studying the liquid inside with intense concentration.

He appeared twenty years younger in the next statue, possessing a fine, robust body. The lines of grief were gone from his face. His eyes focused on an architectural plan spread out on his desk. *The Birth of Pria.*

The display of sculptures continued down the entire hallway. In one he cradled a new baby, another showed him hard at work in his laboratories. Others depicted him holding a sun in one hand and a world in the other, and delivering his Day of Genesis speech, complete with bronze tears on his cheeks. Two significant statues towered over the others, commemorating the hundredth and two hundredth Genesis celebrations. His most recent effigy, marking the three hundredth anniversary, stood outside in the central gardens.

Figure after figure lined the walls, each one handsome, stately, and dauntless. Alina rolled her eyes. *This man is remarkably full of himself.* But she feigned interest in every statue to slow their progress until Sampson stormed back, seized her wrist and yanked her at his pace.

The grandeur of the palace lessened as he dragged her down several flights of stairs and into a bright corridor with a heavy, bolted door. He tapped a code on the lock-screen, and as the door clanged open, Alina held her breath.

They were entering the notorious Gordian laboratories.

CHAPTER 7

Laboratory workers were sworn to secrecy as to what happened behind that bolted door. In school they learned about manufactured food and babies being formed, but explanations were vague. Sampson did not expose such secrets carelessly. She was entering the laboratories never to leave.

The magnitude of the room overwhelmed her, and she stumbled as she looked up. Shiny machinery stretched into the highest turrets, surrounded by a labyrinth of stairs and platforms. The massive room must be deafening when operators were there, but for now, it was eerily silent.

"The workers have the night off for the Harvest Feast," Sampson said, as if reading her thoughts. His lips curved into a cruel smile. "Very convenient, as I'd like no one to know you were brought here tonight."

He guided her onto a steel platform, where she looked down and gasped. The room extended into darkness below her, with more machines and staircases. Rows of doors and lighted windows lined the platform to her left. She glanced into the window closest to her and froze in her tracks.

The room revealed columns of shelves and neatly stacked jars. She leaned in and narrowed her eyes. *It's food. Strange food I haven't seen before. Maybe it's for the next celebration.* But then something twitched.

The jars' inhabitants were black, spiny, and quivering violently. She jumped back and screamed.

A chorus of clicking noises started from the room. Alina darted after Sampson, who continued walking as if nothing had happened. Her legs trembled beneath her. Those creatures did not live in Pria. Only beautiful, pleasant things existed here.

She peered into the next window and saw a table lined with silver trays, panels and tools, as if the workers left without cleaning up. Her body relaxed a little. Nothing surprising was stored there. She expected the contents of the next room as well, but the sight stole the breath from her lungs.

A large, transparent sphere filled the room, drifting with fetuses in varying stages of development: some almost too small to see, others full-sized and squirming. Each baby possessed a glowing tube from its navel to a ball of light in the center, like a small sun, providing energy to grow.

"Beautiful, isn't it?" Sampson whispered in her ear, startling her. "I can create life. Everything you see here are my creations. There's no limit to what I can make, and no power great enough to stop me. I made the beginning, and I could make the end if I chose to. Someday, when I'm tired of it all, maybe I will." He gave a soft, dark chuckle.

Alina shuddered as his breath tickled her neck. She would no longer gratify him by peering into the rooms. She waited, coolly, for him to take the lead, then passed three windows without a glance. But as she passed the fourth, a chill ran through her, and she halted, turning her eyes toward the glass.

The dark room looked empty, but the chill grew colder along her spine. She didn't care to know what the room harbored, yet she stood transfixed, her eyes straining to penetrate the darkness. The fear spread to her heart, paralyzing her muscles.

A pair of beady, red eyes blinked in the darkness. She opened her mouth to scream but released only a rush of air. The eyes bore into her, growing brighter as her terror increased. She could see Sampson from the corner of her eye, watching her with a pleased grin on his face.

"Come with me," he said. "There's a room just for you." When she didn't move, he snatched her arm and jerked her along the platform, releasing her from the spell. She stumbled over her feet as the breath returned to her lungs.

Something had petrified her until she couldn't move. What *was* that creature?

Her courage returned, warming her muscles, and she yanked her arm from Sampson's grasp. He snapped his head to hers and they stopped walking, glaring at each other. He opened the door in front of him and extended his arm, inviting her inside. Her eyes didn't flinch from his as she walked in.

The room had no windows. A tall, shiny machine filled a corner of the room, and next to it was a small slab with restraining straps. The slab looked uncomfortable, but that didn't matter. She wouldn't feel it. This was her permanent resting place.

No one would know she was there.

"It's time," he said with a smug smile, then his face went stern. He motioned toward the slab.

She crossed her arms and walked toward it, glancing over the machinery before sitting down.

"*Lie,*" he snapped. She tightened her jaw and complied.

"Do you know why you're here?" he asked as he wrapped a strap around her wrist.

She saw no point in lying. "Because I'm mortal, and therefore a threat to you."

His eyes flickered angrily. "*You?* A threat to me?" he cinched the strap, pinning her arm to the cold slab. "How could you threaten *me?*"

Alina caught her mistake. "I meant—I'm *different*, so I disrupt your perfect world."

Sampson studied her as he pulled off her heels and strapped her ankles. "Is that what you think?" he asked.

"Yes. I have an awful temper—I yell and scream when I get angry. I cry when I'm upset. These things disturb your peaceful world. I always knew I'd be sent to Carthem. I don't know why I'm here in your laboratories, but there must be some reason."

He glowered at her for a moment, then took a small panel from his pocket and tapped it with his finger.

Alina couldn't see the face on the screen. "Yes?" a male voice said.

"Everything is set here. Is the other matter resolved?" Sampson asked.

"We're finishing the entry now, sir."

"And Rex?"

"He's on his way."

"Good, I'll be in my office in five minutes."

Sampson clicked off the panel and looked at Alina. "We'll see how Rex defends himself this time."

Alina panicked. "Defend himself from what? He helped me yesterday when I was confused and—"

She stopped herself but too late. When she confessed her mortality, she'd condemned Rex. Defending him only implicated him further. She shut her eyes tight. *How could I be so stupid?*

She couldn't meet Sampson's glare. He folded his arms across his chest and spoke calmly. "You know, I should thank you, Alina. My methods are thorough, but I often wondered about Rex. Tonight, you exposed him as the traitor he is. He'll suffer for his crimes and die in Carthem."

"No!" Alina screamed.

"And you" —his voice rose as he gripped the side of the slab— "will begin a new life today. You caught on faster than I expected, but no matter—I'm ready. One last thing to arrange, and I will return." He stormed out of the room, slamming the door behind him.

Alina trembled and squeezed her eyes shut. Tears dripped down her cheekbones and into her ears. She'd be kept alive in this laboratory while her loved ones died in Carthem. Jade would be sent with Rex; she knew too much. No one in Pria would know what happened to her.

Unconscious. Forever. A sad, lonely way to exist. It would be better to die.

Her eyes flung open. Of course! She needed to die. Then Sampson would fall. Why hadn't she thought of it before? Rex probably didn't know how to tell her. She would sacrifice herself and take pleasure in it. Her personal gift to Sampson.

She forced herself up on her elbows and scanned the room. Something sharp should work. Sharp things made her bleed, and if she bled enough, she would die. She was pulling at the straps on her wrists when the door opened.

A worker in a white laboratory uniform walked in, pushing a cart with small, tinkling instruments. A white hood and plastic visor concealed his face.

Alina yanked at her restraints. "Go away!" she ordered, louder than she meant to. "I'm *not* going to sleep!"

"Alina, it's me!"

It took her a moment to recognize the voice. Her mouth dropped in surprise.

"Rex!"

He put his finger to the mask. "Shhh! We have only a few minutes." He lifted his visor and fiddled with the straps on her wrists, cursing under his breath. He snatched a tool from the cart and sliced through them. After freeing her ankles, he took a bundle from the cart and handed it to her. "Quickly, put this on."

She unfolded a uniform and hood identical to his. "What are we doing?" she whispered.

"We're going to Carthem. And don't worry, it's not as horrible a place as you've heard." He paused. "Not that I've been there."

"I don't care if it is," Alina said as she stepped into the suit and zipped it over her gown, then took the shoes Rex held out for her. "Any place is better than this cell for eternity." She slipped on the shoes and placed the visor over her head. Her heart pounded in her chest.

"I'm sorry, Rex," she whispered.

"Don't be. It would have come to this, anyway." He lowered his visor as they walked through the doorway onto the metal platform.

"Sampson acted sooner than we expected. Not long after you arrived at the feast, two men escorted Jade away. When I saw you enter the aircar, I knew I needed to move fast. Our original plan is too risky, so I'm improvising tonight."

"Can we find Jade?"

Rex's shoulders drooped. "I don't know. I hope so."

Alina followed him toward the bolted door, glancing at the window with the red-eyed fiend as they passed, but felt nothing. All the rooms were dark.

She pointed to the windows. "These rooms hold Sampson's creatures, and they're terrible!"

"I know. My rebel friend who got me in here sealed the rooms off so they couldn't affect us. Apparently, some of the creatures mess with your mind."

"Yes, I noticed," Alina shuddered.

They reached the exit and Rex tapped the lock-screen. They cringed as the door clanged open. It seemed loud enough to alert the whole palace.

"Now for the hard part," Rex whispered. "Finding the serum dagger without being seen."

"*Serum dagger?*" Alina squeaked.

"Shhh!" he said as he inched his head out and glanced down the hallway. "I'll try to explain on the way." He slipped out, sliding his body flat against the wall. Alina followed.

"We should walk normal," Rex muttered under his breath. "That's the whole point of the disguise, right?"

"Except Sampson said all the workers have the night off. We'll look suspicious at first glance," she muttered back.

"Having them gone is a good thing. Fewer around to find us. Come on, let's go."

Alina's stomach was in knots. They scurried down the hallway, pausing to peek around each corner. Alina glanced frequently behind her as she followed Rex.

Halfway down the hall, they froze. Voices and footsteps carried toward them, growing louder. Rex scanned the doors, and when he saw one ajar, he dashed into the room and pulled Alina after him, closing the door softly from behind.

The sight of the room made Alina gasp. In the center sat the largest monitor she'd ever seen. Its flat, square screen stretched from the floor to the ceiling. Hundreds of narrow slotted trays lined the walls, filled to capacity with info-discs. A sliding ladder leaned against the right wall, next to the monitor.

"What in the world—" Rex started, but a man's voice from the hallway silenced him.

"Interesting guy, this Zaiden fellow."

Alina's heart stopped.

"Put it back so we can tell Sampson it's done," another man said nervously. Alina glanced at Rex, but he was looking at the floor. She couldn't see his face through the mask.

One of the men chuckled just outside the door. "I love taking Rex down. I always knew he was a fraud." A long pause followed. "That's funny. I could've sworn I left the door open. We've only been gone a few minutes."

Alina panicked as Rex gripped her arm. They darted behind the monitor just as the lock-screen buzzed and the door opened.

Alina held her breath as the men entered, dreading discovery at any moment. Footsteps tapped the marble floor to the ladder near their hiding spot. She peeked around the monitor and caught a glimpse of a sharply dressed man, looking as if he'd come straight from the Harvest Feast.

He pulled the ladder toward him and began climbing, an info-disc in his hand. Alina made herself as small as possible, praying he wouldn't have a reason to access the trays behind the monitor.

Halfway up the wall he slid the info-disc into a tray between the others, then climbed down and turned to the man standing in the doorway.

"You know, Brock, I'm not sure I want this promotion. It's more entertaining here, even if the pay is lower. Access to all the beautiful women I want—it's paid off many times. You'll still let me into this room when I need it, won't you?"

Brock snorted. "Whose girlfriend do you want to steal this time?"

"Well," he dropped his voice as if sharing a secret. "I've been watching Sampson's third woman; you know, the one with the nice body."

"Phil, are you *mad*?" Brock hissed. "You dare try to steal one of his? You know he's the only one who can let them go. Even they can't choose to leave."

"That's what I want to find out," Phil said. "Can you think of anything more thrilling? Is there any woman harder to get? It's a challenge I can't resist. Besides, I'm bored with easy women. I need some danger to get me excited about life again." He chuckled. "I'm sure they get bored with Sampson, too. We all know they're in it only for the fame."

"You know, I never thought of it like that before."

"What about the girlfriend you already have? You know, the one you've lived with for five years?" Phil teased.

Brock grunted with disgust. "Very funny. I need you to become an Emotion Officer so you can take her off my hands."

"Why don't you leave her?"

"It's not that easy. The woman is a master manipulator."

"Yeah, blackmail is becoming more common these days. Have to be careful who you hook up with."

Brock lowered his voice. "Let's get the discs down for all his women. No harm in looking. Then if it doesn't work out with one, you can try the next!"

"Do we have time right now?"

"We'll just take a quick look." Alina heard the sound of discs sliding out of place, and footsteps approaching the monitor.

"Convenient that Sampson likes them accessible," said Phil.

"What, the discs or his women?" Brock joked. "Now, which one do you—" a soft pinging noise interrupted him, and the room went quiet. He swore as the sound came again.

"Well, answer it!" Phil hissed. "It's not like he can see what you're doing. There are no cameras in here. Just keep your face steady."

Alina heard a soft click, and Sampson's voice echoed into the room.

"Are you *trying* to vex me?" he asked. The anger in his voice chilled Alina; he seemed dangerously calm.

"We're done!" Brock sounded nervous. "We're on our way."

"Rex should've been here by now. Get back to the control room immediately. No mistakes tonight. Do I make myself clear?"

"Yes, sir," Brock answered. Alina heard a soft click, then a brief pause.

"Guess this'll have to wait for another time," Phil mumbled.

"Let's hurry," said Brock, a hint of worry in his voice.

They hustled around the room, sliding discs into trays. The light switched off, the door closed, and a lock clicked in place. Footsteps faded down the hallway.

Neither Alina nor Rex moved for a minute. Alina jumped as an info-disc clattered to the ground. Rex felt his way to the door, tapped the light and chuckled. "They were in such a hurry they didn't put the discs back properly."

Alina stepped out from behind the monitor. "Rex, they're looking for you," she said nervously.

He lifted his visor. "It's okay. My goal tonight was to get you to Carthem. Yes, having those two in the control room complicates things since that's where the dagger is kept. I'll have to draw them out. But this can also work to our advantage." He took her arm. "Listen to me, Alina. *You're* the valuable one here. It's crucial you make it to Carthem. Don't worry about Jade and me, we're expendable, but you—"

Alina pushed up her visor and jerked her arm away. "What are you talking about Rex? *I'm* the expendable one! You need to kill me for this whole plan to work, so what are you waiting for? Don't risk any more of the rebels' plans by keeping me alive!"

Rex stared at her for a moment, then understanding dawned his face. "Oh, no, Alina, you have it all wrong! I can see why you'd think that, but—oh I've messed up—we *don't* want you dead; you're much more valuable to us alive! Believe me. You *must* keep yourself safe for the resistance." He clutched her arm again. "Please."

Alina hesitated, then nodded. "All right. Tell me what to do."

"If they're expecting me, then I'll give them what they're looking for. I'll draw them out of the control room so you can reach the dagger and enter Carthem on your own. I'll do everything I can to meet you there."

"But I don't know anything about the dagger!" Alina exclaimed.

"There's ageless serum in its blade. I don't know how it works, but when someone is cut with it, they are transported to Carthem. Simple." Rex took a piece of paper from his pocket, unfolded it and handed it to her. "My friend wrote these directions. They begin at the laboratories, so figure out where we're at now and start from there."

Alina read the note to herself.

Turn left and follow the hallway to your first right, into a large foyer with a spiral staircase. Take the stairs up to the next level and turn left. Follow that hall until you see a door labeled 'Operations and Control.' The code is 469904. Open the door, and proceed to the control room, the third door on the left, code 386022. The dagger is kept in the drawer of the central control desk.

Alina looked up. "Just like that?"

"I hope so," Rex answered. "There may be guards, and an alarm is likely to go off when you take the dagger, so be fast. Get your hands on it and cut yourself."

"Do you think Sampson suspects we'll go after the dagger?"

"He might. That's why my diversion needs to be big enough to empty that room. But hey," he grinned, "I know how to put on a good show."

"Rex—"

"We have no choice, Alina. You *must* make it to Carthem. And keep yourself alive. Unfortunately, I have no advice for you once you're there. But you'll find allies since everyone hates Sampson. Maybe you'll find Camden."

He looked at her and his face softened. "I'm sorry I have to leave you. This whole escape has been reckless, out of necessity. But I think you're ready." He hugged her and whispered in her ear. "Believe in yourself. Camden used to say mortals were stronger than immortals by a thousand-fold. Something about passing through adversity. I never knew what he meant, but if he said it, then it's true."

He opened the door, peeked out, and looked back at her and nodded. "All clear. Stay here for about fifteen minutes while I clear your path. Don't wait any longer." He paused. "And be safe."

She swallowed. "You too, Rex." He pulled the shield over his eyes and disappeared into the hallway.

She closed the door and locked it, then let out a long breath and glanced around the room. The info-disc on the floor caught her eye. The striking woman on the case looked familiar.

She studied the disc for several moments before it came to her. The woman, once Sampson's public girlfriend, now lived on Alina's street. She accompanied him to the Day of Genesis celebration two years ago. He had a different girlfriend now, but Brock and Phil claimed she was still one of his.

Many of his ex-girlfriends didn't fit into society after the breakup, and this one in particular became the subject of fierce gossip after Sampson let her go. People called her a social climber, a manipulator, an inept lover. She threw a tantrum when Sampson broke up with her and was almost *sent*.

Alina shook her head. This woman couldn't possibly be with him. Brock and Phil must be mistaken.

She looked at the cases along the wall and noticed each spine had a name. Since no two people had the same name in Pria, she knew which discs belonged to whom. Scanning the lower trays, she found her name next to Jade's, then grabbed both discs and took them to the monitor. She had a few minutes to spare.

She grimaced at the photo on her case, taken in the hallway at school. The fluorescent lighting illuminated every oily pore on her face. She opened the case and slid the disc into the slit on the monitor. Bold letters flashed onto the large screen, and she backed up to get a better view.

ALINA
born: March 22 (DOE)
caretaker: Jade

What did DOE mean? Was it a code for the year? No one kept track of years in Pria, except in their minds. But the date puzzled her most. She celebrated her commencement on June tenth. March twenty-second was the day following the Day of Genesis.

She found the remote and swiped through the pages, then let out a startled cry. She glanced around the room. *Is he watching me now?*

She never knew her life had been so closely monitored. Hundreds of video links and pictures filled the screen. She smiled at a photo of Jade holding her, tickling her tummy and watching her laugh; then at six years old, grinning a toothless smile. Other pages showed her sitting in class at school and on outings, or sleeping in her bedroom, taken from the angle of her window. That one unsettled her.

Her disc even included a photo from the day before, when she ran to the school bathroom after the encounter with Eris, and then as she talked to Zaiden in the hall with puffy, red eyes. She cringed with humiliation.

She had to get moving, but couldn't resist taking a peek at Jade's disc. She slipped the disc into the monitor and as the first picture flashed across the screen, she gasped.

The woman bore no similarities to the one Alina lived with.

Thick eyeliner and lipstick shaped Jade's eyes and mouth. Twisted, kinky black hair fanned out around her face. She looked so much happier, even younger. The bold letters read:

JADE
commenced: August 5
caretakers: Marcos and Thea
caretaker to Alina; SD in occipital lobe

SD. Surveillance device?

Alina didn't know a couple had raised her. How strange Jade never mentioned them before.

She seemed a happy child. Videos with her caretakers showed a handsome couple doting on her at parties, school activities, and celebrations. Hundreds of photos were taken with friends. Her appearance altered over the century of her life. Alina giggled at the stiff hair, heavy jewelry, skin-tight clothing, and other fads. Did she know this woman at all?

Then Alina reached a photo that made her jaw drop in disbelief. A dark-haired, handsome man had his arms wrapped around Jade, who looked more beautiful than Alina had ever seen.

But Jade doesn't like men!

This one seemed different—rugged and flawed. Attractive, but not like men of Pria. One blue-green eye was slightly higher than the other. His teeth were faintly yellow, and his hair carried flecks of gray. She read the caption below the picture.

Jade with J'koby Yates—Enemy #1

Who was he?

Alina removed the disc from the monitor, put it in its case and set both back in their trays. She hunted through the discs for one that read *J'koby* but found no sequence to their order. She climbed the ladder and after skimming several rows, found another that caught her attention. *Zaiden.*

She had no time to search his disc now. She chewed her lip for a moment, hovering on the ladder, then snatched the case and scrambled down. She'd take it with her to Carthem to remember him.

A disc was nothing without a panel, however. Did they have them there? She scanned the room until her eyes settled on the remote underneath the monitor.

She picked up the small panel and examined it. The screen was small but contained a slit in the side for an info-disc. She unzipped the laboratory uniform and shoved the disc and panel into the bodice of her gown.

She pulled the visor over her eyes and had just touched the doorknob when a loud explosion echoed through the palace, shaking the walls. She froze as footsteps thundered down the hallway.

"Clever fink. He's in the laboratories!" Brock shouted as he passed the door. "We've got him!"

Alina's heart raced. *What did Rex do?*

She turned the knob, peeked into the hallway, and crept out. She pulled the paper from her pocket and unfolded it. *Turn left, then right into a large foyer. Take the staircase up to Operations and Control.*

She reached the foyer, but nearly cried out when she saw the staircase. It swirled in the center of the room, exposed, without walls or rails. She gritted her teeth and dashed for the staircase, crouching on her hands and knees as she climbed. She inspected the horizon as she came to the next floor, then scrambled up the last few steps and hurried to the hallway on the left.

She fought back tears. Rex was caught, she knew it. But what happened to Jade? Alina hadn't lived a day without her, and now she must go to Carthem alone. Everything depended on her.

The paper shook in her hands as she reread the instructions. She snuck down the hall until she found the door with large, black letters.

OPERATIONS AND CONTROL

She exhaled and tapped the code into the lock-screen. It clicked, and she slid through the door. This hallway differed from the other areas of Gordian. It wasn't grand and lofty but gleaming white. The floor, ceiling, doors, and walls were all the same sterile color.

Third door on the left. There might be guards. An alarm will sound. Find the dagger and use it before Sampson gets there.

She found the door and put her finger above the lock-screen, then paused. Something nagged at her. Sampson's most valuable possession shouldn't be this accessible. She heard no sounds behind the door and saw no sign of the guards. Entry seemed too easy. Maybe Rex had been misinformed.

She'd come this far and shouldn't leave without being certain. She set her teeth and tapped in the code, expecting a shrill siren the moment it registered. But the door opened without a sound. A dim light flickered through the crack.

The door flung open, and strong hands seized her, pulling her in and yanking the hood from her head.

Guards! She wrestled with all her strength until a voice cut through the darkness, turning her blood cold.

"Welcome, Alina. We've been expecting you."

CHAPTER 8

L ight flooded the room, and Alina let out a startled cry.

Hundreds of monitors blinked around her. She glimpsed Rex's street, lit up in celebration with tangled lovers and wild dancers. Other screens revealed the inside of homes, the front gate of Gordian Palace, and the foyer with the exposed staircase she had just ascended. She swallowed.

Sampson, always watching. Even now, he glared at her as he ran his fingers along the hilt of a sheathed knife.

He stood up and walked to her. He lifted a long finger and stroked her cheek. She didn't blink.

"Well done," he whispered. "You played your part well."

She held her voice steady. "What are you talking about?"

"Crome, make sure her wrists are tight." The man holding her wrapped a rope around her wrists and fixed it into a hard knot. She winced.

A ping rang out. Sampson kept his eyes on Alina as he lifted a small panel and tapped it. "Yes?"

"Rex is in the dungeon. Everything went as planned."

Sampson flashed his white teeth. "Perfect."

He clicked off the screen. "Yes, well played. Although, I am a little disappointed. I expected more rebels to show up in a vain rescue attempt. I know Rex doesn't work alone."

Alina's nostrils flared, then her eyes darted to the knife in his hand.

Sampson raised the dagger. "If you think I'd leave this in a room available to anyone in my palace, you highly underestimate my intelligence."

Alina opened her mouth, but nothing came out.

"When I take you down to your friend Rex, you can tell him he's far too trusting. I also have my spies." Sampson smiled coldly.

Alina bit her tongue. *I walked right into a trap. I should've stopped when something felt wrong.* But if Sampson carried the dagger himself, no plan would've worked.

"Do you always carry that with you?" she asked.

"Oh no, that would be too dangerous. It travels around my palace, and security moves with it. *I am the only one who wields it.*" He returned the knife to its sheath on his belt. "That will do, Crome. I'll take her now."

He grabbed Alina's arm and pulled her out of the room and down a maze of hallways and stairs. As they moved deeper into the palace, the floor changed from marble to stone, and the light in the corridors dimmed. They reached a high arched door where Sampson tapped in a code, then entered a narrow stairwell. Sampson turned sideways as he descended, and Alina's shoulders brushed the walls. Her chest felt tight.

The tightness moved to her throat and closed in, like the stone around her. She wrenched out her arms to stop the enclosing walls, and the rope loosened and almost fell from her hands. Alina stiffened with shock, then lifted her chin and smiled. Either Crome didn't know how to tie a knot, or he'd helped her.

The passage opened into an empty antechamber, and Sampson turned, fixing his stern eyes on her as if waiting for her to speak. She didn't meet his glare but stared at the ground. Her hands would help her only if she caught him off guard.

Strange sounds echoed from the darkness: a deep, guttural growl, and an unintelligible chatter, like a woman speaking two octaves higher than normal. A man's voice sang a hollow, choppy song, as if something pounded his back. A cold chill tickled Alina's spine.

"Who are they?" she rasped.

Sampson's eyes flashed in the dim light. "Do you think I'd make life pleasant for my traitors? That with one painless swipe of this dagger, I'd send them to Carthem without paying for their crimes? Now, don't misunderstand me—the stories of Carthem are true. It *is* a terrifying place because *I* make it so. They suffer here, then are sent there to suffer more." He heaved an inflated sigh. "If people would just believe what I tell them—that they're lucky to live in Pria, life would be so much better for them."

"What can *you* do to them?" Alina scoffed. "They're immortal! You can't starve them or hurt them—they can't feel pain! What do you do—*bore* them to madness?" Her heart stopped as she spoke the words.

Sampson flashed a dark, knowing smile. "These people have been coddled their whole lives," he stressed. "They've had one thrill after another: party after party, tryst after tryst. They're accustomed to beautiful scenery and people. You put them in a dark place like this, by themselves, and before long they start to break down. You see, Alina, while I have full control over the body, I have yet to conquer the mind."

"I don't understand what you mean."

"I have created a true utopia where no one is in want. Physically speaking, that is. The needs of mortals are simple: they must eat, drink, and sleep. When these basic needs are met, as they are for immortals, they move onto more addictive, sensual needs: refreshment, entertainment, gratification for the eyes and body. If it's a carnal desire, Pria can grant it, but beyond those pleasures, things get tricky. Mental and emotional desires create chaos. To be a ruler with absolute power, one must control *all* the cravings of its subjects."

"I see," Alina realized. "You control them by focusing so much on carnal needs, they don't think about deeper ones."

Sampson chuckled. "Yes, but the best part is, everyone worships me as a wise and peaceful ruler. As long as I keep Pria pleasant and satisfying to their bodily pleasures, they rely on me. Instant gratification makes people weak—easy to govern and manipulate.

The unfortunate ones who end up here are begging for mercy within minutes. They promise not to think again if I let them go back to their lovely homes and shallow relationships. But do they ever leave after seeing things here?" He laughed darkly. "Of course not."

He noticed Alina's glare, and his features hardened. "My greatest obstacle can be my greatest weapon, when used wisely."

"And what's your greatest obstacle?" Alina asked.

"I've told you. *The mind.* It threatens me every day. Although I generally succeed in making people selfish and passive, occasionally one thinks outside the box. They believe something is missing in their lives, though they don't know what it is. They become increasingly dissatisfied until, before they know what happened, they're here in my dungeon begging to go home."

"And how is that your greatest weapon?" Alina hoped to keep him talking as she twisted the rope behind her into a ball.

He rolled his eyes. "Don't you get it? I meddle with their pampered brains. I can't hurt them physically, but it's easy to hurt them mentally. Mind torture is much more effective. I've learned quite a bit about the immortal mind through my experiments."

Alina took a step away from him. "How many prisoners do you have?"

"Oh, a decent number. But I can't hold them here forever. Carthem is vital—I need a place to send them if they're of no use to me. How else would I keep Pria from overpopulation? I send them to Carthem before they go completely mad, so they have some awareness of their suffering once they're there. Otherwise, what's the point? But I admit, once or twice I've waited too long." He chuckled.

Alina felt sick.

His smile vanished. "Now, are you ready to see your friends for the last time?"

She lowered her head and whispered, "Yes."

Darkness filled the hallway ahead, but as Sampson led her, dim lights brightened their path as if responding to a silent command. The wailing grew louder as they passed the small, barred windows.

Many hands shoved through them and Alina heard anxious, unintelligible requests. She clenched the rope at her back and looked ahead, too frightened to meet the feverish eyes around her, until she heard her name.

"Alina!" a woman's voice screamed, her white knuckles gripping the bars. Stunned, Alina stopped and stared at her.

"Do you know this woman?" asked Sampson.

Alina looked closer. She possessed the beauty of an immortal, but her eyes glared with the wildness of a madwoman. Alina knew those eyes back when they were gentle. Miss Vivian.

Alina faced Sampson. "Yes. She was my teacher. You've kept her locked up all these years?"

"She's a tough one to crack. Very valuable. I don't think I'll ever let her go. She has kept her wits much longer than most—as you see, she even remembers you."

Alina seethed as Sampson studied her with a smug, conceited smile. When he turned back down the corridor, she glanced once more at Miss Vivian. The hollow eyes stared at Alina, as if trying to remember how they knew her. "You're right. I'm Alina," she whispered, swallowing hard. "You were once the only friend I had."

She blinked back tears as she followed Sampson and focused her eyes on the dagger's hilt, secured at his waist.

Jade's scream erupted from a cell window. "NO! Alina, get out of here!"

Another face appeared across the hallway from her. Rex gripped the steel bars and clamped his teeth. "Not you, too," he squeezed out.

Alina wanted to run to Jade but couldn't turn away from Sampson. She needed to wait for the right moment.

"You aren't the only ones I've captured tonight," Sampson gloated. "I've saved the best for last."

"Who?" Alina sneered. "There's no one else I care about."

"Are you sure?" Sampson raised an eyebrow, hiding a smirk.

He pointed to the cell next to Rex. Alina glared at him as she shuffled to the door with her back against the wall. A boy huddled inside with his face hidden.

"Turn into the light," Sampson demanded. The prisoner shifted, and Alina started, almost betraying her loose hands.

"Zaiden!" she exclaimed. "What's he doing here? He hasn't done anything wrong!"

"Ask him yourself," Sampson responded.

Alina looked at Zaiden in shock. She could feel the disc inside the bodice of her gown, his life's story secure against her pounding heart. She hadn't expected to see him again, but now hope fluttered inside her. If she did this right, he could come to Carthem with her, and they would be the same: mortal and flawed.

"Zaiden?"

He didn't answer but stared at the ground in front of him. The light from the hallway cast a shadow under his eyebrows.

Alina whipped back to face Sampson. "Do you mean you imprisoned him because I—" She broke off. She couldn't confess her feelings, not where Zaiden could hear.

"Certainly not," Sampson chuckled, "though anyone who catches your eye is worth watching. We took him because he came here tonight. After he peeled Eris off, he followed you the entire way. We knew what he was doing, of course, but we humored him a bit before catching him. Too bad he didn't get a chance to rescue you."

She glowered at Sampson. Was he toying with her? Did Zaiden come to rescue her?

She peered back into his cell and found him staring hard at her, as if he wanted to memorize every part of her face. His gaze made her knees go weak, and she shuffled to maintain her balance.

"I'm sorry, Alina," Zaiden said.

Sampson smirked at her, reading every emotion on her flushed face. His haughty smile and the adrenaline from Zaiden's gaze gave her the push she needed.

She snatched the dagger from Sampson's waist and placed it against her wrist.

"Let them out. Now. Or I'll cut myself."

Sampson's eyes widened at the sight of her unbound hands. Then he went rigid and forced a laugh. "You wouldn't leave without your friends."

"Oh, yes she will!" Rex blurted out. "Do it, Alina!"

Panic flickered in Sampson's eyes. "If you choose to leave Pria now," his voice trembled, "then they never will. They'll be driven to madness in these cells, with no escape. Forever."

"Don't listen to him, Alina," Jade insisted. "Just do it."

Alina shook, but held the blade steady. She knew what Rex told her to do. She had to get to Carthem, on her own if she must. But she couldn't go without them. Not while she could see them and hear their voices.

"Let's come to an agreement," Sampson said smoothly.

"Alina," Rex begged. "Please go, before he tricks you out of it. Don't worry about us!"

Alina stared at Sampson. She could see the fear in his eyes.

"I have a proposal for you," he said in a honeyed voice. "You stay here with me and share my power. I'm at your mercy. You know I'll do anything to protect you. I'll destroy the machine—come with me now and watch me. You'll have me in the palm of your hand. I can make you famous, beautiful—whatever you like."

Alina laughed. "Remember my 'pathetic act'? You know I hate Pria and care nothing about being famous."

"You don't want to go to Carthem," he said. "Trust me."

"And why wouldn't I?"

He grinned smugly. "There's no one there for you. Your father is dead. I killed him myself."

Her heart paused, but she didn't move. "Unlock all of them," she demanded. "Then we'll talk about this proposal."

Sampson set his jaw and glared at her.

"NOW!" she screamed, her knuckles turning white around the dagger's hilt.

He lurched forward and punched the code on Rex's cell, then

moved to Jade's and Zaiden's cells. Alina didn't take her eyes off Sampson, but from the corner of her eye she saw Rex and Jade join her in the corridor. As Zaiden exited his cell, her eyes flickered in his direction.

Sampson pounced on her and she leaped back, thrusting the dagger at him. He dodged it, and she ducked and spun around, swiping the legs of Rex, Jade, and Zaiden. She felt Sampson's fierce hands grasp her hair and yank her back, and as the dagger fell from her hands, she stretched out her leg to catch it. The blade grazed her ankle before clanging to the ground.

Sampson's eyes widened in horror and his scream filled the dungeon. He fumbled for the dagger and lunged at Alina, but she felt nothing. He looked beyond her, and his lips twisted into a triumphant grin—the last view she saw before everything went dark.

CHAPTER
9

A sharp burst of light flashed around Alina. She felt the comfort before she opened her eyes—a warm tingling in her veins that invigorated her. She blinked twice, sprang to her feet, and found herself in a field of tall, wiry grass. The wildflowers were pale compared to the vibrant ones of Pria, and the sky was a bleak gray, but Alina considered it the most beautiful place she'd ever seen. Carthem had a raw, unrefined beauty, accepting her as one of its own.

A deep moan broke her from her reverie. Rex writhed in the grass, blood saturating the leg of his uniform. Jade lay still, the blood from her wound trickling through a tear on her dress.

"Rex, Jade, are you okay?" Alina asked. She glanced around. "Where's Zaiden?"

She dropped to the ground and rolled Jade onto her back, then gasped at her chalky white face.

"Jade!" Alina screamed, shaking her.

Jade gave a soft mumble, and Alina pressed her hand over her heart. "What do you need?" she asked.

"Water," Jade whispered.

Alina looked around. They would have to walk to find some. She cradled Jade's head in her lap. "We'll get some. I'll go, or Rex—"

Rex interrupted her with a loud shriek. She jumped, bouncing Jade's head. "What is it, Rex?"

He was on his back with his eyes closed, releasing a low, continuous moan.

"Are you okay?" Alina asked him.

He opened one eye. "I think I'm dying."

"What do you mean?"

He sat up and coughed, hacking dramatically, then collapsed back on the ground. "My mouth is sticky—it must be bleeding! And my leg—" he paused, trying to find the right word. "It *hurts*! I think you cut it off! You sliced me too hard and my leg is gone!"

Alina rolled her eyes and smoothed Jade's hair. "Sorry, Jade. I thought it was something more urgent."

"What?" Rex hollered. "This *is* urgent! I—" A look of terror crossed his face. "I'll never walk again!"

"Rex," Alina said, but he couldn't hear her through his wailing.

"REX!"

He stopped. Alina spoke calmly. "Your leg is fine; it's just a cut. And the stickiness in your mouth means you're thirsty." She stifled a laugh. "You've been watching too many horror shows."

Rex cracked his eyes open to glare at her. "Have not," he mumbled.

"Jade needs water, too, and she seems worse than you, if you can believe it. Zaiden's not here; do you think he ended up somewhere else?"

Rex pushed himself to a sitting position and looked around. "Are you sure you cut him?"

Alina stiffened. "What do you mean? I sliced him, like you two."

"Did the dagger break the skin?"

"I heard something tear, it must have—"

"Maybe it tore only his pants."

Alina stood up and looked around, chewing her lip. "No. You're wrong—he was right there. I felt the blade cut something." She closed her eyes and pictured herself swiping Rex, Jade, and then Zaiden. Sampson pulled her hair, and she stuck out her ankle to catch the blade. Zaiden was standing next to her—no, behind her.

Then Sampson flashed his horrible smirk. As she faded from Pria, he noticed Zaiden behind her, solid and present as ever. Zaiden wasn't as valuable as Alina, but Sampson could make good use of him.

Her heart tightened with panic. "Y-you don't think he might've landed somewhere else?"

"I don't see how," Rex said. "We all came here. He should be with us."

Alina's legs shook beneath her. She dropped to the ground and pulled her knees to her chest, hiding her face in her arms.

Zaiden risked everything to follow her when she was taken. He had looked at her from his cell as if—she wanted to believe—he felt something for her. And she'd left him in Sampson's dungeon, where he'd be mentally tortured until—no, she couldn't bear the thought. Tears sprang to her eyes.

Rex put a hand on her shoulder. "I'm sorry, Alina. He seemed like a great guy. He showed a lot of courage following you to Gordian." He gave her a playful nudge. "Showed a lot of interest in you, too."

Alina burst into tears. Rex coughed.

"Sorry, what I meant to say—he's a smart guy. He may still get here. There are rebel spies working at Gordian who can help him."

"You think so?"

"Yes," he affirmed. "It's very possible."

She wiped her eyes and looked at Jade. "Let's get moving. Jade is too weak to walk. Can you carry her?"

"I think so. Let's look for water. I'm so thirsty, and this heat might be the death of me. I remember hearing how hot the sun is here, but I didn't know it was a big ball of fire that would burn the flesh right off my bones."

Alina looked at him, astonished. "You're hot?"

Rex scowled. "Don't tell me you feel all cool and comfortable in that heavy jumpsuit, with this brutal sun beating down on us."

"Actually—I do." She paused. "In fact, I feel the best I have in my life. *And* I'm wearing a tight gown under this suit."

Rex stared at her with wide eyes, then glanced at her legs. "Where did you cut yourself? Where's the blood?"

She looked down, pulling up the leg of her jumpsuit. There was no trace of a cut.

Rex gasped. "Alina!"

She jumped. "What?"

"The dagger changed you."

"What do you mean?"

"You're immortal!"

Her jaw dropped. "No—" She flipped her hands in front of her as she examined them, then looked down at her legs. "I can't be."

"It's the only explanation."

"Am I really beautiful, then?"

Rex grinned. "Do you mean in that perfect, Prian way? Hmm, it's hard to tell." He studied her for a moment. "It could be a gradual process. Your blemishes are gone, for one."

Alina ran her fingers over her face. She felt comfortable and contented. Not a pain or itch irritated her.

A bead of sweat dripped from Rex's scalp as he struggled to lift Jade. "I'll carry her," Alina offered. Jade gave a soft moan as Alina pulled her onto her back.

"Where should we go?" Rex asked.

"To the trees. There should be water next to growing things, don't you think?"

He shrugged. "Sounds good to me."

They walked in silence. Rex seemed too labored to speak. When they reached the shade, he leaned against a tree, took a long breath and sat down. Alina set Jade beside him.

"I'm going to have a look around," she said. "You stay with Jade and rest."

Rex gripped her arm. "Don't go far! People get lost and die in the woods."

Alina turned to him, surprised by the fear in his voice. Rex, who was scarcely afraid of Sampson himself, was terrified.

She gave him an encouraging smile. "Don't worry, I won't go out of hearing distance. Then I can call for you if I can't find my way back."

He nodded. "Hurry."

She walked through the forest, sticks snapping at her feet. Sampson's words echoed through her mind: *Carthem is dangerous, mostly because I make it so.* She thought of the creatures in the Gordian laboratories. Rex shouldn't be left alone with Jade for long; he wouldn't respond well to terrors like those. She moved faster, trusting his scream to alert her if needed.

The trees' bark flaked from the trunks like a fruit peel, so different from the smooth, polished wood of Prian trees. She found no signs of water. They would have to travel farther. As she turned back, her eye caught a twitch on the forest floor.

She stared at the ground. Could rocks move here? She crouched down and studied the gray, smooth stone, so well-proportioned it stood out from the jagged rocks around it. After several minutes with no movement, she decided she must have imagined it and stood up to leave.

Something whistled and bounced off her forehead. A second whistle followed, hitting her chest. She spun around and saw the hard shell sinking back to the earth.

The rock was alive! She dropped to her knees, scanning the ground for what had hit her. Two long, gray quills lay in the dirt, the tips oozing a red liquid, like blood. She picked them up and tapped the tips with her finger. They seemed sharp, and heavy for their size. With their speed, they could pierce any mortal to the heart.

She slid them into her pocket, then scrambled to her feet and ran back to Rex.

He sat with Jade's head in his lap. "What did you find?" he asked.

"There's something out there that shoots deadly quills! It looks like a rock but has an outer shell that lifts up when it shoots—and it seems to sense movement!"

Rex stared at her with wide eyes. She nodded. "This wilderness is dangerous. Sampson sends in creatures from his laboratories. I saw some of them—one left me so terrified I couldn't move."

"We need to find Stormport soon then, and water and food. Jade isn't well. The transition has put her in some state of shock."

"What's Stormport?"

"The nearest town to the portal."

"Do you know how to get there?"

"No."

Jade stirred, and Alina knelt beside her. "How do you feel, Jade?"

"You have to leave me," she mumbled.

Alina looked at Rex. "Does she understand what's going on?" she whispered.

He furrowed his brow as he looked at her, then gasped. "The surveillance device! Sampson could be watching us! And he may send something in to kill us."

"But the last thing he wants to do is kill me—"

"Shhh!" Rex hissed. "He can probably hear everything we say. She's right. She can't stay with us. It'll be too hard to keep our plans secret."

"But we can't abandon her, she'll die!"

Jade reached for Rex's hand. "Don't worry about me. I'm a survivor." Rex gazed at her, tears glistening in his eyes.

Alina shook her head. "We can't leave her. She survived Sampson's cruelty, yes, but surviving Carthem is different. No one can make it here alone."

Rex chewed his lower lip. "She could close her eyes the whole time, but Sampson could still hear what we say."

"Then we don't speak to her, or to each other, while she's near. We move away when we need to discuss our plans. It'll work." Alina turned to her. "Can you do that, Jade?"

She closed her eyes and nodded.

"Will you carry her this time?" Alina whispered to Rex. "I want to walk a few steps in front to be a shield. We have no idea what's out there."

"Sounds like a good idea," he answered, and grunted as he hoisted Jade onto his back. "I have this gnawing pain in my stomach. Am I hungry?"

"Yes, most likely," Alina answered. "The pangs get worse the longer you wait to eat."

"How bad can it get?" Rex sounded worried.

She shrugged. "I don't know. I never went long without eating in Pria. Food was always around."

"Do you know what can or can't be eaten around here?"

Alina looked around. "Not really."

"What about the leaves on the trees?"

"Maybe, but I suggest looking for fruit first."

They edged through the trees, Alina scanning the horizon for signs of movement. Jade looked pale as she clung to Rex's back. He kept his eyes on the ground, his brow wrinkled. Jade could be dying, but Rex seemed more fixed on his hunger pains.

After several minutes, they reached the top of an incline, and Alina heard rushing water in the ravine below. She raced down the slope toward the sound.

Large rocks broke the surface of the shallow river, clear enough to see the stony bottom. "Come, Rex!" she called.

Rex shrieked behind her and a cascade of pebbles tumbled down the slope. "HELP!"

Alina dashed up to where he and Jade lay motionless on the hill.

"If I move, I'll fall," Rex whimpered, barely moving his mouth. Alina suppressed a laugh.

"It's okay. I got you." She picked up Jade and put her on her back, then reached out to Rex. He lifted his hand, then screamed as the pebbles slipped from under him and he tumbled down to the riverbank.

He lay on his back and pointed up at Alina. "Don't ever run off like that again!"

"Sorry," she called. He wobbled as he stood and brushed the dirt from his clothes.

"Jade, we have some water for you," Alina said as she reached the bank. "We don't have anything to scoop it with. We'll have to help her," she told Rex.

Rex helped Jade lie down near the stream and then flopped onto his belly and brought his cupped hands to her mouth.

Alina walked along the bank, eyeing a clump of prickly bushes with flecks of red inside the leaves. She thrust her hands into the center and felt around, then pulled out a handful of berries. She tasted one and made a face.

She brought them to Rex. "I found these. Do you want to try them?"

Although he'd complained of his starving belly only minutes before, Rex backed away from her outstretched palm. "Are they safe?"

Alina shrugged. "How should I know? Anything here can kill you, I suppose. But who knows how long it will take us to find Stormport? Do you want to be hungry the whole way?"

"I'll have some," said Jade, holding out her hand. Alina gave her a few berries.

"Jade, no!" Rex shrieked. He flinched as the berries ruptured under her teeth, then grabbed her arm. "Do you feel sick? Is your stomach going to explode? Your eyes are closed! Are you dying?"

"Rex, I'm supposed to keep my eyes closed, remember?"

Alina stifled a giggle. Jade couldn't contain herself, and soon the two of them roared with laughter. Jade wiped a tear from her cheek. Rex glared and frowned.

"I'm fine, Rex. They aren't bad. Why don't you try some?" Jade suggested.

He took a berry from Alina, studied it for a moment, then popped it in his mouth. He spat the pulp out a few seconds later, his tongue hanging over his lips.

"That's the worst thing I've ever put in my mouth! How can you eat those?"

"Yes, they're nothing like Prian fruit," said Alina. "I suppose we'll have to get used to lots of changes here."

"Easy for you to say," Rex grumbled. "You don't have to eat them if you don't want to."

"True, but I think since you *have* to eat them, you'll come to like them," Alina replied. She looked around. "We should follow the stream so we have water, and it will probably lead us to Stormport."

"Good idea, Alina," said Jade. "I feel better now I've had some water. Are there any more berries?"

"There's plenty along the river," Alina answered. "Another reason to stay near it. However, we may run into more creatures." She dropped her voice as she addressed Rex. "Can you lead Jade? I still want to be a shield in case something happens."

Rex chuckled. "I'm sure Sampson hadn't planned on this."

"Does this mean I'm no longer a threat? Did we solve his biggest problem?" Alina asked.

Rex frowned. "We'll talk later, when Jade isn't around."

"You mean when *Sampson* isn't around." Alina pinched her lips together. "I hate the control he has over her."

"Maybe something can be done about that here."

They continued along the path, Rex leading Jade as she walked with her eyes closed. Alina offered to carry her, since they'd seen no creatures, when a splash of water and a rustle in the bushes stopped them in their tracks.

Alina took out the quills from her pocket. She didn't know how she'd use them, but they were better than nothing.

After a long silence, she heard a hard gulp, and the sputter of coughing. *I've done that before. Water down the wrong part of the throat. Do animals cough?*

"Who's there?" she called out.

Another long pause followed, then something rose from the bushes. Rex gasped.

"Stan?" Rex narrowed his eyes. "Is that you?"

The pale, skinny man looked frightened. He gave a small nod.

"What are you doing here?"

Stan coughed again. "S-Sampson sent me here when he found out I h-helped you," he stammered.

Rex started toward him. "Are you okay?"

"Yes, I'm fine," he snapped. "I just have the jitters. I've seen some crazy things already. When I heard you approaching, I thought it was more wild creatures."

"Well," Rex chuckled, "we *are* pretty wild, traveling through the woods like this. But I'm sure we're safer in a group, so why don't you join us?"

"Rex," Alina interrupted. "Can I talk to you for a minute? In private?"

He raised his eyebrows. "Okay."

Rex followed her to a nearby tree, where she turned to him and dropped her voice. "I haven't told you what happened after we separated at Gordian. Sampson was waiting for me in the control room. He said he had spies, implying whoever helped you find me in Gordian was actually working for him. Would that be Stan?"

Rex frowned. "Yes. He gave me the directions and codes to the control room."

"Then we can't trust him. What do you think he's doing here? Did he upset Sampson, or is there another reason?"

Rex's nostrils flared. He puffed up his chest and marched back to Stan.

"Tell me the truth, Stan," he demanded. "Are you working for Sampson?"

Stan's eyes widened. "No! No," he repeated. "I mean, it's not what you think." He cleared his throat. "I've, uh, been playing both sides to help the resistance—"

Rex interrupted Stan by slamming his fist into his jaw. As they both bellowed in pain, Alina couldn't tell if the punch hurt Stan or Rex more.

"Stop, Rex," said Jade, her eyes closed. "Let him explain."

"He almost ruined everything!" Rex hollered, massaging his

knuckles. "Alina was captured, we were imprisoned, and Zaiden left behind—"

"And we're here!" Jade cut in. "We made it! Alina might be here by herself if Sampson hadn't caught her. I think the scheme worked better than we'd hoped. You know the odds we had against us. If he's not a traitor" —she nodded in Stan's direction— "then we should thank him."

Alina turned toward Stan. "We're interested in hearing your explanation."

A stream of blood trickled from Stan's mouth as he spoke. "I'm a loyal member of the resistance, I swear it." He looked at Rex. "Do you know what Sampson did to Mira? All these years I thought she'd been sent to Carthem—he had her in his dungeons!" His voice trembled. "I've been spying on him for years now in hopes of finding her. I misled you because he was watching me as I wrote the instructions. I didn't want to blow my cover."

"What—so it doesn't matter who gets locked up in Gordian as long as your *cover* is safe?" Rex snapped.

"I'm sorry! I didn't know what to do. I hoped things would turn out okay, and they did—like Jade said! How did you escape, anyway?"

"Alina is brilliant," Jade said, grinning.

"Sampson was waiting in the control room when I arrived. He said you were spying for him," Alina said, ignoring his question.

"That's what *he* thought. Besides, why else would I be here?"

"Good question," said Rex. "Why *did* Sampson send you here?"

"He found out I led you to Alina's room in the laboratories, though I don't know how. He was so angry, he cut me with the dagger almost the moment he saw me." Stan squirmed under Rex's eye. "Come on! I led you to Alina, didn't I? Can I still tag along with you?" He glanced at Alina and Jade.

Rex glared at him. "Fine, but don't expect any of us to talk to you."

"Fair enough," he said.

"Let him carry Jade for awhile," said Alina.

"No way," Rex scoffed. "He'll plunge some secret knife into her the minute our backs are turned. He was probably sent here to finish us off."

Stan marched over to Jade and lifted her onto his back, then glowered at Rex. "If I kill her, you can kill me. You know I don't stand a chance against you and an immortal."

Rex stole a glance at Alina. "Uh—what are you talking about?"

"Come on, Rex," Stan said, wiping his brow. "I've lived with immortals for two hundred years, and you think I wouldn't recognize one? Look at her, she's gorgeous!"

Alina blushed to the roots of her hair, which embarrassed her further. Immortals were extra attractive when they blushed.

"I suppose if you won't risk your cover in Pria, you won't risk your life in Carthem," Rex said bitterly. He turned to Alina and muttered under his breath, "But I still don't trust him."

"We'll keep an eye on him," Alina whispered. Stan marched ahead of them with Jade on his back. He seemed well recovered from the edginess he had when they first found him. Alina frowned.

THEY TRAVELED INTO THE EVENING, and when the sky grew too dark for them to follow the river, Rex and Alina decided to rest for the night and continue the search for Stormport in the morning.

"It's fortunate we haven't met any Prian creatures," Alina said.

"Yes, but also peculiar," Rex pointed out.

"It's also a good thing I don't sleep. I can keep watch."

Rex nodded, then sighed.

"What's worrying you?"

"Oh, nothing. I just wish there was something to eat besides berries."

Jade felt her way to the ground, eyes still closed. In all of their travels, she hadn't peeked once.

"Are you hungry?" Alina asked her.

"I'll have a few more berries, if there are some."

"*Please*, take them all," Rex said as he sprawled out on the ground and rested his head on a log. He closed his eyes, and before long, began to squirm. "How am I ever going to fall asleep here?"

Alina smiled. "Not like sleeping on the night of Genesis, is it?"

He rolled to his side. "What I'd give for a pillow."

Stan lay down on the dirt, rested his head on his arm, and didn't move again. After a few minutes, a harsh noise vibrated through his nose at regular intervals.

Rex sat up in horror. "What's that?"

"Mortals breathe like that when they sleep sometimes," Jade answered. "I heard Alina do it from time to time."

Alina grimaced. "I sounded like *that*?"

"Heavens, no. You were soft and dainty. Stan sounds—"

"Foul," Rex answered. He rolled over and moaned. "I'll never sleep tonight."

"How about you, Jade?" Alina asked.

"I'm fine," she said, and yawned. "This spot of dirt is softer than it looks." But she writhed for a few minutes before settling down.

"You're always so positive, Jade."

"That's not a bad thing, is it?"

"No," Rex spoke up. "In fact, it might save us."

AN HOUR LATER, after Jade had fallen asleep, Alina listened to Rex wiggling on the ground and thought it safe to ask him a question.

"Rex?"

He grunted as he shifted. "Yeah?"

"What did Sampson mean back in the dungeon, about my father being dead? What was he talking about?"

Rex stopped moving and went quiet for a moment.

"Do you know what a father is?" he asked.

"I've only heard Sampson referred to as Father. That's why I'm confused."

Rex pulled himself to a sitting position against the log. "Remember Alina, you were *born*, not manufactured in the Gordian laboratories. You had a real mother and father, something no one in Pria can claim, except Sampson himself." He paused, and a broad smile stretched across his face. "It's called a family."

"A family?"

Rex went on, as if he didn't hear her. "Camden told me about families at times, when it didn't pain him to talk about them. He wondered why Sampson didn't banish him from Pria sooner, considering the threat he was."

"Why was he a threat?"

"He knew the truth about life in Carthem, before Pria."

"What do you mean?"

"You've been taught Carthem is an awful place. But this world has many beautiful things that can't be experienced in Pria. Camden had a wife and family when he lived here." He paused. "Do you know what a wife is?"

"No."

"Of course not, because you've never heard of marriage. Here in Carthem, when a man and a woman love each other, they get married. I suppose it's similar to how women and men live together in Pria, except, as Camden explained, marriage requires commitment—solemn vows of loyalty. The two are bound together until one of them dies, or at least they're supposed to be. One of Sampson's arguments in favor of dissolving the family unit was it created so much heartache. People couldn't stay true to each other—they were too selfish. He claimed it was better not to make the vows in the first place so they couldn't be broken."

Rex smiled again. "But Camden's marriage was a happy one. He got emotional when he spoke of his wife, so he didn't share much. I always wanted to hear more, though. I could tell his relationship with her was different."

"From what?"

"Well, from those in Pria. People there can't think beyond themselves. They go from lover to lover without moving past the physical aspect of love. Sure, that part is fun, but passion can't sustain itself forever—believe me, I've tried. Camden never had a relationship in all his years in Pria. How could he, when he knew what real love was like?" Rex shook his head. "I'm afraid I couldn't settle for a shallow relationship either. Not that I didn't try."

Alina asked, "Is it true Sampson killed my father?"

Rex paused. "I don't know. But—" he took a deep breath, "most likely."

"And my mother?"

In the darkness, Rex crossed his arms and rubbed them. "She didn't make it."

CHAPTER 10

Rex finally drifted to sleep, and though Alina could see well in the dark, nothing could stave off the boredom. She kept her eyes peeled for any movement around them, but the night was still. How strange that the trip had been uneventful. Maybe Sampson didn't have as much power here as he claimed. The thought lifted her spirits.

Stan's snoring halted, and he shifted on the ground. Alina glanced in his direction and saw him sitting up.

"Alina, are you there?" he whispered harshly.

"Yes, I'm here."

"Oh, wow, I can't see a thing—can you see me?"

"Yes. My eyes are pretty good in the dark."

"In that case, I think I'll go behind a tree to do my business. Can you direct me?"

"Come on, Stan," she rolled her eyes. "I won't watch you."

"No, no, I'm new at this, and it makes me self-conscious. I need to know no one can see me."

She sighed. "Fine. Stand up and move to your left. Start walking straight. Good. Now stop. Reach out to your right and you'll feel a tree."

He found the trunk. "Thanks," he said, and disappeared behind the tree. After a moment, Alina heard the sound of urine hitting the ground.

She expected he'd need help walking back, and as she waited, she ran her hands through her hair. The fine strands slid through her fingers like silk. No matter what Rex said, she looked different. Her legs were trimmer, especially around her thighs. Her face felt smooth, without blemishes, and her teeth straight and even. She chewed on her bottom lip, wishing she had a mirror.

After several minutes with no sound from Stan, she looked at his tree. What was he doing?

"Stan, are you okay?"

Silence.

"Stan?" she called louder. When he didn't answer, she stood up, feeling nervous. She'd heard nothing, not even a rustle since the urine stopped. She crept toward the tree.

"Stan, you still there?"

She stepped over a rock and peeked around his tree. No one was there.

"Stan!" she called out. She scanned the area, then looked at the ground. She saw a wet spot in the dirt, the only indication he'd been there at all.

Alina hurried back to the others, trembling. What happened to him? She thought of waking Rex but decided not to. It had taken him so long to fall asleep, and besides, what could they do? They couldn't search in the dark, and she wouldn't leave them alone. They'd have to wait until morning.

She searched the woods for any sign of movement. Something dangerous could be lurking nearby, ready to take those she most loved. She might not be able to protect them.

She looked at the dark sky, littered with stars. *Come quickly, morning.*

CHAPTER 11

She didn't have to wait long. Within an hour the sky brightened, and Alina relaxed her shoulders. They'd encountered no serious dangers so far. Perhaps Sampson thought she was mortal and wanted her kept from harm. She clung to the thought.

Rex and Jade moaned and stirred in their sleep as if realizing their discomfort. Alina studied them as the light touched their faces. They looked so different from their immortal selves. Jade's hair twisted in tangles around her face, and her features seemed slightly unbalanced. Rex's face had turned cherry red from the sun. Freckles dotted his arms and hands.

Rex opened his eyes and grimaced as he sat up. "Wow, that sleep did nothing for me. I feel worse than before. Every part of my body hurts."

"Stan disappeared in the night," Alina blurted out.

He snapped up his head. "*What?*"

She explained what happened. He stared at her with wide eyes. "Show me where you last saw him."

They walked to the tree, examining the area around it. "Hmm," Rex said. "Nothing looks out of the ordinary."

"I know. It's so odd," she said.

A rustle shook the bushes not far from them. They heard a soft growling noise. Alina met Rex's eyes.

"Up a tree. Quickly."

Rex dashed to Jade and yanked her up, shaking her from her restless sleep. "Which tree?" he hissed.

"Right here—I'll push you both up." Alina heard the low growl again. "Hurry!"

"What's going on—" Jade started.

Alina boosted Rex to the nearest branch then pushed Jade up. "Reach out, Jade!" Alina shrieked. "Grab his hand!"

Something tore through the dirt behind them, snarling. Alina forgot about her invincibility and screamed as she scaled the trunk, grabbing branches and hauling herself up. The creature snapped at her heels.

Rex froze in place. "What in Sampson's name *is* that thing?" he whispered.

Alina didn't look down but grabbed Jade and pulled her higher into the tree. "Keep moving, Rex! Is it climbing?"

"No, but it's trying to. It's jumping and clawing the trunk."

Alina looked down at the creature and gasped. A barbed snout and sharp fangs gnashed at her below its bloodshot eyeballs.

"What is it?" Jade hissed, her eyes closed.

"Be glad you can't see it!" Rex replied.

"It's huge," Alina said. "And look, its tail is spikier than its nose!"

"At least it can't seem to climb."

The creature lifted its head and let out a long, chilling howl. "What's it doing?" asked Alina in a hushed voice.

They heard a matching howl in the distance, and minutes later, an identical creature ripped across the ground and jumped on the other's back. It sprung on its sinewy legs and clawed at the trunk, growling.

"They're working together!" Rex exclaimed in horror.

"How fast can you run?" Alina asked him.

"What—do you think we can outrun them?"

"No, I'm sure we can't. But I have these." She pulled out the quills from her pocket. "Maybe these will hurt them. Once they're out of our path, we'll have to jump and run along the river as fast as we can. I'll carry Jade."

He nodded. "Something tells me our safe travels are over. We need to get to Stormport as soon as we can."

"I'll drop the quills, and if they work, then we jump from this tree and run. Let's hope nothing else meets us. Got it?"

Rex darted his eyes around the base of the tree, then nodded again. "Whenever you're ready."

She took one of the quills between her thumb and forefinger, aimed, and shot it toward the creatures. It whizzed through the air and hit the first one on the nose. They heard a guttural groan as it tumbled backward onto the ground and went still.

"Hurry—the other one!" Rex ordered. She leaned forward and pitched the quill. The creature hissed as it pierced its eyeball.

"Go!" Alina shrieked. Rex slid down the tree and jumped over the creatures, and Alina leaped into the air with Jade on her back. After landing on her feet, she took off running.

Rex kept up with Alina at first, but after a minute, started to lag behind. "Times...like this...miss being...immortal," he panted. After a few minutes he stopped and bent over, clutching his side. "Can we rest for a moment?" he asked.

"Okay," Alina agreed, glancing around them. "I wish I could carry both of you. It's not that I get tired—I don't know if there's enough room on my back."

Rex waved a dismissive hand. "I'll be fine in a minute." But he held his stomach and winced. "If I could just get some decent food to eat!" he mumbled.

"We can't be too far," Alina reassured him. "If only we knew which way—hey, do you feel something?"

A breeze picked up, rustling the branches and blowing dirt from the forest floor. Alina looked into the wind. A dark shadow crept through the woods, clouding the trees from view.

"What *is* that?" Rex croaked.

"Jump on my back," Alina ordered, and he obeyed. "Jade, open your eyes and jump on Rex's back. Hurry!"

They both leaped on and clutched her, and Alina broke into a sprint. She moved ahead of the shadow until Jade shouted, "I'm slipping!"

Alina slowed to help Jade regain her grip. The mist moved closer, billowing like a massive storm cloud.

She couldn't run fast enough and keep them on. As the vapor surrounded them, Alina felt Rex and Jade stiffen on her back.

"I'm burning!" Rex screamed. "Help! Oh, Alina help!"

She gritted her teeth and ran faster, tears streaming down her cheeks. Rex's scream halted in his throat as they writhed and groaned on her back. Alina ran harder until unexpectedly, the forest cleared. Through the vapor around her, she could see buildings and homes on the horizon.

"We're here! We made it to Stormport!" Alina cried.

Rex and Jade didn't answer but slid down her spine, no longer trying to hold on.

CHAPTER 12

A moment before she reached the city, Alina felt something vibrate through her veins like an electric charge. The vapor disappeared and a shrill siren rang out just as Rex and Jade fell to the ground. Rex gasped for breath, but Jade lay stiff and motionless.

"Help!" Alina screamed as two men raced toward her from the street.

"Don't move!" one of them yelled.

Alina obeyed but spoke as they approached. "We need help. Please!"

They eyed her suspiciously, then glared at Rex and Jade. "Two refugees with a spy. An interesting combination," one of them muttered.

The other man spoke to Alina. "You'll come with us and do exactly what we say, or we'll stun you as well." He gestured to Jade. Alina stared at the men, puzzled.

They lifted Jade and carried her to the street. Alina picked up Rex and put him on her back. "Rex," she whispered. "Are you okay?"

He gave a low moan. "My leg."

Alina looked at his leg and gasped. The wound from the dagger was green and frothy, and his leg was beginning to swell. She ran to catch up with the men.

"Please, my friend here is hurt. He needs help."

"Of course he's hurt! You ran through the black mist!" one of them exclaimed. "How did *you* come out okay?"

"What's the black mist?"

The man studied her. "You must be fresh from Pria."

She nodded. "We are."

They reached the street and he opened the door to a small car. "Get in," he commanded. Alina helped Rex inside, and they pulled Jade across their laps.

"Is she going to be okay?" Alina asked.

"Depends on why she's here," he said, slamming the door. The men slid into the two front seats.

Alina jumped when the vehicle moved, jerking them almost out of their seats. A low rattling noise grew louder as the car gained speed. It didn't glide above ground like the sleek aircars of Pria. The men's heavy silence didn't welcome conversation, so Alina said nothing but looked at Rex. He rested his head against the window and breathed heavy with his eyes closed. Every few seconds he held his breath and tightened his muscles. "It hurts so bad," he groaned. His leg had doubled in size, stretching the fabric of his uniform.

Alina took his hand. "Hang on, Rex. We're in Stormport."

He gave a soft but eager grunt.

Alina gaped out the window as they drove through the streets. Carthem wasn't what she expected. Her school teachers claimed everyone had brown teeth and wild hair and lived in run-down shacks. But the homes were well kept and pleasing, though much smaller than those in Pria.

People were outside working in the yard and playing with animals, and groups of children climbed trees and threw balls to each other. A man and woman sat on a bench near the street, tickling a baby on the woman's lap.

Alina elbowed Rex. "Look," she whispered. "It's a family."

Rex opened his eyes. "Where?"

She pointed, and he stared until they passed. Then he let out a small sigh. "Are we really here?"

"Yes."

He closed his eyes and licked his cracked lips. "Carthem is the most beautiful place I've ever seen."

Alina smiled. "But the sky isn't bright blue. There are no perfect, six-petaled flowers. The homes are small, and the people—well, they're nothing to look at."

Rex gave a weak snort. "Don't remind me of that accursed place. Mortality is a rough adjustment, no doubt," he stiffened in pain, "but it's paradise compared to my life in Pria."

"Don't talk, Rex, save your energy," Alina said, but she reflected on his words. Pria, with all its pleasure and beauty, seemed the perfect paradise. But for Rex and many others, freedom made a paradise. Freedom to choose love, pain—even death.

Yet that same freedom brought chaos, suffering, illness, and heartache.

On the edge of the street, a child stumbled and fell on the gravel. As he started to cry, a woman helped him up and held him close, smoothing his hair with her hand. Alina remembered Jade, ten years earlier, doing the same for her. Tears came to her eyes. She'd choose the chaos any day if it created more of those memories.

THE MEN PARKED the car next to a large building, then stepped out and opened the back doors. Jade was still unconscious.

"Please, let me carry her," Alina begged. "She's not well."

"*We* will carry her," one of them snapped. They picked her up and motioned for Alina to follow. She ran around the car and helped Rex out, then lifted him onto her back.

They walked through double glass doors into the building, where a woman stood up from behind a desk.

"Is everything okay?" she asked.

"Call Baylor and Dr. Scott and send them to the debriefing room immediately," one of the men said. The woman nodded and sat down.

Alina followed them down a hallway and into a small room, where three metal chairs surrounded a small table. "Stand against the wall," they ordered.

Alina complied, still carrying Rex, who felt heavy and limp on her back. One of the men pulled a small square device from his pocket and scanned it an inch above Rex's body. After a satisfied grunt, he turned to Alina and did the same. The device gave a loud, long beep. He scratched his head as he read something on the screen. "Interesting," he murmured. He nodded to the man holding Jade and they started from the room, taking her with them.

"Wait—" Alina called out. They responded by slamming the door behind them.

Trembling, she placed Rex on a chair and propped his leg up, then knelt down next to him.

"How are you feeling?"

He made a face. "Not my best. My leg—"

A man interrupted them by barging into the room. Dressed in white with a circular tool dangling around his neck, he observed Rex for a moment, then set a leather bag on the table and rummaged through it.

He knelt on the floor next to Alina and cut Rex's pants with scissors, then dripped a purple liquid onto his leg. Rex gave a soft moan, and the man began wrapping the leg with a bandage.

"I'm Dr. Scott," he said. "Don't worry, you're going to be fine."

Alina relaxed a little. "What did that black mist do?"

"It's a lethal gas that infects any opening in the body. Usually it goes straight into the lungs. Most don't survive. He was lucky it wasn't worse."

Alina went pale. "Our other friend—where have they taken her?"

"To the hospital wing."

"Is she okay?"

"I don't know. I'm going now to examine her." He stood up and handed Alina a vial of purple liquid. "This medicine treats the infection. Have him put it on his leg every day for a week. Here are some clean bandages."

"Thank you," Alina said. He nodded, grabbed his bag and left the room.

Alina took Rex's hand. "How do you feel?"

He blinked his eyes. "Much better."

"They took Jade to the hospital wing. I'm worried about her."

Rex licked his lips. "It's okay, I'm sure they're helping her. We're lucky to be here. Their security seems strong—" he broke off as the door opened again and a tall, black-skinned man entered. Alina gave a small gasp. She'd never seen someone without hair before. Smooth, shiny skin stretched over his bony skull.

He nodded at Alina. "Have a seat," he said, motioning to the chair next to Rex. She sat down.

He stood with his arms folded. "I think you both have some explaining to do."

Alina glanced at Rex. She didn't know what was safe to disclose.

Rex cleared his throat. "As you probably know, we've come from Pria."

The man gave a curt nod.

"We are enemies of Sampson and had a difficult time leaving."

"He didn't send you?" the man asked with raised eyebrows.

"No. This girl is of interest to him, you see, and I was in danger of being imprisoned, so we fled. We almost didn't make it."

"She seems very unscathed for one fleeing Pria." He studied Alina.

"Well, she—" Rex broke off.

The man raised one eyebrow. "Yes?"

"The wilderness wasn't too dangerous. We didn't meet anything threatening until this morning, and we arrived mid-day yesterday."

"Nothing during the night?"

"No, but someone in our party did mysteriously disappear."

The man looked back and forth between them with eyebrows furrowed. "The wilderness between the portal and our city is the deadliest in all of Carthem. It's the only area Sampson can unleash the mist, which he did today. Most from Pria don't make it here at all. If they do, they're *always* injured, unless they're Sampson's spies, who all seem to arrive unharmed. But his cast-offs are at his mercy. If he wants someone to die in Carthem, he usually makes it happen. Did you meet *any* opposition on your way?"

"I saw a rock that shot deadly quills," Alina said.

He nodded. "We call them killing stones, but they're animals. It didn't hit you, I presume, since you're still alive?"

"Uh—right."

"Anything else?"

"Some horrid-looking beasts with spiky tails chased us," Rex mentioned.

"And?"

Alina paused and glanced at Rex. "We were able to get away," she answered.

The man's face hardened. "They sound like monyxes to me, and those are impossible to outrun. If you're truly enemies of Sampson, you better have a good reason why he didn't finish you off."

Alina looked at Rex, waiting for him to explain.

The man continued. "And how do you explain the woman in your company with the hidden spying device?"

"You can detect those?" Rex asked.

"Of course! Our lives depend on it! An alarm signals when something Prian-made crosses our borders. A sensor also stuns those carrying a spy chip."

Alina felt a wave of relief. "She's only stunned?"

"Yes. She'll be fine. Who is she?"

"Her name is Jade," Rex said deliberately, watching the man's face.

He started. "Did you say *Jade?*"

"Yes. Have you heard of her?"

The man looked back and forth between them. He pointed his finger at Alina. "Are you *Alina?*"

Rex broke into a broad smile. "Yes."

The man beamed and put out his hand. "I'm Baylor Simms. And you are?"

Rex shook his hand vigorously. "I'm Rex. I'm so glad you know who we are."

"Well, it's no accident our town is set up close to the portal," Baylor said. "We're the border control, so to speak. We want to examine all who come from Pria. There's not another town for miles, so the wilderness drives them here."

"How—?" Alina began. She had so many questions, she didn't know where to start.

Baylor grinned as he turned to her. "Alina! I'm so happy to meet you. You'll find your name is well known here. And such a beautiful young lady, for a mortal."

"Uh, actually, she's not mortal anymore," Rex piped up.

Baylor's mouth dropped. "What do you mean?"

"Somehow the entry into Carthem reversed her."

"Does Sampson know?"

Rex looked at Alina. "I'm not sure. If he doesn't, then he might be trying to protect her. That could explain why we met so few dangers in our travels. But I don't know how much he can control."

"What does this mean for us?" Baylor asked.

"I don't know yet. I was hoping to find answers here. Any chance Camden is alive?" He winced, as if afraid what the answer might be.

"Yes, he is. And J'koby too."

Alina's eyes widened. *J'koby?*

Rex grabbed Baylor's arm. "You mean it? Camden's alive?"

"Yes."

"Is he here in Stormport?"

"No, both of them live in Jaden, a city about three hundred miles from here. Jaden and Stormport are the two headquarters of Carthem."

"Jaden? Is the city named after—"

"Her? Yes."

This information seemed to bother Rex. He frowned. "What do you plan to do with Jade, anyway?" he asked.

"She's being prepared for the operating table," Baylor said. "Her chip must be removed. Don't worry," he added, noticing their expressions. "We've done this operation many times before. It isn't without risks, but it must be done. There's no other option. Leaving it in is too dangerous. Sampson is constantly trying to infiltrate Stormport. He would destroy the whole city if he could."

"Why?" asked Alina.

"Because one of his top enemies lives here: Lance. He entered Carthem as a spy for Sampson soon after Camden left Pria. Once he arrived here in Stormport, he joined the resistance."

"I remember him!" Rex exclaimed. "Sampson gave some strange excuse for his disappearance."

"I'm sure he did. Lance was valuable to Sampson, and no one suspected he was conspiring against him. Even Camden thought him loyal to Pria because he took no part in the resistance there."

"How did he get here?"

"He volunteered for a secret mission to find the hidden portal in the Blue Forest. Sampson wanted a way to enter and return so he could control both worlds better. Lance was one of Pria's best scientists and worked for two hundred years in the laboratories. But after entering Carthem, he joined the resistance and established the security around Stormport. He's a genius. Sampson is aware of this treason, so you can imagine his anger, but none of his attempts to penetrate Stormport have succeeded."

"How did you ever function *without* Lance?" Rex asked.

"I've often asked the same question. But Carthem wasn't as dangerous before he came here. After Alina was born and Lance left Pria, then Sampson, in his anger, became aggressive about matters in Carthem."

Alina asked, "Are there other cities besides Stormport and Jaden?"

"No, Carthem is sparsely populated. We have a few people who come from Pria, but most are descendants of survivors from the Last Great War. So, the population grows slowly. Jaden is equipped with the same security as Stormport, which keeps them safe from Prian dangers. Most of our population lives in these two cities, but there are a few smaller towns as well."

"Are there any wild savages?" Alina asked, thinking about what she'd been taught in school.

Baylor chuckled. "There are some distant towns, I hear, where the people live without electricity or modern conveniences. We don't travel much because the wilderness is so dangerous. The nearest settlements are all similar to ours, minus the extra security. In time, we hope to implement this security in all of our towns, but it's expensive and the resources hard to come by. If we could explore Carthem we could find all we need, but Sampson has kept the wilderness deadly to stop this kind of progress. You'll find his iron hand squeezes us tightly here, which is why overthrowing him is our top priority."

"Let's get moving, then!" Rex said, slapping his good leg. "Will Jade's surgery take long?"

"After the operation, it'll take a week before she's fully recovered. There have been some repercussions in previous surgeries, when the brain did not heal properly. But after five days she should be out of danger."

A rock formed in Alina's stomach. "Do those repercussions happen often?"

"You know, I'm not the one to ask. You can visit her and talk with Dr. Scott tomorrow. He's too busy today. We have rooms for you to stay in, and food and donated clothing, but we expect you to work and contribute while you're here. Many people fresh from Pria become helpless and depressed. Mortality is overwhelming for them, so they curl up in a ball and shut down. It's expected every newcomer will go through this, so we have counseling for it. We call it 'mortal shock syndrome.' I personally believe the best antidote for it is work."

Baylor led them from the room and Rex leaned on Alina's shoulder as he limped down the hallway to the foyer. Baylor raised his palm. "Wait here while I see if your rooms are ready for you." He walked to the woman behind the front desk.

Alina helped Rex settle into an armchair, then strolled over to the sprawling glass window. She recoiled as a small creature with eight legs skittered across the floor in front of her. She'd seen similar creatures in the woods when they traveled from the portal, but they were outside. Could those creepy things get *inside* buildings? Or bedrooms? Even beds? She shuddered and walked to the other end of the window.

The cars fascinated her. Round wheels spinning over the ground seemed such a slow, inefficient way to get somewhere. At times, people walking on the sidewalks moved faster. Unsightly brown and white spots covered most of the cars' doors and roofs, and they rattled and screeched as if they might malfunction at any moment.

A young man walked past the window and Alina gasped as she noticed bright red bumps sprinkled over his face. *The bumps are normal!*

He caught her staring at him and halted, his eyes widening. She felt a kinship to him, so she smiled.

His jaw dropped, then he shut his mouth and hustled on, blushing up to his ears. He glanced back at her as he walked away.

Alina crossed her arms and rubbed her jaw with her fingers. She *must* look different, because she'd never caught a boy's eye like that before.

"We're ready for you," Baylor called to Alina. She hurried to help Rex out of his chair, and they hobbled after Baylor to the elevator. They went up three stories to a quiet floor, where Baylor unlocked one of the doors and nodded to Alina.

"This is your room. Rex will be next door. Food will be brought up shortly, and feel free to call the front desk if you need anything else. They know you're here. Although, they don't know *Alina* is here." He grinned.

"Please don't spread the word yet," Rex said. "I think we should keep her identity concealed until I consult with Camden."

Baylor nodded. "That's wise. I'll certainly keep her secret." He glanced between both of them and smiled. "I'm honored to meet you.

My father was expelled from Pria, and he carried a deep loathing for Sampson until the end of his life. I honor him by working to overthrow Sampson."

"Who was your father?" asked Rex.

"Xavier."

Rex smiled softly. "Camden told me of him. They were close friends in Pria. I hope they shared some time here before he died."

"A little. His life was cut shorter than it should've been, but he accomplished a lot during his time."

"It's a pleasure to meet you, Baylor. Thanks for your help."

"Always."

Rex hobbled with Alina into her room. She shut the door and looked around. "This isn't bad," Alina noted. The walls were covered in flowered paper, and she had a single bed with a blanket, a table and chair, a monitor, and a small bathroom. "Everything you need, right? Except a change of clothes. We should've planned this trip better," she joked.

"We'll be fine. I think *Miss Alina* will have the entire city at her disposal," Rex teased.

She rolled her eyes. "So, what are we going to do?"

"Well," Rex sat on the bed, stretching his leg gingerly. "We stay here until Jade is recovered. I hope to talk to Camden soon." He went quiet, staring at his bandaged leg. "It'll be so good to see him again. I didn't think he'd be alive when I got here."

Alina sat down next to him. "It's wonderful news. I'm excited to meet him." She paused. "But how does everyone know me?"

"They must know of the plan. Lance and Baylor seem to."

"What plan?"

"There are some things I haven't told you. Perhaps now is a good time." Rex took a deep breath.

"As you know, Camden was my caretaker in Pria. He was one of the original founders and the last one to be banished. About thirteen years before you were born, Sampson approved Camden's request for a ward, and he got me. His sole purpose was to train me for the resistance. All growing up, I knew that would be my life."

"But I don't understand," Alina cut in. "There are so many who enjoy life in Pria, or at least seem to. Are there enough people to organize a resistance?"

"It's taken two centuries to gather them, but yes, there's enough. Sampson has made his share of mistakes and angered many people. When you live forever, it's easy to get disgruntled and restless. His world hasn't been as easy to rule as he anticipated."

"Who is J'koby?"

Rex released a long breath and looked her square in the eyes. "He's your father."

Alina stared, her mouth hanging open. "But—Sampson didn't kill him?"

"Apparently not. He must have been bluffing when he said that in the dungeon, maybe to catch you off guard. I admit, I believed him. I don't know how J'koby survived."

Alina clutched Rex's arm. "Remember the room full of info-discs in Gordian? I looked at Jade's disc after you left the room. I saw a picture of J'koby with her, and they seemed to be in love. But Jade can't be my mother—you told me she died."

"Yes. You're right, Jade is not your mother."

"But she and J'koby—"

"Yes, they were together," he snapped. "J'koby came into Pria on a strict mission and got distracted by her. He couldn't resist, I guess." Rex seemed angry. "So many fell for her, you know, because she's different from other women. But she didn't give anyone a chance until he—" Rex broke off.

"What is it?"

He paused. "Nothing."

"Come on Rex, you can tell me," Alina prodded.

He stared at his hands, clasped in his lap. After a moment he whispered, "I also fell in love with her."

Alina smiled, unsurprised by his confession. "Did she ever return your love?" she asked.

"I was only twelve when she came to our house for rebel meetings, and too young for her, but I hoped when I came of age her feelings would change. They didn't. I had flings of my own, which distanced her further. So, I stopped dating altogether to prove how much I wanted her."

"But she loved him."

Rex nodded, tightening his jaw. "Which was cruel, because he knew he couldn't stay with her. He broke her heart, and she was never the same afterward."

"And now they'll see each other soon."

Rex stared blankly at the wall. "Yes."

He looked tired, with dark circles under his eyes. Though still handsome, he no longer fit the dashing socialite from Pria. He seemed —older.

"Go take a nap, Rex. You need some rest."

He smoothed the bed with his hands. "That's right, I can sleep in a real bed and forget my troubles for awhile. What a great idea! Don't plan on seeing me again today. I may sleep till morning. No, wait, I want to eat first."

As if on cue, a woman knocked on the door and walked in holding a tray of food. She set it on the table. "You must be Rex," she said to him. "I left your food in your room."

"Thank you," Rex said.

"You're welcome. I'll get some clothes sent up. Do you need anything else? Extra pillows, perhaps?"

Alina smiled. "No, thank you, one is fine for me."

The woman left, and Alina glanced at the tray and sighed. "I'll probably eat, too, just to stay busy. I don't like being awake while everyone else sleeps."

"Yeah, that's rough, you're on your own," said Rex. "At least in Pria, company was around, even if they were boring and shallow. Maybe the monitor will pass the time?"

She glanced at the small, boxy screen. "Funny-looking thing, isn't it? How do you turn it on?"

Rex pursed his lips and scratched his head. "Beats me."

"Can you make it to your room okay?"

Rex rose carefully, testing his leg. "I'll be fine. I feel much better."

"Goodnight, Rex."

"'Night." He gave Alina a hug and limped out of the room.

The moment the door closed, Alina unzipped her uniform and retrieved Zaiden's info-disc and the panel from the bodice of her gown. She reddened as she realized how often she'd thought of him that day. There were plenty of more pressing things to worry about. Perhaps she'd reverted to him as an escape.

She took the disc from its case and turned the panel in her hands. She'd waited for almost two days to look at it, terrified it wouldn't work outside of Pria. She inserted the disc into the panel and clicked it on.

A rush of excitement surged through her as the panel lit up and Zaiden's handsome face filled the screen. She smiled, then narrowed her eyes as she studied his features. His dark eyes looked troubled under his heavy eyebrows, and the smile on his lips forced and feeble. Alina suspected him of being somber and mysterious, but in this picture, he looked disturbed. She swiped the page and read the bold letters.

ZAIDEN
commenced: December 30
caretaker: Arton

His young photos showed an adorable boy with ash-blond hair and dimples when he smiled. His hair had darkened since then, but his eyes were the same—deep brown, the color of chocolate. He didn't appear a happy child; he frowned more than he smiled. He was a sports star in grade school, in Sampson's Young Scientists Club, and voted "Most Self-Absorbed" in his class at age twelve. All three pages showed him sulking.

His caretaker, Arton, was a rumored womanizer, and the pictures confirmed it—almost every image showed him with a different girlfriend. Usually that vice corrected itself, as philandering damaged a man's reputation until women avoided him, but it seemed Arton hadn't reached that point yet. The more photos she saw, the more Alina disliked him. Zaiden seemed to echo her feelings because as he grew older, there were fewer pictures of him and Arton together.

His coming-of-age had the usual transformation, from child-like charm to defined, stunning features. His dimples became mature indentations in his square jaw and his hair went from ash blond to golden brown. She loved how his light eyelashes framed his dark, mysterious eyes.

She closed her eyes, and for about the hundredth time, visualized him staring at her in the dim light of Sampson's dungeon. What drew her to him? Did she like him because he was the first boy to notice and be kind to her?

She shook her head. No. She liked him because he was different. His eyes longed for more in life than Pria offered.

She reached the page of his fifteenth year and found several photos of him with two boys who looked familiar. At the bottom of the page a bold caption stated:

Zaiden with Chet and Lorenzo—extent of affiliation unknown

Alina gasped. She remembered Chet and Lorenzo. They created a scandal by running away from home. It took three days to find them, deep in Pria's mountains. Sampson called their actions revolutionary and dangerous and declared they must receive his therapy to cure them. Otherwise they might slip again, with more dire consequences.

His therapy. Sampson used that term when a child became too disruptive, and she understood what it meant now. *His indoctrination*. Chet and Lorenzo were pulled from school for months, and when they returned, they were model Prian citizens. She'd never seen them with Zaiden, but dozens of pictures revealed a close friendship around the time the boys rebelled.

Other pages showed Zaiden at school and athletic events, at city celebrations and outings with Arton and his pretty women. There were no photos of him with girls until she swiped and saw herself, talking with him on the street the day she walked home from Rex's house.

She recoiled at the picture. The angle, probably taken by the officials following her, caught an unflattering view of her profile. Her face glistened with nervous sweat. She looked like this as she declared to Zaiden she'd be a beauty one day. He must have thought her delusional.

She pressed her lips as she studied his wrinkled brow and downcast eyes. He pitied her.

He didn't gaze at her from the cell in Sampson's dungeon. She imagined it. A perfect boy like him, surrounded by beauty, couldn't be attracted to the girl in that picture. Alina swiped again and found a close-up of him and Eris kissing at the Harvest Feast. She flung the panel across the room where it smacked the wall and landed on the floor with a thud.

She sprang off the bed, grabbed an apple from her tray and took a bite. Everyone in Pria ate when they were upset. No matter how much they ate or drank, no bad effects came from it. Food wouldn't bring any lasting satisfaction, but for now, it comforted her.

She chewed furiously, tossed the core in the garbage and walked to the bathroom, where curiosity drew her to the mirror above the sink.

Trembling, she walked in. *Why am I nervous?* She shut her eyes, flipped on the light, then flung them open. Her hands slapped over her mouth.

She didn't recognize the girl in front of her or the striking blue eyes blinking in shock. Her nose looked the same, but smaller. Lush, thick eyelashes settled on her pink cheeks, which were smooth, like porcelain. Though she'd been traveling all day, her honey brown hair looked soft and glossy. Her full lips revealed straight, white teeth when she smiled, and her figure was both slim and well proportioned.

She stared in the mirror for a long time, shifting angles and smiling, trembling with excitement. Out of all her regrets for Zaiden that day, one now tormented her most—he wasn't there to see her.

CHAPTER 13

The next morning when the sun peeked through her window, Alina made a mental note to acquire more reading material as soon as possible. Zaiden's info-disc was all she had, and she perused it until she knew each picture intimately, except the one of him and Eris. She watched the monitor for a while, but entertainment in Carthem was not the big industry it was in Pria. She picked up only three streams through the static: a news report discussing local weather, an educational program about Stormport's laboratories, and a drama with such exaggerated and stilted acting, she couldn't turn it off fast enough.

Alina opened her blinds to let in the sunlight just as someone knocked on her door. "Come in," she answered.

The same woman from the night before entered with a new tray of food. She set it on the table and took the nearly full tray from the day before. She gave Alina a worried glance as she left.

"Thank you," Alina called after her.

She sat down, picked up her fork and took a bite of the eggs on her plate. Though somewhat bland, she enjoyed the simple, fresh taste. Prian food had a flavorful but artificial nature about it. This food attempted to be nothing more than nourishment for the body.

Another knock sounded at the door. "Come in," Alina said.

Rex hobbled through the door, holding his breakfast tray and smiling. "I slept great! I think I'm getting the hang of mortality now." He sat down and dug into his eggs. "The aches are annoying but sleeping and eating—wow! Immortals don't know what they're missing! Sampson's smart to keep them ignorant. If they knew, they'd be coming over by the thousands."

"I take it your leg feels better," Alina said.

He grunted affirmatively through his full mouth, then gulped the eggs down. "I put more medicine on it this morning. It works fast."

Alina watched with envy as he gobbled his bacon. She nibbled a piece of toast and swallowed some juice. It seemed pointless to eat. She put the toast back on her plate.

"Rex, I looked in the mirror last night. Why didn't you tell me how much I'd changed?"

He studied her, as if seeing her for the first time. "I guess you do look a little different."

"A little? I hardly recognized myself!"

Rex rolled his eyes. "You girls are all the same. You think one blemish or bad hair day will be noticed by everyone you meet. No one really pays attention." He paused to swallow another bite of eggs. "I suppose I'm not the one to ask, though. Growing up around beautiful women has made me blind to them. I like to look past that. But the truth is, I haven't noticed anyone except Jade for years."

Alina smiled. She liked that about Rex. He saw her as Alina, not as beautiful or ugly.

"Let's go see Jade," she said.

"Sure—just let me finish eating." He scraped his plate, drained his juice and wiped his mouth. Then he leaned back and let out a loud belch.

"Whoa, excuse me," he said. "Man, these mortal bodies are disgusting!" He kept a tally on his fingertips. "They smell, they leak, they itch—"

"Rex," Alina interrupted, "I'd rather not hear it. Let's go."

"Oh, okay."

They left Alina's room and started down the hall to the elevator. Rex took his time, but Alina barely noticed his limp.

"Do you know what this building is?" she asked.

"I don't, but I wonder if Lance works here." He dropped his

voice. "I'm interested to meet him. I'm wary of any of Sampson's former allies. I don't know which ones truly want to help the resistance. Some only wish for power themselves. Many of his highest in command are simply waiting for the right moment to take his place."

Alina raised her eyebrows. "But Baylor speaks highly of him."

"Yes, well—I'd like to get Camden's opinion. I don't trust people easily." He muttered under his breath, "I'm not like Jade."

They took the elevator down to the lobby, where a gray-haired woman sat behind a counter. "Good morning," she said, showing unnaturally straight teeth. "I'm Eleanor, the receptionist here." Alina's jaw dropped as she viewed the woman's small, shriveled body.

"Are you okay, dear?" Eleanor asked.

"I-I'm fine. Excuse me," Alina stammered, mortified by her rudeness. She tried to look at Eleanor's eyes, rather than the wrinkled skin sagging from her bones.

"We'd like to visit Jade if we can," Rex said.

"Of course. She's in room 127. Let me call Dr. Scott first and see if she can have visitors right now." Eleanor picked up a device on her desk.

While they waited, Alina walked to the double doors and took in the outside view. Stormport had the raw, imperfect beauty she loved about Carthem.

A child was running on the pavement, matching the energy of the dog racing alongside her. Alina saw her young self in her. The girl had scrapes and bruises on her legs and hair flying in knotted tangles. An older woman called after her to slow down and watch for cars.

Others bustled along the street: some short and overweight, others tall and lank, or, like Eleanor, wrinkled and gray haired. Alina glanced back at Eleanor and noticed her pleated skin jiggling as she laughed with Rex. How grotesque that people lived long enough to look like that! But Eleanor seemed cheerful and happy in a way Alina hadn't seen in Pria.

"Good morning," a man called into the foyer, addressing Rex. "I'm Dr. Scott, if you remember from yesterday. You look better. How's your leg?" Alina left the window to join them.

"It's much better, thank you. The medicine works great. I'm Rex, and this is Alin—Ali," he shortened.

"Yes, I talked with her yesterday—nice to see you again, Ali. Will you both come into my office for a moment?"

"Certainly."

They followed him down the hall and into a room, where he motioned for them to sit down. He closed the door and took a seat behind a desk. A framed photo of himself with a woman and two young boys hung on the wall.

He peered at them over rectangular spectacles. "I'm afraid you can't visit Jade at this time. She's ill, and we won't perform the surgery until she is well."

"Ill?" they said at the same time. "From the black mist?" Alina asked.

"No. She had the same infection on her leg as you, Rex, but that is all. You must not have been exposed to the mist for long. But she's caught a virus, and it's made her very weak."

Rex and Alina exchanged stunned glances. From what they knew, mortal illnesses were serious and often fatal.

"Oh, don't worry," Dr. Scott said, "it's nothing serious. Many newcomers from Pria pick up viruses, fresh hosts as they are. I'm surprised you are both looking so well, actually."

"She'll recover, then?" Alina asked.

"Of course. She's a little miserable, but we've given her medicine, and if she shows improvement in the next twenty-four hours, we'll begin the surgery."

"Is the surgery dangerous?" Rex asked.

Dr. Scott leaned forward, clasping his hands under his chin. "Yes and no. Our medical care is exceptional, thanks to Lance. This particular procedure has caused death in some instances, which makes it one of the riskier ones, but that happens rarely." His mechanical approach bothered Alina, but he seemed confident in his knowledge, so she put her mind at ease.

"How long will she stay in the hospital wing?" she asked.

"She can be released after a week, if all is well. You two can stay upstairs in our guest apartments and ask Eleanor how to work for your stay."

"Of course, thank you," Rex said, as someone knocked at the door.

"Come in," Dr. Scott called.

Baylor poked his head in. "Eleanor said you were here," he said to Rex and Alina. "I need to speak with both of you right away."

Rex looked back at Dr. Scott, who nodded. "We're finished. I'll keep you updated on Jade's condition."

Baylor looked nervous. He led them to the same room where they met the day before. "Have a seat," he said as they entered.

Rex and Alina sat down. Baylor pulled up a chair close to them and dropped his voice.

"You mentioned yesterday there was someone in your group who disappeared. Who was he, and what happened?"

Rex's eyes narrowed. "His name is Stan. He was part of the resistance in Pria. I thought I could trust him, but he led us to Sampson in Gordian Palace, then claimed he didn't mean to do it."

"Do you still suspect him?" Baylor asked.

Rex thought for a moment. "I do. The resistance has traitors who have complicated things in the past. There is fierce loyalty among the true members, who would give themselves up before betraying another. Something about his story doesn't seem right."

"When did he disappear?" Baylor asked.

"At night," Alina said. "He went behind a tree, then vanished. I never heard a sound."

"What does he look like?"

Rex wrinkled his eyebrows. "He has black hair and greenish, hazel eyes. His ears are big for his face. He's short and scrawny, too." Rex chuckled. "He sure didn't keep his looks."

Baylor stood up and started pacing the room, his hand stroking his chin. "I think we've spied him."

"What?" Alina exclaimed.

"Our security guards have spotted a man on our northern border with dark hair and a smaller build, like you described. He came through the security shield and set off the alarm, then ran back into the wilderness."

"What's he trying to do?" Rex asked.

"We're pretty sure he's testing the system. Sampson frequently sends spies to do just that. What's disturbing about this, though, is he wasn't stunned."

"But Rex and I weren't stunned, either," Alina pointed out.

"True, but Rex carries nothing from Pria in him. You have the serum, which is why the alarm went off, but since you're immortal it probably felt like a small buzz. Jade was stunned because she carries a surveillance chip. We monitor everyone who crosses our borders, but the high-pitched alarm only goes off when something Prian-made is entering. That in turn activates the stunning mechanism. One shouldn't happen without the other."

"So, you're saying Stan might have a surveillance device, like Jade?"

"Most likely, yes. But his seems to be more advanced."

Rex cursed Stan under his breath. "He *is* a traitor! Sampson sent him in to follow us!"

"Yes, that's the only explanation," Baylor said. "Lance is extremely concerned by this incident. He believes Sampson may have found a way to penetrate our security. You'll be meeting with Lance soon—he wants all the information you can give him about Stan."

Rex nodded. Baylor stroked his chin for a moment then said, "That's all for now. I'll let you know when Lance wants to see you."

"Is there any way I can speak to Camden?" Rex asked.

Baylor nodded and pulled a small device from his pocket. "Here's a phone you can use. I'll write down the number for you."

Rex eyed the device curiously. "A what?"

"A phone," Baylor repeated. "I forget you're not familiar with our technology. This is what we use to communicate. You dial a number, put this part against your ear and speak. Its range is limited, but it reaches Jaden. You can take it back to your room. Hit this button and type in this number, and Camden should answer." He scribbled a chain of numbers on a piece of paper and handed it to Rex.

"Thank you," Rex said, taking the phone and paper from him. "Let us know what else we can do to help."

Baylor nodded. Rex and Alina followed him out of the hallway. They waved goodbye to him and Eleanor in the foyer, then headed to the elevator.

"Wow," Alina said. "My mind is racing, trying to remember everything Stan learned about us that Sampson now knows. What should we do?"

"We wait for Jade to recover and learn as much as we can from Baylor. I'll ask Camden's advice too." Rex fingered the phone in his hands.

Alina smiled. "How long has it been since you've spoken to him?"

"Since the day of your birth. Almost eighteen years."

Several minutes later, in Alina's room, Rex trembled as he waited for someone to pick up at Camden's apartment in Jaden. Within moments, Camden and Rex were enjoying a tearful reunion over the phone.

"We're here, we all made it!" Rex exclaimed. "Yes, Jade and Alina are with me. Jade is waiting for surgery. Sampson put a surveillance chip in her when she became Alina's caretaker." He paused. "I agree. It couldn't have turned out better."

Except for Zaiden, thought Alina.

"Yes, she's in the room with me. She's doing great," Rex glanced at her and cleared his throat. "She's immortal now. The dagger changed her somehow...yes, I think he knows by now. What does it mean for us?" He paused. "I suppose that's good news...no, it'll be at least a week, when Jade gets well. How dangerous is the road? Yes—let's hope so. I'll send word as soon as we know. In the meantime, the ball can start rolling. Can we trust Lance?" Rex smiled at Camden's answer. "Good, I'm glad to hear."

He glanced at Alina again. "Of course, I will respect his wishes." The room went quiet, and Rex scrunched up his face and covered his eyes with his hand. Alina turned her attention to her fingernails.

"I've missed you, too." He could barely speak. "See you soon."

He tried a few buttons on the phone until it turned off. Alina waited for him to talk first. She jumped when he blew his nose.

"They're ready for us whenever we can get there." He gave a stuffy laugh. "They've been ready for years."

"Ready for what?"

"For you. For the overthrow of Sampson. Everyone wants him gone. He has a lot of power here—you saw what we encountered in the forest." Rex released a shaky breath. "Camden said the journey to Jaden is very dangerous."

"Then how can someone like him, with so much power, be overthrown?" Alina asked.

"When you meet Camden and J'koby, your doubts will go. They've been conspiring for centuries. They planned you—and look at what a success you have been."

Alina looked at the ground. "I'm nothing special. I get nervous when you say that. What does everyone expect from me?"

He placed a hand on her shoulder. "You *are* special, Alina. And you're the best hope Carthem has."

She wanted a new subject. "Tell me about my mother. How did she die?"

Rex frowned. "I knew you would ask about her. But J'koby wants to explain everything to you about your birth and your mother. It's his wish, and his place. Plus, he'll do a better job. I don't know the whole story. I was only thirteen."

"What *can* you tell me, then?"

He laughed. "Not much. I wish I'd paid more attention. Camden tried to teach me things, but it's hard to care when you're young."

"But you know *some* things about my mother, right?"

"I remember her, yes. She came to our house for rebel meetings, held under the guise of poker nights. We set up the table and held cards and everything. Moved chips around as we discussed top secret things."

"You participated?"

"Yes, when I was old enough to understand what was going on. On one of these nights, Jade and I decided she'd send you to me if you discovered your mortality too early. You're lucky I remembered anything we talked about. I had a huge crush on her." He laughed.

They heard a knock on the door and Alina slid off the bed to answer it. Dr. Scott stood in the hallway in his white scrubs, his spectacles perched on his nose.

"Hello, Doctor," she said. "Come in. Rex is with me."

"Oh, good. I tried his room first with no answer. I have some good news. Jade's symptoms have improved enough for us to operate. The surgery is scheduled for this evening."

"Can we see her before the operation to wish her well?" Alina asked.

"No. I'm sorry. We can't risk exposing her to any new viruses you might be carrying."

"But I don't—" Alina started, but Rex hushed her with a glance.

"Her recovery should take about a week, then?" asked Rex.

"At least. Longer if there are complications. The healing of the brain is a critical process. Problems can arise without warning."

Alina and Rex exchanged worried looks.

"Feel free to come down in the morning to ask about her progress. We'll keep you informed as best we can and let you visit as soon as she's ready."

"Thank you," they answered. Dr. Scott nodded, then left the room.

Alina looked at Rex. "At least things are moving quickly."

"I'm scared," he said.

"Me too."

"The thought that someone you love could die is a scary thing. How do mortals deal with it? I suppose that's why Sampson's ideology is so persuasive," Rex said.

"Yes. In Pria there is no death, but ironically, there isn't enough love to make it scary."

"That reminds me of something Camden used to say," Rex mused. "He said in order for love to exist, there must be death."

"What did he mean?"

"The possibility of death increases love, and love makes death devastating. They are interdependent. He even went further and claimed that without death, people don't truly love."

"But don't you think *some* people in Pria love? What about your feelings for Jade?"

"I thought I loved her there, but now that I'm faced with the possibility of losing her to death, I have a better understanding of what love is. But yes, I believe immortals can love. In Pria, loss comes through banishment. I was devastated when Camden was sent away. I suppose he meant that the finality of death makes love more poignant and real."

They were silent for a moment until Rex spoke again. "I meant to ask you—how did you overcome Sampson in the dungeon? Why were your hands free?"

"Oh! One of the guards, Crome, helped me. Sampson ordered him to tie my wrists. The knot felt tight, but when I moved my hands, it came loose."

Rex beamed. "Crome, huh? He's one of the best—Sampson never suspected him. He made a big sacrifice for you. His cover is ruined now, and that's a big blow to the resistance. But I know he believes getting you into Carthem was worth it."

"Do you think Sampson knows he helped me?"

Rex pressed his lips together and nodded. "It's obvious. He was ordered to tie your hands, and they went free. He's in the dungeons as we speak, I'm sure of it."

Alina sighed. "I hate to think people are in that awful place because of me."

Rex touched her arm. "Don't think of it like that. Think how happy they are that *you* are in this wonderful place because of *them*."

CHAPTER 14

For five agonizing days, Rex and Alina fretted as Jade's condition fluctuated. One hour she moved her body and tried to speak, the next she lay still and unresponsive. Dr. Scott frowned and shook his head when he examined her, and this put them in a near state of panic. Jade needed her rest, but each time her eyes closed, Alina worried they wouldn't open again.

She and Rex kept themselves occupied by completing jobs for their room and board. They stripped beds and washed windows throughout the building and cleaned the public bathrooms. Before long, Alina couldn't decide which was worse—scrubbing the smelly toilets or having Rex as her cleaning partner.

The first time they cleaned the men's bathroom, Rex held a cloth at arm's length as he wiped the urinals down. His other hand he kept over his nose.

Alina looked at him and rolled her eyes. "Rex, that's not working. You have to scrub to get them clean, you know."

"Ughhh!" he wailed. "This bathroom stuff is the most revolting part of mortality. Men are especially disgusting creatures."

Rex claimed this dirty, unpleasant work brought on his first cold; for two days he stayed in bed and was miserable company. At first Alina told him to grit his teeth and toughen up, then tried to be more understanding after he hotly reminded her that she'd never been sick and didn't know what it felt like. Viruses didn't exist in Pria, as they had no hosts, so until she experienced it herself, she could keep quiet. True, she hadn't been sick before, but she knew the sore throat wasn't bothering him most. He was worried about Jade.

Despite his illness, Alina envied him; immortal life was starting to drag. She missed sleeping. The night hours made her lonely and anxious, with nothing to do but worry. Though her body never tired, her mind needed a respite.

One morning after a particularly hard night, she put off her chores and asked Eleanor where she could get something to read. She didn't expect there to be discs for her panel, since she'd seen nothing similar in Carthem. But she needed *something* to occupy her mind while everyone slept.

"Yes, dear," Eleanor answered her. "You can walk to the library from here. Go out this front door, take a right, and it's two blocks down on your left. You'll see a sign in front, 'Stormport Library.'"

Alina thanked her and stepped outside into the fresh morning air, grateful to escape the hospital wing and smelly bathrooms.

Children played across the street in the park, with dogs barking and running at their heels. The small restaurants and clothing shops along the street fascinated her. After she and Rex wore the same dirty uniform for two days, Eleanor bought them clothes from the best store in town. Alina liked the fashions of Carthem; the moderate colors and styles differed from the flashy trends of Pria. She hoped her simple clothes would help her blend in, but every head turned and stared at her as she walked down the street.

The library had faded brick walls and cracked, white columns. She skipped up the crumbled steps to the front door, and, ignoring the lingering eyes around her, walked to the front desk.

"May I help you?" a bespectacled woman asked.

"Yes, I'm interested in reading about Carthem's history. Can you direct me?"

"Certainly."

The woman led her to an aisle near the corner of the library, where a cozy set of armchairs faced a charred fireplace. She pointed to three shelves. "This is all we have, but I think you'll find a good selection."

"Thank you," Alina said, as she reached out and pulled one from the shelf. "What are they?"

"Why, they're books!"

She opened it up, and a sweet musty smell reached her nose. The paper was yellowed, and the outside leather scratched and worn. The book seemed a perfect emblem of Carthem: rough, defaced, and comforting.

"Can I take any of them with me? Just to borrow?"

"Of course. Choose the ones you'd like to read and bring them to my desk."

"Thank you. And—one more question, please."

"Yes?"

"Can people write freely here?"

The librarian looked puzzled. "I'm not sure I know what you mean."

"Can someone write what they think, and people can read it? Or are there restrictions?"

The woman raised her eyebrows. "Yes, anyone can write and publish a book. But when it comes to Carthem's history, we take the truth very seriously. Nothing is published without verification."

"Good. Thank you," Alina said. The woman nodded and left.

Alina was glad to hear this. In Pria all reading material, stored on info-discs, was strictly regulated, supposedly for the author's protection. After all, he or she might say something offensive, and this could land the author—and others, if a feud erupted—into Carthem. 'Unchecked words lead to unchecked wars' was one of Sampson's popular slogans.

Alina tilted her head and scanned the titles. *People, Policies, and Politics of Carthem; Life after Pria; Life as an Immortal: From the Mouth of an ex-Prian; The Man with the Iron Hand: Sampson and his Lies;* and *The Connection between Carthem and Pria.*

She took the two about Carthem, then plopped into a chair by the fireplace and picked up *The Connection between Carthem and Pria.*

She flipped to the back cover and read about the author, Miles

Cedarwood, who was one of the founders who helped Sampson establish Pria, and one of the first exiled. Three hundred years stretched between the first edition's publication and the latest one. Camden's endorsement on the back confirmed it as the most recent edition. She opened the book, crossed her legs and started to read.

The first chapter introduced the discovery of a new substance before the Last Great War. Ageless serum, as the substance was later called, brought rapid advancements in technology, science, engineering, and medicine. One person was prominent in every area of this innovation: a young, brilliant, and charismatic scientist named Victor Sampson.

Sampson's innovations and inventions made him popular at a time when cultural, political, and economic divisions sparked discord across the territories of Carthem. Yet access to these advancements became limited through government interference and escalating costs. Sampson seemed apart from the conflict. His popularity established him as a spokesman, yet his neutrality as a scientist and innovator spared him any direct blame.

The historians couldn't say who initiated the first attack. The outlying territories appeared to target the central government. Retaliation was swift, and soon all of Carthem was embroiled in a major civil war, the Last Great War—the war Sampson referred to at every Day of Genesis. Key infrastructures were devastated, leaving the outer territories without critical necessities, and cutting off lines of communication and transportation. Ironically, all of Sampson's hard-earned innovations—the things that initiated the unrest—were destroyed, along with the government.

From the ashes, Sampson arose as a natural leader. The people were so broken, they embraced his leadership without question.

Alina glanced at the clock, then hastily gathered the books and took them to the front desk. Jade's visiting hours had begun, and as of yesterday, her condition was still uncertain.

She hurried back to the hospital lobby and found Rex waiting in a robe and slippers, his hair ruffled and his nose chapped red.

"You're out of bed!" she exclaimed.

"I'm too worried about Jade to rest. Where have you been?"

"At the library. Look at these!" she dropped the books in his lap. "They're called books! You've got to try them."

"Sounds great," he said, waving her off. "Now, go see Jade!"

She laughed at his gruffness and hurried to Jade's room. Alina froze as she stepped into the open doorway.

Jade was sitting up in bed, sipping juice through a straw. The needles were gone from her wrists, and her lips and cheeks flushed with color. She held the small cup and drank her juice with ease. Alina let out a cry and dashed to the side of her bed.

She kissed Jade's prickly, shaved head, then grasped her hand and knelt down. Jade wiped a tear from Alina's cheek and laughed. "You cry so beautifully now," she teased.

"It's because they're happy tears," Alina replied.

They beamed at each other for a moment. Alina felt shy. She and Jade hadn't been free to grow close before. Could the wall between them break down simply because of an operation?

Jade's eyes twinkled. "Tell me what's happened since I passed out. Last I remember, I was on your back in the forest and Rex was complaining about food for about the thousandth time."

Alina burst into laughter, then went into an animated account of Rex's back-and-forth complaints and raves about mortality. Jade squeezed her eyes shut as she laughed and clutched her sides.

Her heart and tongue loosened, Alina unloaded into Jade's willing ears everything about Stormport: Eleanor and Baylor and the news of Stan, the mundane tasks of earning their keep, and how worried she and Rex had been about her. She confessed her crush on Zaiden and the joys and annoyances of being immortal. When she demonstrated how the boys on the street gawked at her, Jade burst into such hearty laughter that the nurse dashed in and scolded Alina, then sent her off so Jade could rest.

As Alina leaned in to hug her, Jade whispered in her ear. "We have a lot of years to catch up on. Someday I'll make it up to you."

The tears came back to Alina's eyes. "It's been only an hour, and you already have."

As she walked out of the hospital wing, Jade's laughter ringing in her ears, Alina realized she had talked the entire time and still knew little of her caretaker. But Jade seemed delighted, as if Alina had given her the time of her life.

She wouldn't let that happen next time. Alina wanted to soak in every detail of this woman who was as dear to her as a sister, or mother—or whatever they were called.

Family, she remembered. Jade was family to her.

CHAPTER 15

J ade left the hospital wing the following day and moved into Alina's room. They talked into the night until Jade could no longer keep her eyes open. Alina wished their conversation didn't have to end, but Jade needed her rest.

Alina considered their reversed places and how often Jade must have been lonely in Pria as Alina slept. Jade endured so many solitary nights; Alina could endure them too.

She sat in the armchair and picked up *The Connection between Carthem and Pria* but didn't open the book. Instead she reflected on her discussion with Jade, who had been forthright and honest—answering Alina's questions without the hesitation of her earlier years. Alina respected her father's wishes and didn't ask about her birth but wanted to know how Jade felt about him.

Jade smiled. "I knew you would ask that. I hope I'm ready to talk about him. It's been so long."

"You don't have to tell me if you're not ready," Alina rushed.

"No. I've always wished I could tell you. There was *so much* I wanted to tell you. It tortured me to raise you so distantly. Horrible years I'm glad are over."

She looked thoughtful for a moment before she began. "I met J'koby by accident. He was living—or hiding, I should say—with Camden."

"He lived with Camden?"

"Yes. He's his son."

"His what?"

"His child. Born to him and his wife."

Alina's mouth dropped. "Rex never told me that!"

Jade raised her eyebrows and nodded. "I'm not surprised. He's not a big fan of J'koby."

Alina suspected she knew why but asked anyway. "How come?"

"Imagine being the number one person in your caretaker's life, and then his long-lost son appears out of nowhere and moves into your home. J'koby is Camden's own flesh and blood. Rex couldn't compete with that."

"Oh—that *is* sad," Alina murmured. And J'koby took Jade, too. No wonder Rex wasn't a fan. "So how did you meet?"

"Well, one day I went over—" She paused and her cheeks turned red.

"What?" Alina asked.

"I'm ashamed of my friends at the time. I had one who was interested in Camden. He was top of the 'desirable list' because he was so impossible to get. Only Sampson ranked higher than him."

"They wanted him because he was hard to get?"

"Of course." Jade cleared her throat. "So, this friend of mine— which I shouldn't call a friend, because she wasn't nice, and I shouldn't have put up with her—"

"It's okay, Jade," Alina cut in. "We've all done things we're not proud of."

Jade smiled. "Well, she was desperate to get Camden's attention. He was one of the few real gentlemen in Pria, you see—so honest and respectful of women. He had a lot of female friends but never dated. He didn't even flirt, and it drove them crazy. One day my friend told me she wanted to try something different. She reasoned so many women failed with him because they tried to be polite and courteous, like he was. Gentility never got them anywhere. She decided to be aggressive."

Alina broke in. "But there are plenty of aggressive women in Pria. Surely one had tried that before?"

"Not like this," Jade said. "She was planning to force herself on him. Make him—well, you know."

Alina's jaw dropped. "But how?"

"Let's just say blackmail, in a twisted kind of way. She thought it would turn him on." Jade shuddered. "Anyway, she asked me to get Rex out of the house so she could carry out her plan. Rex was about ten or eleven at the time. She told me to drop in and ask if I could take him to a Young Scientists' function I was in charge of. Camden and I were good friends with mutual respect for each other. I knew he would be mortified if my friend carried out her plan. So, I decided to warn him instead.

"I knocked on his door, and he invited me in but seemed nervous. He kept glancing up the stairs. I was hoping to speak to him privately, but Rex came running to see who was at the door. I told Camden I had something to tell him that wasn't appropriate for Rex to hear, and he was about to take me outside when J'koby came bounding down the stairs, without his shirt on." She giggled.

"He hadn't heard the doorbell and didn't know I was there. Camden panicked. It was too late, though, we'd seen each other. J'koby, who should have fled, was glued to the spot, staring at me."

Alina leaned forward, smiling, and put her hands under her chin. "What did he say?"

"Camden tried to make excuses for him, but they were pointless. I could tell right away he was different. He was handsome but obviously wasn't immortal."

"How could you tell?"

"Well, he was half naked, and while his chest wasn't unsightly, he wasn't sculpted like an immortal. He had flaws; I could see them. And I liked that."

"What happened next?"

"Camden tried to send me away, but J'koby stopped him. He whispered to Camden that since I'd seen him, they must convince me to stay quiet. Camden was uneasy, but for the most part, he trusted me. He knew I needed to be informed so I didn't talk to others about the mysterious man living in his home. He introduced us to each other, then made me swear not to tell anyone, which I never did.

J'koby insisted I come visit them often. He claimed he needed to keep tabs on me, but of course we both knew the real reason.

"After several weeks of visits, and when I'd come to know not only J'koby but Camden and Rex very well, they felt they could fully trust me. So, they told me their secret."

"What was that?"

"J'koby was a mortal from Carthem and Camden's biological son —which was amusing, because J'koby looked older than his father. Camden thought he'd been killed with the others in his family. Sampson intended to kill him, but J'koby escaped and fled for his own safety. When things settled down after the war, and he returned to find Camden, J'koby learned his father had followed his enemy— Sampson—into an immortal world. So J'koby devoted his life to learning everything he could about immortality in hopes of finding his father. He lived in Carthem for over three hundred years before he entered Pria."

"But you said he was mortal!"

Her eyes twinkled. "He *was*. In Pria, that is. He's a brilliant man. He knows more about immortality than Sampson and can switch between the two."

Alina furrowed her brow. "But if he was mortal in Pria, why did they need me?"

"I asked him that question, too, when he was planning your birth. He said a mortal must be *born* in Pria to have the power to collapse it. He discouraged my questions for my safety. I didn't push it."

"I see," Alina said. "So, you two fell in love?"

She smiled. "Yes. Perhaps I was foolish because I loved him partly because he was mortal. I didn't trust immortals, and because he wasn't one, I believed he was safe to love."

"Did he ever prove you wrong?" Alina whispered.

Jade paused, tears forming in her eyes. "No. He lived up to all the good things I saw in him. But as you know, our story did not end happily. We spent two wonderful years together before he was caught and sent back to Carthem." She looked down at her hands.

"And now I will see him again. I hope he likes bald women." She brushed a tear from her cheek and smiled.

"Oh, your hair will grow fast. Or you can do a short, barbed hairdo."

"Yeah, I never liked those!" she laughed. Alina had more questions, but Jade looked so exhausted, Alina encouraged her to go to bed.

Now she sat with the unopened book in her lap and thought of J'koby and Rex. Alina was fond of Rex and hoped one day, Jade would love him back. But the more she learned of J'koby, the more she cared for him. It was exciting to have a father, and if he and Jade loved each other, the three of them could be like a real family.

But Rex was like a father to her, too, in his own way, and his devotion to Jade was solid and unwavering. She wisely mistrusted immortals but must be convinced of his loyalty by now.

Jade slept soundly; the small rise and fall of her chest the only indication she was alive. Dark blood pooled into the veins of her hands and black fuzz covered her head, but despite her flaws, she was the most beautiful woman Alina had known. Maybe she, like Rex, was learning to look inside to find real beauty.

Alina glanced at her own smooth hands and fingernails and ran them over her lean, shapely legs. She knew the power of her beauty by the hard gazes that followed her, but was she beautiful where it counted most? If mortality found her again, would she—and others— still find her remarkable?

Earlier, she asked Jade how she dealt with the stares as an immortal. Jade's clear answer surprised her.

"They never stared at me in Pria. Unless someone is exceptionally unique, no one notices."

"But no one stared at me in Pria, though I was obviously different," Alina answered. "They avoided me—except for Eris and some of the kids at school."

"That's because you were different in ways they didn't want to see," Jade explained. "Their eyes were accustomed to perfect things.

You upset their world—the only world they knew. To deal with this, they ignored you and looked away, making you nonexistent in their minds. But here in Carthem, you are the most stunning person they've ever seen. Even those who came from Pria may have forgotten what it's like to see someone so perfect."

"But I feel my beauty is becoming my identity—something no one can look past."

Jade leaned forward and kissed her forehead. "Then you must *give* them a reason to look past it," she said, smiling. "You are very bewitching, my dear. It will have to be something big."

CHAPTER 16

The next morning, after Rex joined Alina and Jade in their room for breakfast, Baylor poked his head in and announced they must all complete a wilderness survival course before traveling to Jaden.

"Lance's orders," he emphasized. "But Jade, you're permitted to observe the exercise portion since you're recovering from surgery."

"Do we *have* to do this?" Rex complained. Alina knew how much he wanted to get to Jaden and see Camden.

Baylor glared at him. "You have no idea how dangerous it is out there."

An hour later they met in the basement of their building, in a large gym surrounded by mats, climbable walls, and shooting ranges. Baylor, dressed in electric blue sweats and white running shoes, was already running laps. He ordered them to follow.

Alina sprinted off gracefully and enjoyed the exhilaration of being good at something. She'd hated to run in Pria, where kids made fun of her. Now she knew why. Rex looked angry as he ran with arms flailing, his face twisted into a grimace. When he passed Jade on the bench, she smothered her laughter with a towel.

They spent the morning learning first-aid skills and shooting poisonous darts similar to the quills from the killing stones. Baylor explained how the darts killed creatures and humans instantly, and as there was no antidote, they must handle the guns with care. This did little to help Rex, who became too nervous to shoot straight. Jade fared slightly better. Alina hit every target dead in the center, and Rex kept calling her a show-off.

They took a break for lunch, and as they sat on a mat eating, Baylor walked to a woman on the other side of the gym and kissed her on the lips. A young girl hugged him, and the three of them chatted lively, their voices echoing across the room. Baylor glanced in their direction, then made a discreet but accurate impression of Rex running. The woman and girl broke into laughter. Rex was so hungry he didn't notice.

"Do you think that's Baylor's wife?" Jade asked, which got Rex's attention. He stopped chewing and looked at them.

"And maybe the girl is his daughter," Alina said. "She looks about my age."

Jade nodded. "Come, let's go introduce ourselves."

They polished off their lunch, stood up and started across the gym. Baylor walked to meet them halfway.

He introduced them to Janet, his wife, a handsome woman with smooth, dark skin. Her jet-black hair was pulled into a spiky bun, and her exercise clothes flattered her fit, muscular body. Their daughter, Trinee, was a year younger than Alina. She had clusters of blemishes on her cheeks and full lips above her bright teeth.

Trinee smiled at Alina. "My father says you're doing great—you've mastered the course and it's only been a few hours."

"Well, it's easy when you're—like me." Alina didn't know if she should speak about her immortality. But Trinee already knew.

She leaned in to whisper to her. "Don't worry, I know about you, and I'm not jealous. My dad said being immortal isn't as great as it seems. Is it true you can't sleep, or enjoy food?"

"Kind of," Alina admitted. "Food tastes good, but I have no hunger to satisfy, so it's not the same. And I don't sleep at all. I miss that."

Trinee grinned. "Come with me for the afternoon. Dad says training is pointless for you. I'll take you around town and introduce you to my friends."

Alina hesitated. She longed for friends, but the thought of being around people frightened her. "I don't know—"

"What's wrong?"

She didn't want to admit her fears but felt she could be honest with Trinee. "I'm not very good at making friends. It's not that I don't want them, I just don't know what to say around people."

Trinee smiled warmly. "No problem. How about you and I hang out?"

Alina beamed, close to tears. She hadn't had a friend since Pierce. Unless she could count Zaiden. "That would be great."

Trinee told Baylor of their plans and Alina laughed as Rex moaned, with a twinkle in his eye, about the unfairness of her getting the afternoon off. The girls left the gym chatting and giggling as if they were longtime friends rather than new acquaintances.

Alina was curious about everything in Stormport, while Trinee wanted to hear about Pria. They took turns sharing experiences, first Trinee explaining what the school, boys, and families were like, then Alina doing the same.

"You don't have families?" Trinee gasped when Alina told her.

She shook her head.

"But—who takes care of you? And when you need to talk, who do you go to?"

"Most people go to their guardians. They're called caretakers. Some have great relationships with them, others don't. I couldn't talk much to Jade. She was under surveillance, you see, although I didn't know at the time."

Trinee shrugged. "I suppose it's no different here. Not the surveillance part, but the mix of good relationships and bad. Not every family is as close as mine."

This surprised Alina. "Really?"

"Yeah. They treat their pets better than their family members, sometimes."

"Now that sounds a lot like Pria."

"Yes. I'm lucky my parents are happy together. Mom worries about Dad, though. His job is demanding, and he has to travel to

Jaden a lot, which is very dangerous. She frets the whole time he's gone."

Alina's eyes softened. "I'd love to have a marriage like that one day. And a family. Jade is my family, and I've never been happier since she's opened up to me. My life in Pria was so lonely—there was no one I could talk to."

"No friends?" Trinee asked.

"Well, maybe one."

"Who?"

Alina blushed. "A boy was nice to me, but I hardly knew him. I can't really call him a friend."

"But you can call him your *true love*, right?" Trinee teased, linking arms with her.

Alina's eyes sparkled. "Of course!" she exclaimed, and they burst into laughter.

They spent the afternoon in town, where they ordered milkshakes at the soda shop and flirted with the cute waiter, then scoured the department store for fancy dresses to try on. Trinee showed her the historic district of Stormport, where they window shopped and kept a tally of the boys who stopped to stare at Alina.

"You should talk to some of them," Trinee prodded. "Let your hair down, like you did with the waiter in the soda shop."

"I only flirted with him because *you* did. I couldn't talk to him on my own—I don't have anything to say."

"That's the lucky thing about being pretty. Boys are interested no matter what you say," Trinee sighed.

Alina studied Trinee for a moment. She had long eyelashes that almost touched her eyebrows. Her black hair was slightly frizzy, but the way she pulled it back made her look older and sophisticated. Alina noticed the graceful curve of her jaw and how confidently she held her shoulders and neck.

"Trinee, you are *beautiful*," Alina raved, her sincerity so convincing that Trinee looked hopeful for a moment, then grinned.

"You don't have to build me up. I wasn't fishing for a compliment."

"I know. But I really mean it."

"Well, thank you. And you are too—inside, as well as out. I can tell you're worried about that." Trinee smiled, her white teeth bright against her ebony skin. "And I *am* trying to build you up. But I'm being honest too."

Alina smiled and dropped her eyes so Trinee wouldn't see her tears.

I have a friend.

She loved Carthem. This broken world gave her everything Pria never could.

CHAPTER 17

The days flew by after Alina found a friend. She spent most of her free time with Trinee, who occasionally invited other friends along. Alina soon felt at ease around them even as they peppered her with questions about Pria. At Baylor's request she concealed her immortality, as did Trinee, but otherwise spoke freely and found it liberating. The girls were appalled that century-old men dated teen girls and babies were left alone to crawl around mansions while their caretakers went out. They seemed impressed by Alina's ability to endure such a place.

She and Trinee spent many afternoons downtown, revisiting the same landmarks and stores, including the soda shop where the cute waiter worked. He greeted them the moment they walked through the door, poised behind the counter with a grin on his face. After a few visits, Alina heard more about him than she cared to know. His name was Pierre, he was the star of every sports team in his high school, of which he graduated early through excellent marks. Scores of girls came in regularly to see him, as he made the best Sweet-n-Nutty malt shake in town. But they were silly girls, and he was looking for a serious relationship—someone he could spend the rest of his life with. He leaned against the counter as he bragged, twitching his biceps beneath his rainbow-striped shirt. When Trinee mentioned the customers waiting in line, he didn't seem to hear but continued to pester Alina for her name. The customers came to her rescue when they started yelling at him. Pierre jumped up to take their orders and the girls made their escape, bursting into laughter as they exited the shop.

Alina loved having friends to laugh with, and felt reluctant when Baylor finalized their travel plans to Jaden. He oversaw their preparations by filling their packs with food, water, sleeping gear, clothes, weapons, and first-aid supplies. Early summer in Carthem meant traveling in the heat, and to alleviate this, Baylor secured the best vehicle in Stormport—one with large tires, four-wheel drive, and air conditioning.

Two days before their planned departure, Baylor informed them that Lance had rearranged his schedule to meet with them at last.

They had expected Lance to call for them earlier—Alina was famous, after all. But whenever Rex pointed this out to Baylor, he shook his head and mentioned Lance's busy schedule. This time, however, he revealed a little more.

"You may find Lance a bit—" He paused, thinking of the right word. "Eccentric."

"Why is that?" asked Jade.

"He's brilliant," Baylor assured them, "but as Sampson's top target, he's paranoid about being assassinated. He doesn't meet with anyone fresh from Pria for weeks, sometimes months—when he's sure they're loyal to Carthem. He's made an exception for Alina."

"Took him long enough," Rex said dryly.

"You can't blame him for being careful," Baylor replied. "He's convinced if he dies, the fight against Sampson will fail. And he's probably right."

The next morning, Baylor drove them across town to the tallest building in Stormport. The guard at the front door frowned as he scanned them with the same device they'd seen when they first arrived. It emitted a long beep as it went over Alina.

"Serum runs through her veins," Baylor explained. "It's going to beep every time for her."

The guard looked surprised but nodded to permit their entrance. Their footsteps echoed as they walked into the tall foyer. On a railing above, a worker passed in a white laboratory outfit with a plastic shield over the eyes. Now she understood why the building was so large—it housed Carthem's laboratories.

Baylor led them into an elevator and tapped a button. The elevator clanged shut and lurched them up seven stories, where they exited into a quiet, empty hallway. They walked to the end of the hall to a shiny metal door with a monitor in the center.

Baylor placed his hand on the screen. It hummed and scanned, then gave a soft click.

"Come in," said a deep voice from inside.

They entered a large room full of bookshelves, a few empty chairs, and a meticulously organized desk. A short heavyset man stood up when they entered. Large glasses magnified his green eyes as he reached out his hand.

"Welcome!" Lance said, his round belly jiggling as he shook Rex's hand. "You must be Rex, and Jade, and Alina. I'm glad to meet you at last. I'm sorry I didn't call for you sooner. Stormport and Jaden's safety is a huge responsibility, but perhaps someday all the security will not be needed."

They nodded their hellos, and Lance smiled at Alina. "We've waited a long time for you. Your birth encouraged me to leave Pria. You bring purpose to the resistance."

Alina forced an uncomfortable smile as they sat in the chairs around his desk.

Lance ran a hand over his bald head, then stroked his beard with his fingers. "I understand you had an interesting journey from the portal to here."

"Yes," Rex said. "The wilderness didn't get dangerous until we were close to Stormport. Maybe Sampson was concerned for Alina's safety."

"Perhaps he was at first, but the black mist is sent directly from him, so he must have known about Alina's immortality by then and was trying to kill the two of you." He pointed to Rex and Jade.

"How does anyone survive out there?" Rex asked.

Lance sighed. "It's a constant fight. When we find a way to

overcome one thing, he unleashes something new. And this time Stan is that new threat. What can you tell me about him, Rex?"

Rex's eyes flashed with anger. "He's a traitor, and, unfortunately, knows a lot about the resistance because he was part of it. He played both sides well—I had no idea."

Lance put his elbows on his desk and interlocked his fingers. "This is bad news. Sampson may have found a way to penetrate our security. The stunning mechanism should have knocked Stan out cold." He closed his eyes for a moment, then slammed his clenched fists on the desk and cursed. Jade and Alina jumped in their seats.

"Just when we get you" —Lance nodded at Alina— "he forces our energy back into protecting ourselves so we can't proceed with our plans."

Jade spoke calmly. "We can still proceed. We'll go with Alina to Jaden while you take care of the security concerns here."

He stroked his chin again. "It will be difficult to spare Baylor."

"Then keep him here. We'll be fine."

"No," Lance said. "You need him more than I do. I only hope Jaden is secure when you get there. Not to mention Millflower and the other towns—" He rested his head in his hands and rubbed his temples.

"Are there towns along the way?" Jade asked.

"There's one between here and Jaden," Baylor explained. "Millflower—a farming community and the hub of our food production. It has some security features, but not like Stormport and Jaden."

"Yes, hopefully it holds," Lance said, and sighed. "The time is here—we knew when Alina showed up. Time to unite and get everyone in Carthem involved in the Cause. They'll be scared—no one is prepared for something like this." He gave a small smile. "But it's exciting, too."

He met Alina's eyes. "You need to be aware—Sampson will do whatever he can to bring you back to Pria and under his control. There's a portal in the Blue Forest, so it can be done."

"Do you know why Alina became immortal when she left Pria? Does the dagger reverse one's condition?" Rex asked.

Lance leaned back in his chair. "I've been thinking about that since I heard. I don't know why she changed, but I believe J'koby may have some ideas. He's the expert on immortality and the serum dagger."

"Can I ask a question?" Alina spoke up.

"Of course."

"Rex told me the resistance doesn't want me dead, even though my death would cause Sampson's downfall. Why is that?"

Lance and Rex exchanged glances. Lance nodded. "How J'koby explained it to me," Rex said, "is if you die, everyone who originated from the serum would also die."

"So, people like Camden, J'koby, Trinee, and Baylor would be fine," Lance said. "They were conceived by a mortal mother and father. But me, Jade, Rex—we'd die. Not to mention everyone in Pria, including the entire resistance. A tragic death toll. We hope to avoid that."

"And Sampson would live?" Alina asked.

"Yes, Sampson would live. Pria would cease to exist, and he'd be mortal and vulnerable, but he could still slip through our fingers."

"Is there any other way to weaken him?"

"Yes," Lance said. "Camden and J'koby have developed a plan, and you are at the heart of it. If the plan fails, then there may be no other option than to let you and all those others die to save Carthem. But I want to live to see the end of Sampson's rule if I can. How about all of you?" He forced a chuckle, and Rex and Jade laughed nervously.

"I will do whatever I need to. I want to help Carthem also," Alina said. "Does this plan free those in Pria as well?"

Lance nodded. "Those who wish to be. Many of them fear mortality and will not want to leave. We won't force them. The important thing is they *have* the choice." He leaned towards her. "Your immortality is a blessing to us *and* to Sampson. Camden and

J'koby were concerned about keeping you safe once you got here, and it's a relief not to worry about that. Sampson's world is getting shaky, and now our biggest concern is keeping our people safe as he tightens his hold." He rubbed his forehead. "I'll be honest, this worries me. Carthem has always been a necessary thorn in his side. He'd wipe this world clean and start over if he could."

They went quiet as Lance tapped his fingers on his desk. "Well, you must leave tomorrow as planned. I'm happy to put you in Baylor's hands. There's no better guide."

"Thank you, Lance," said Jade.

"One more thing," he said as he slid open a drawer in his desk, pulled out a book, and held it up for them to see. "This is our wilderness guidebook. We wrote it specifically for those new to Carthem, and it covers all the dangers we know of. I'm sorry I didn't get this book to you sooner, but I wanted the content to be as accurate as possible, so I've spent the past two weeks updating it. I suggest you read it all before leaving tomorrow." He handed the book to Rex, who eyed it nervously.

Lance continued. "Baylor will take our best radio, which will allow you to communicate with us during the first part of your journey, then with Millflower and Jaden for the last half. Phones work only in the towns."

He smiled at them, then stood up and reached out his hand to shake theirs. "I'll let you finish your preparations. Thank you for meeting with me. Please, travel safe."

Rex and Jade thanked him, and as they stood up to leave, Lance turned to Alina. "Can I speak with you for a moment in private?"

"Oh—of course," she answered.

The others left the room, and when the door closed, Lance sat down at his desk. "Alina, I have something to ask of you. It's up to you, but if you're willing, it will help our cause tremendously."

"I'll do anything to help," she agreed.

He gave her a crooked smile, the first that seemed genuine. "Thank you. Will you donate some of the serum that runs in your veins? You must know by now how powerful it is. With it I may be able to create an antidote to the poison in Sampson's creatures."

"Yes, of course! How do I donate it?"

"The only release is through tears. Your skin can't be punctured." He pulled a small vial from his desk drawer. "We don't need much. The serum replicates rapidly under the right conditions, which is why Sampson has an endless supply of it. Try to release some before you leave tomorrow. Think sad thoughts, laugh until you cry—whatever it takes."

She grinned. "A little more notice would've been helpful."

"I apologize, but I'm sure you'll do fine. Reading that guidebook can bring anyone to tears."

CHAPTER 18

That evening after they finished packing, Rex knocked on Alina and Jade's door with the guidebook in hand. They agreed to study, together, all they could about Carthem's dangers before facing them. Alina and Jade sat on the bed with their backs against the wall. Rex plopped down in the chair and opened the book.

The preface, written by Lance, warned that the book became outdated almost the moment it was printed, as new dangers arrived daily from Pria. He encouraged anyone who survived any new encounters to report them immediately so they could be added to the next edition.

"That's reassuring," Rex muttered. He cleared his throat and began to read.

"'Carthem's wilderness is a deadly place, thanks to Victor Sampson and his desire to eliminate all who live here. Some threats, however, are natural and do not have Prian origins. This book will discuss both dangers, with emphasis on the serious and common. We do not guarantee it will cover all dangers. Our best advice: if something looks suspicious, get away.'"

Rex looked up and snorted. "Valuable advice indeed."

Jade giggled.

He read on. "'The most threatening of the natural dangers is severe weather, and each season holds some risk of exposure, such as hypothermia, heat stroke, and dehydration. Travel is recommended during the mild seasons of late spring or early fall, and be prepared with plenty of water, warm clothes, and fuel in case of unexpected extremes.

"'Other natural dangers include wild beasts native to Carthem. They are not confrontational like the engineered beasts from Pria; however, death can occur when people underestimate their instinctual power. Some of the most dangerous are bears, wild cats, and moose in the northern mountainous areas, poisonous snakes and scorpions in the desert, and blood-sucking insects in the eastern rainforest.'"

Rex looked up, confused. "I've never heard of any of these things, have you?"

Jade and Alina shook their heads.

"How are we supposed to recognize them? Some guidebook. And blood-sucking insects? I don't like the sound of those." But the next page answered Rex's question, with a picture of each native creature above a descriptive caption.

"'Be wise with these animals, but don't fear them,'" Rex continued. "'Generally, if you don't seek them out or threaten them, they will avoid you. The creatures to be feared are the ones contrived in Sampson's laboratories.'" Rex shuddered.

"'Sampson releases animals of his own creation into Carthem. He makes these creatures innately aggressive. Their instincts are to kill. Wilderness travelers must carry a weapon at all times and should consist of parties of four or fewer. The larger the group, the easier they can be tracked. It's common for lone travelers to elude all creatures, but we recommend a party of two or three so there can be a guard every hour of the night.'"

"Great!" Alina cut in. "I'll be the guard every night!"

Rex and Jade smiled, but her words did little to ease the tension in the room. Rex handed the book to Jade. "I can't read any more."

"Try to relax," she encouraged as she took the book and cleared her throat. "'Prian-made creatures locate to the climate most conducive to their survival. Sampson has picked up on this, so he creates animals fit for certain regions. As a result, we have dangerous creatures throughout all of Carthem. We will describe creatures by region so travelers can prepare according to their routes.

"'The southwest area of Carthem is a dry desert. It's the least traveled region as there are few settlements. Only one Prian-made creature thrives here, the skin-sucking carber. This scaly, sand-burrowing animal is about the size of a small cat, has large eyeballs and a long, skinny snout. The carber attacks by latching onto its victim and sucking water from the body. This dehydrates the victim within minutes and leaves the carber replenished for several months, sometimes years. Since no one has survived a carber attack, no one knows how painful the experience is, but the victims' screams imply a horrific and excruciating death.'" Jade grimaced. "Ugh, look at that thing!" She held up a picture of a scaly beast with sand colored eyeballs.

Rex's teeth chattered. "We're not going through the desert, are we?"

Jade glanced at the map. "No, thank goodness."

"No wonder nobody lives out there!" Rex said.

"Well, from the looks of it," said Jade, her eyes skimming the page, "the carber seems to be one of the tamer creatures."

"What?" Rex cried.

"Let's only read about the areas we'll be traveling through," suggested Alina. "Hearing about all of Sampson's creatures is not going to boost our morale."

"Good point," said Jade as she turned the page and continued reading. "'The most traveled route is the road between Stormport and Jaden, a distance of three hundred miles. A majority of the path is through the prairie. It's hot in the summer with little shade.' Hmm, good thing we have a vehicle. 'The biggest threat is a small maggot-like creature called a brainwaste.'"

"*Brainwaste?*" Rex exclaimed.

"Stop interrupting, Rex. 'Brainwastes are tiny insects that flourish in the tall prairie grasses. They cannot fly, so they crawl up the grass stalks and cling to vehicles or travelers. Once they have found a victim, they enter through the ear canal and drill through the skull, where they feast on the brain. Victims rapidly lose their senses, hallucinate, and become violent. There are no warning signs until the creature burrows through the skull, which makes removal impossible. Victims become delirious and attack anyone within their proximity. If someone in your company complains of a painful drilling sensation on the side of the head and becomes incoherent, it is best to flee immediately. This is difficult but necessary to protect the lives of those nearby.'"

Rex smothered a squeal from his mouth.

"But there's good news!" Jade read on. "'Thanks to our scientists in Stormport, we have an effective method of eluding these creatures. Tight metal patches, called ear shields, snap around the head and cover the ears completely. These patches have proven effective against brainwastes. A thorough examination of the body, particularly the head, should be done before the ear shields are removed.'"

Rex slapped his hands over his ears. "Okay, I'm not removing mine until we get to Jaden. What else do we have to worry about?"

Jade read on. "'Most of Sampson's creatures carry the same danger—serum poison.

"Ageless serum is what makes Sampson's world possible. He can manipulate it into a potent, deadly toxin, which is then carried through a host. When his insects or animals transfer this poison through bites, scratches, or blood-sucking, it kills their victims slowly and painfully. The inner organs fester, secreting the toxin through every orifice. This can then infect anyone who comes in contact with the victim.'"

Alina flushed with anger. "What an interesting pattern we have here. First, Sampson's victims always suffer—death can't be quick or painless. And then he makes sure anyone who comes to their aid also dies. This prevents others from helping."

"What choice do they have?" Rex asked.

"None. That's what makes it so sad. Abandoning loved ones in their agony. At least I know I can stay and comfort anyone who dies by my side."

"I hope you won't have to," Jade said.

Alina's voice caught as she spoke. "I'm terrified of these creatures, and they can't even hurt me. I worry about all of you."

Jade reached out and rubbed her back. "At least nothing can hurt *you*."

Alina didn't look at her. She grew tired of them emphasizing her value.

Jade returned to the book, but the list of creatures was so extensive, she only skimmed through them. They included bloated, crusty millipedes and other bulbous insects that oozed poisonous serum, birds that attacked in swarms and pecked poison into people's brains, cat-like animals with venomous claws that shredded the skin, and of course the killing stones—hard-shelled creatures that expelled deadly quills.

Rex's face turned a pale shade of green. "Why does everything have to be so gross? Oozing and festering and crusting over?"

"Speaking of gross, look at this, Rex," Alina said, studying the book over Jade's shoulder. "Here's the creature that chased us up the tree." She pointed to a picture of the bizarre-looking beast, with its spiky body, sagging jowls, and gnarled fangs. "It's called a monyx and can sense warm blood from over a mile away."

"Huh?" Rex asked. "You mean freshly spilled blood?"

Alina scanned the page. "No—warm-blooded animals, including humans. The monyx smells the blood in their veins. Wow, we were lucky. The spiky tail releases serum poison that paralyzes the victim. When he can't move, the monyx continues to slash until he finds an artery, then drinks the pool of blood that follows."

Rex clapped his hand over his mouth and ran to the bathroom. Alina and Jade grimaced over the retching sounds.

"You okay, Rex?" said Alina, after he went quiet. "I've done that before. It's not fun."

"Yes, I remember," Rex moaned. "After you rode the coaster at the spring festival."

Alina cringed. "You saw me? I ran away after I got off and threw up my lunch in a bush. I was so worried someone noticed!"

"I was always looking out for you. But don't worry, I'm pretty sure no one else saw."

"You know, I'm done reading about these creatures," Jade said, flipping through the pages. "Our defense strategy will be the same for all of them—"

"Yes. Running for our lives," Rex called from the bathroom.

"—Let's read about the other dangers, the non-poisonous ones."

"You mean Sampson uses something besides serum poison to kill people? I didn't think his brain could stretch that much," Rex scoffed as he came out of the bathroom, wiping his mouth.

"Yes. They're humans."

Alina knitted her eyebrows together. "Huh?"

Jade continued reading. "'A particularly dangerous—and mysterious—group of creatures are called mirages. Little is known of them, as no one who has attempted to study them has survived.

"'According to eyewitnesses, mirages are usually seen in the haze of dawn or dusk, at what appears to be a great distance from the traveler. The sight of the mirage is alluring and captivating because of an aura they emit to ensnare their victims. If one succumbs to the aura, he will seek out the mirage to his ruin.

"'Only those who recognize and immediately resist a mirage have lived to share their experience. Because of this, anyone who beholds one *must* flee at first sight; if they look twice, they will succumb. This has proven true—and fatal—100% of the time.'"

"What do these mirages do to their victims?" Rex wondered.

Jade raised her eyebrows. "No one knows. The bodies are never found." She shivered as she continued reading. "Because of their intrigue, these creatures draw the attention of the curious and are a popular method of suicide. However, they are *not* to be trifled with. Some have sought them out, thinking they could escape after the first glance. *Under no circumstances should you seek them out.* Only inadvertent encounters have produced survivors, and the best defense is to flee the moment one is seen.'"

"Whoa," Rex said nervously. "How do we recognize them?"

Jade pursed her lips and scanned the page. "'There are no pictures of them because no one who has attempted to photograph one has lived. But survivors describe them as intoxicating, more than anything experienced before. Their strong aura stirs a warning only to those on guard. Different survivors have different accounts. The important thing to remember is if you pause to consider the temptation, you will fall.'"

A long silence followed. "That's pretty freaky," Rex said.

"Listen, this is even freakier. Sounds like they aren't the worst," Jade said, reading on. "'The most dangerous of all creatures is the nightstalk. It's so named because of how it hunts its prey. The nightstalk attacks at night and uses fear to capture its victims. Nightstalks are human in origin. They're a puzzle to scientists because of their deadly nature, yet they carry no poisonous serum. Their terrifying features, combined with their gruesome killing methods, have made them the most feared of Sampson's creatures. They haunt all regions of Carthem. People describe them as living nightmares, and some believe it is this reputation that gives them their power.

"'The first sign of an approaching nightstalk is sudden and unwarranted fear. If possible, flee immediately, while you can still move. The fear paralyzes the muscles and slows the brain, allowing the nightstalk to overpower the victim. It then skins the victim's body with its long nails and consumes the heart in a slow, painful death. They also have a mysterious telepathic connection, so if one nightstalk is killed, others are alerted, and they unite to find and kill whoever threatens them. Though it hasn't been proven, Carthem scientists believe these creatures can be defeated if one can overcome the fear.'"

Jade stopped reading, and a chilling silence filled the room. Alina knew this creature; she'd seen it in the Gordian laboratories. She'd felt its paralyzing terror and how difficult it was to overcome. Would being immortal make it less overpowering, as there was no possibility of death? She didn't know.

"Does the book explain if Sampson uses people from his dungeons?" Alina asked. "He mentioned something like that to me."

Jade stared at Alina for a long moment, then picked up the book and cleared her throat. "Alina, I should warn you—" she broke off.

"What?"

"Just—prepare yourself." She hesitated and took a deep breath.

"'Sampson uses his prisoners in Gordian as puppets in Carthem. These victims' minds have been altered by his experiments. Their mental conditions differ, so they are unpredictable in their behavior, but some of the most common traits we see are self-mutilation (though never to the point of death) and aggression toward others. Like the animals, this seems to be ingrained in them. Sampson often equips them with weapons, and, despite their incoherence, they are powerful fighters because of their hostile nature.'"

Jade looked up and met the wide eyes of Rex and Alina. "I'm not as surprised as you because I knew this already. He's an *evil* man."

She turned back to the book, her hands shaking as she held the pages. "'Sampson exploits his prisoners to enact revenge. Occasionally one will be found haunting the outskirts of a town, only to be recognized as a beloved friend of someone living there. If any of Sampson's traitors left a lover behind in Pria, they can almost be certain to meet him (or her) as a deranged killer sent to finish them. If a confrontation takes place, they are left with a heart-wrenching decision: kill the loved one, or be killed *by* him or her.'"

Alina jumped off the bed and darted to the bathroom, her sob escaping her mouth before she could close the door behind her. She crumbled to her knees and muffled her cry in her tight fist.

The repercussions for leaving Zaiden behind were worse than she imagined. Endless life in a dungeon seemed merciful now. She gripped her hair at the scalp and wept.

The serum! I'll get back at Sampson by helping Lance. She took out the vial from her pocket and held it against the side of her nose until it spilled over.

Rex left the apartment, his fingers tapping on the door as he passed, and a few moments later she heard a soft knock.

"Come in," Alina choked out. Jade entered and gently pulled Alina up, leading her back into the room. She helped her onto the bed and sat crossed-legged next to her.

"Maybe I read too much tonight," she whispered.

Alina shook her head. "You can't hide the truth from me. The sooner I know, the better. The hardest part is, I finally accepted I might never see him again." Her voice shook as the tears returned.

It was true, she had accepted this, but Zaiden still occupied her mind every free moment. "I–I don't think I could bear seeing him like that when it's my fault he's imprisoned in the first place. Even if he doesn't care about me—but I can't help wondering, you know, if he would, now that I look different..." she trailed off.

"You think he'd only like you if you're pretty?" Jade asked.

Alina shrugged. "I know it's vain. But I always felt that was why boys never paid attention to me."

Jade stroked her hand. "You put too much emphasis on beauty. I understand why—you had a different experience in Pria than the rest of us. But when everyone is beautiful, the meaning of the word changes. It's a matter of opinion. Once or twice, I heard people say how unforgettable you were because of your unique face."

Alina rolled her eyes. "Of course—I had red blemishes and crooked teeth and other things they hadn't seen before. But here—well, you've seen how people react."

"Yes, but remember, they have a different opinion of beauty. If Zaiden *did* make it here, he might be attracted to the simple girls of Carthem the same way he was drawn to you in Pria."

"You think he was?"

Jade grinned. "I don't know his reasons, but yes, he definitely was."

"It doesn't matter, anyway. If he makes it here, he'll be a crazy killer, stalking me." She tried to laugh but dissolved into tears.

Jade rubbed her back, and after allowing her to cry for a moment, spoke gently. "I'm not sure if this will help you feel better, but can I tell you my story?"

Alina looked at her and nodded, wiping her cheeks.

"You probably haven't thought of this, but isn't it peculiar Sampson didn't release me into Carthem as a violent crazy woman after J'koby was sent back? To this day, he remains the worst of Sampson's enemies, and Sampson knew we loved each other."

"But since J'koby was mortal, why didn't Sampson kill him?" Alina asked.

"I don't know for sure, but my guess is he wanted more. He's a cruel man. He wants his enemies to suffer and feel oppressed under his power. That's the ultimate satisfaction for him."

"Did he try to make you insane?"

"Yes. I believe he imprisoned me for that purpose. And to hasten this, he put you—a newborn baby—in a dark cell next to mine, so I would be tortured by your cries and my inability to do anything about them. This was temporary, though, until he could decide what to do with you. He needed to keep you secret. But naturally, no one in Gordian knew anything about mortal babies—not even he, who once lived in a mortal world. He never had children of his own. Or if he did, he didn't know them.

"But during those two years that J'koby lived with Camden, he taught me everything about caring for babies. He didn't have children himself, but he knew a lot, having lived among mortals for so long. The plan was, if Sampson discovered you and killed him and your mother, I would become your caretaker."

"The plan worked, then!"

Jade nodded. "It wasn't easy, though. Your cries and my helplessness *would* have driven me mad if I didn't take action. Sampson knew how you threatened him, so he searched desperately for a way to keep you alive. He always sent one of his indoctrinated guards down to feed you—he never came himself, because he was terrified of you. You threatened him so much, he got anxious just being near you."

She took a deep breath. "When I heard your cries, I got an idea. I told the guard you might be ill and to send for Sampson right away. He came down immediately. I told him I believed your cries indicated you were dying. Sampson didn't believe me at first. He knew viruses and germs didn't exist in Pria and thought as long as you ate, you'd be fine. His naiveté was so extreme, it was almost easy." She grinned.

"I told him there were many ways a child could die without germs or infections. They could die if neglected or isolated without affection. Their body organs and brain could shut down, and so on. Everything I said was true, and he must have remembered some from his mortal days, because he believed me.

"So, he turned on a light, and holding me firmly, led me into your cell where he told me to examine you for signs of illness. He knew you'd need a diaper, so you had extra layers down there, but his guard didn't have the slightest clue how to change your bedding, much less how often. You were lying in a small cradle, soaked in urine and feces. I took off your clothes and wiped you clean enough to reveal a flaming red rash from your upper torso down to your knees. Not only was this alarming to see, but you were screaming at the top of your lungs and Sampson went into a panic. He thought you, and therefore his precious kingdom, were heading for a quick and painful death."

"The rash—was it serious?" Alina asked.

Jade chuckled. "No. J'koby told me about them. Any small detail might get you into my custody, so he told me everything specific to babies. This worked. I told Sampson I knew how to treat the rash, but you couldn't live in a dark dungeon and survive—you needed to be nurtured to thrive. The better life he gave you, the longer you would live, and the more time he would have to find a solution. I offered to be your guardian and he consented, on one condition—I was put under surveillance. He didn't want you to know who you were. Who you *are*."

Jade paused and looked down at her hands, tears trickling around her nose. "That was the best moment of my life, the day I became your caretaker and was spared being sent into Carthem to murder my love."

Alina was crying, too. She reached out to hug her.

"Don't give up hope for Zaiden," Jade whispered. "It takes a long time—years—to make someone crazy enough to murder a loved one. Sampson doesn't have that kind of time."

CHAPTER 19

At six o'clock the next morning, Alina dressed in her traveling clothes and placed the last of her things in her pack. She buried Zaiden's disc and the panel at the bottom, where no one could see it, then slid the guidebook into a side pocket where it would be accessible. The book didn't seem as ominous to her now. Jade's words soothed her, and Trinee brought a welcome diversion when she called after Jade went to sleep. The girls chatted and giggled late into the night, and when the dawn came, Alina felt ready to face the journey ahead of her.

Rex tapped on the door and entered, dressed in similar khaki-colored pants and waterproof boots.

"Is Jade awake?" he asked.

"Not yet."

"We need to wake her. We're supposed to meet Baylor in the lobby in fifteen minutes." He looked at her bag on the floor. "Did you pack the guidebook?"

"Yes."

He sighed. "I suppose we better take it, though I'd soon burn it for all the good it does."

Alina walked to the bed and rubbed Jade's arm. "Wake up, Jade. We need to leave in a few minutes." Jade stirred for a moment, then swung the covers off and went into the bathroom. Alina put on her pack and followed Rex into the hallway. He leaned against the wall and closed his eyes.

"Did you sleep okay?" she asked.

He shook his head. "Not a wink."

"Maybe you can sleep on the drive."

"Baylor said the road's pretty bumpy. Lots of ruts and dips."

"Well, think of how good you'll sleep tonight when we're in the wild. You'll be glad to be tired then."

"I hope so."

"At least we don't have to clean bathrooms anymore," Alina said, trying to perk him up. He forced a smile.

They said nothing more until Jade joined them in the hallway in her traveling clothes. She hoisted her pack onto her back and straightened her hat. "Are we ready?" she asked.

"Let's go," said Rex.

A small crowd gathered in the lobby to say goodbye: Dr. Scott and Jade's nurses, Lance, Eleanor, and Baylor's family. Trinee surprised Alina by being there so early after their late night. Her eyes looked puffy, but she smiled as she linked arms with Alina.

"Promise me you'll look after Dad?" she whispered.

Alina's face softened. "Of course."

"Mom's really worried this time, more than usual."

Alina glanced at Janet. She looked sick.

Trinee furrowed her brow. "This trip will be the most dangerous he's been on."

Alina's heart sank. *She* was the reason their journey was so dangerous. "You know I couldn't live with myself if anything happened to him."

Trinee's eyes widened. "That's not what I meant—I don't want you to feel responsible. We all know fighting Sampson is dangerous. I'll never blame you if something goes wrong."

"I know. But I'll do everything I can to keep him—all of them —safe."

"I know you will."

"I'll miss you, Trin."

"I'll miss you too."

They hugged tightly. Trinee turned back to join her parents, and

Alina walked to Lance, who stood on the side by himself, observing the group. He smiled at her as she approached.

"You know, Alina," he said when she reached him, "despite what people say about me being the best hope for Carthem, the truth is, *you* are. I'm glad you're immortal so you'll be safe. But there may come a time when you have to change so the mission can progress. Be prepared and learn all you can so when the time comes, you'll be ready."

Alina didn't understand him, but she nodded as if she did.

"Baylor will get you there safely. I hope you have a wonderful reunion with your father and grandfather."

"Thank you, Lance." She pulled out the vial of serum tears and handed it to him.

He beamed as he took it from her. "Thank you. I knew you could do it."

The crowd followed them out the door, with Jade and her nurses the lively ones of the group. Tears rolled down Janet's face as she held Baylor's hand. He had his other arm around Trinee, who forced a smile.

Their vehicle sat in the parking lot, loaded with supplies. Baylor threw their packs in the back, hugged and kissed his family one more time, then hopped into the driver's seat.

Jade and Alina climbed in the back, leaving the front passenger side for Rex. The crowd waved as they drove away. Janet and Trinee held each other, both in tears. Baylor didn't look back, but his eyes were wet.

As they turned a corner and pulled onto the main street, Alina's mouth dropped in a startled gasp. Despite the early hour, the entire town lined the street, waving and cheering as the vehicle came into view. She grabbed Baylor's shoulder.

"Do they know about me?" she asked.

He turned his head and smiled. "Yes. Lance made a public announcement last night. It's time for people to know you're here.

You need some encouragement as we head off—it helps us remember what we're fighting for."

Large signs and banners waved with the crowd.

Good luck Alina!
We're fighting with you!
Make Carthem free!

The roof of the vehicle was down, and Alina scrambled over the packs and stood to wave. Children jumped up and down when they saw her, and others blew kisses, eagerly returning her waves.

"We love you, Alina!" they called to her.

She blinked back tears as she looked into each face, these people who had lived under Sampson's oppression all their lives. J'koby's mission, her birth, the Cause—brought them hope for a better life. She swallowed and tried to smile. If they knew her, they wouldn't dare put so much faith in her.

The cheers grew more exuberant as Baylor drove to the end of the street and crossed through Stormport's protective shield. Alina climbed as high as she could, waving until the paved road changed to dirt and the people became small dots on the horizon.

"Time to put up the roof," said Baylor, and as Alina sat down, the car enclosed around them. "We should also put on the ear shields. Brainwastes can sneak into cars, no matter how tight they are." He put one around his head and snapped it on.

Alina felt a twinge of guilt for her immortal comforts. The shields looked tight and uncomfortable. Jade grimaced as she snapped hers in place. "Interesting," she said. "I can hear the same as before."

"Another tribute to Lance's genius," said Baylor. "Shields would be worthless if they kept people from hearing other dangers." Baylor revved the engine over a large sandy patch. One of the back tires sank in, and he switched to four-wheel drive.

"Wow. This is going to be a long trip," Rex commented.

But Baylor soon got into a rhythm, and he kept the car at a steady if bouncy pace. He seemed to know the road well.

A restless mood settled over the group. "Tell me about life in Pria," Baylor said, trying to disperse the tension. "Are all the women as beautiful as you, Alina?"

"Oh yes," Rex said. "And if they had brains and personality like she and Jade, Pria would be a paradise indeed. But most of them are shallow and vain."

Baylor chuckled, and Rex began elaborating on the many women who tried to seduce him over the years. Baylor shook his head in disbelief, but Rex didn't exaggerate—women did outrageous things in Pria to get attention. Alina leaned back in her seat to enjoy the view outside. The prairie lands stretched out before them: flat and golden.

Before long, Alina heard a strange noise, which grew louder as she put her ear to the window. She furrowed her brow. Could something be wrong with the car?

"Baylor?" she said, but he was engrossed in Rex's story.

"There I was at home, having barely escaped her, when I heard a knock at my door," Rex prattled. "Well, I wasn't about to answer it. The next thing I knew this woman was peering through my bedroom window—"

"Quiet!" Baylor hissed.

They stiffened. "What is it?" Rex asked in a hoarse whisper.

Baylor didn't answer but cracked his window and removed the dart gun from his pocket. He held it steady through the gap.

A shrill cry broke out, and Rex, Alina, and Jade screamed and cowered in the car. Baylor fired, silencing it.

"What *was* that?" Rex panted.

"A grimalkin," Baylor answered. "Vicious feline creatures with poisonous claws. They pounce and scratch their prey. If a claw draws blood, the poison is pumped to the heart in minutes."

"We wouldn't last five minutes without you, Baylor!" Jade exclaimed. "How did you hear it?"

"They give a strange hiss when going for the kill. It's not very loud, but distinct enough I usually notice it."

"I heard it, too," said Alina.

Baylor nodded at her. "I'm sorry to put an end to the only relief we have, but I don't think we should talk. Not that your story isn't engaging, Rex. I definitely want to hear the ending another time. But for now, we should speak only when necessary and in whispers. I've never encountered a creature so close to Stormport before."

"Keeping the windows closed should help, right?" Rex asked.

"Glass can't stop anything Prian-made, just so you know."

More edgy than before, they strained to hear any unusual sounds outside. Baylor's driving became erratic, and he pushed on the gas to get the tires out of ruts along the road.

A few moments later, Alina heard the noise again, this time strong and disjointed, like a chorus hissing all at once. She panicked.

"Baylor!" she cried, "I hear the hissing, and there's a lot of them this time!"

"I don't hear anything—"

"I heard it before you did last time, too."

Baylor stopped the car. "Guns out, everyone," he said, cracking the windows so the guns could fit through. "This could be bad," he warned as the hissing met their ears.

A moment later, the battle cry of grimalkins cut the air, drowning out the whizzing of darts around them. Thirty or more, with vomit-colored fur and ink-black eyes, stalked the vehicle. Jade shrieked as several jumped on the roof, their sharp claws screeching over the metal. One poked its head over the edge and swatted through the window crack. The creatures fell to the ground when hit, only to be replaced by more of them. Alina gritted her teeth and prayed the darts wouldn't run out. Had the guns been tested like this before?

An unusually large grimalkin clawed at the window with a horrible grating noise. It lay low on the roof where the guns could not aim. "Smart creature," Alina muttered.

"Hit its paw—anything!" Baylor shouted, sweat dripping from his forehead.

After several unsuccessful shots, Alina could see the glass about to shatter. Numerous grimalkins remained, and if they penetrated the car, she'd be the one person left alive.

She leaned against the window and slipped her hands through the crack, seizing the animal around its neck. It scratched ferociously at her hands and arms, but with one strong twist, she broke its neck and flung it to the ground.

One by one, she killed each creature on the car until she could open the door, then slipped out and slammed it behind her. She ran from the car, screaming at the top of her lungs. The diversion worked. Fifteen sets of claws sprung on her at once, and in less than a minute, a heap of mangled grimalkins lay on the ground around her.

She flipped back her hair and ran her hands over her arms. Her sleeves were in shreds, but her skin was smooth without a scratch in sight.

Jade and Rex burst into cheers, and despite Baylor's instructions not to leave the vehicle, they scrambled out and ran to her, almost knocking her to the ground.

"Alina, that was incredible!" Rex exclaimed, squeezing her against him. "I'm not afraid of anything now!"

"Maybe we'll be safer than we thought," Jade agreed. Alina beamed, but when she looked at Baylor, her smile faded.

He seemed relieved, but with a hint of sadness in his eyes. She knew then, as he did—defending themselves wouldn't always be that easy. Larger and more dangerous creatures than grimalkins haunted Carthem's wilderness.

CHAPTER 20

They drove through the prairie all afternoon. After several hours without any encounters, Rex reached a cheerful mood and Jade napped peacefully on Alina's shoulder. Baylor, however, was on edge. His shoulders tightened as he drove, and his eyes didn't blink. The absence of creature sightings made him jittery, as if he expected something to pounce on the car at any moment. He kept repeating, both to others and himself, how they must reach their destination before dark.

Careful not to wake Jade, Alina stretched her neck to peer out the window. The sun dropped low on the horizon, an orb of gold glistening on a wide, lazy river, snaking through the grass. A gentle breeze combed through the tall stalks, rustling over mounds and hills to a dense forest in the distance. The sky glowed in a way she'd never seen in Pria; the orange and pink hues spreading like veins across the sky.

Baylor parked the car on a bank overlooking the river and nudged Jade awake. "Go outside and use the restroom right now, both of you, before the sun goes down," he commanded. "Return quickly to the car."

They obeyed, but after relieving himself, Rex lingered and stretched his limbs. The sun soothed them, and Alina feared when it would set. The darkness would be cold and hostile.

Baylor kept muttering about their peculiarly benign trip. He yelled for Rex to get back in the car, and once inside, ordered them to recline and keep their heads below the windows. As they ate dinner in this position, the sky went dark.

"These travel bars aren't bad," Rex tried to sound cheerful. "So fruity and crispy. Do you like them, Jade?"

"Yes, I do."

After a short pause, Rex asked, "Are these, um, all we'll be eating on the road?"

"Pretty much, so I'm glad you like them," said Baylor. Rex gave a small sigh.

Alina spoke up. "Can't we keep traveling through the night? You can teach me how to drive the car. I think I'll go crazy sitting around waiting for something to happen."

Baylor set his jaw. "You're right. Something *will* happen. The creatures are waiting for the night."

Alina cleared her throat. "That's not what I meant. And you're not very encouraging."

"You need to be aware of what's out there."

"So why can't I drive?"

"It's too dangerous."

"And it's not dangerous sitting here, waiting for something to find us?"

"Traveling through the forest is worse. More creatures come out in the dark."

Alina rubbed her hand over her face. "So, what should I do if I hear something coming when all of you are asleep?"

"Stay out of sight. The nocturnal creatures rely on their night vision to find victims. They use their sense of smell, too, but unless they see you, they won't attack."

"But they'll see the car and smell us in it."

"Yes, and this confuses them. We use this tactic every time we travel, and it works. If we stop and lie low while we sleep, creatures may come and sniff the car, some may even attempt attacking it, but once they see it's not alive, they move on—*unless* they spy movement. Even a brief pop of the head will set them off, and they won't stop until they've broken in and killed us all."

Rex coughed on his crispy fruit bar.

"I don't mean to scare all of you. Try not to worry. Like I said, this system works. We've had only one death at night in two years, when a man got out to urinate."

"So, we can't get out to use the bathroom?" Rex asked.

"Of course not!" Baylor exclaimed. "I told you to go earlier. No leaving the car at night, period. And no popping your head up to look out the window, no matter how curious you get."

"No worries there," Rex said, shuddering.

"But what if someone really has to go?" Alina asked.

Baylor held up an empty water bottle. "Rex, I have one for you."

Alina rolled her eyes. "What about Jade?"

"Sorry, Jade, it's tough being a woman sometimes. But trust me, it's better to wet your pants than to leave this car at night."

Jade laughed. "I'll be fine."

"I apologize to you too, Alina."

"What for?"

"You can't do anything. No lights, no reading. You must stay as still as possible. This will be one of the most boring nights of your life."

"You know, I hope you're right."

"Keep your gun close," he said. "We'll be sleeping with ours."

"Can the darts run out?"

"Yes, but there's plenty. You can shoot for hours."

"What about the human prisoners from Pria—you know, the ones Sampson experiments with. Can they find us?"

Baylor paused before answering. "Yes," he whispered. "I didn't want to mention them because I want everyone to sleep soundly tonight."

"But we need to know how to defend ourselves!"

"It's the same—the dart guns. But humans are more intelligent and less instinctual than the animals, so keep that in mind." Baylor settled back into his seat. "Call for me if you hear anything. But remember, don't move."

Rex wasn't sleepy; he made light conversation with all of them, but before long only Alina responded. She engaged with him, dreading the moment he fell asleep and left her to face the long night on her own.

He shared some memories of Camden and J'koby, and then unexpectedly brought up Zaiden.

"Did you know he tried to join the resistance not long before the Harvest Feast?"

Alina forgot to stay still and cocked her head in surprise. "Really?"

"Yeah. He approached someone in the resistance, and they referred him to Satina, the woman who accepts new members. It's unusual for someone so young to know about the resistance, but apparently, he had connections. But many of us were concerned Sampson had his eye on him because of the incident with Chet and Lorenzo. They were his friends, and we can't afford to take such risks."

"I remember them. Were they rebels too?"

"No, they were too young. They had the rebel spirit, but were angry, zealous, and pretty stupid. They may have planted some of those seeds in Zaiden. Sampson took Chet's caretaker away, and he ran away with Lorenzo before Sampson could bring him in for indoctrination."

"Where did they go?"

"The Blue Forest. They tried to find the portal. I don't know how they heard about it, but I think Lorenzo knew some people in the resistance who might've told him. He tried to talk Zaiden into going with them, but he refused. He was the smart one."

"They were looking for Carthem?"

"Yes, but the portal in the Blue Forest is complicated."

Alina chewed on her lip. She mustered up the courage to ask Rex one more question.

"Did Zaiden know I was mortal?"

"Of course not," Rex answered. "Your mission is top-secret information. But he must have known you were valuable somehow because he followed you all the way to Gordian after those men took you away."

"I see," Alina said quietly.

Rex heard the disappointment in her voice. "Oh! I don't think that's why he followed you, though. Seems like he was interested in you, too..." He trailed off, leaving an awkward silence.

She didn't feel like talking anymore. Rex sensed this, so he yawned and said good night. He tossed and turned for several minutes before settling down. Alina knew he felt bad, but she wasn't angry. It was best to hear the truth from a friend.

She blinked her tears back. *It doesn't matter how he looked at me in Sampson's dungeon. I will no longer imagine he has feelings for me.* But she'd take him in an instant if he found her and was whole and wanted her.

She forced her mind to other things: to Trinee, Janet and Baylor and their happy marriage, to Rex and Jade, Jade and J'koby, J'koby and her mother. She didn't even know her mother's name. How nice it would be to hear the full story from her father's lips. Her heart lifted, but the warm feeling lasted only a few minutes.

A cold fear crept over her, and she wrinkled her brow, confused. Her instincts told her to flee, and as she opened her mouth to call Baylor's name, a sound outside made her go rigid. She had felt this once before.

She heard the noise again, footsteps crunching on grass and sticks, making no attempt to silence its approach. The steps stopped outside the vehicle. Alina lay still and prayed the others wouldn't shift in their sleep.

She knew this creature but was unprepared when its beady red eyes blinked through the window, examining every corner of the car. Terrified, she couldn't move even if she wished to. The nightstalk looked directly at her, then disappeared.

She waited for her body to relax, indicating it had left, but when she tried to release her clenched fist, she didn't budge.

A slashing noise echoed outside, and with a whistle the car

settled unevenly on the ground. She heard a rustling around the car, another slashing noise and whistle of escaped air. Alina panicked. The tires! They couldn't get away!

The nightstalk reached the last tire and the car sank to the ground. Alina needed to wake Baylor, but this creature had frozen every muscle in her body.

She listened, but heard nothing, no sound of footsteps or sticks snapping. The silence frightened her more than anything else so far. She tried to speak, but her teeth fused together. She focused on separating them.

A weak chatter, barely audible, escaped her teeth. "B-B-Baylor."

No answer.

"Bay-Baylor!" she tried again, louder.

Nothing. Maybe he was also frozen with fear.

A sudden crash of glass shattered the silence. Screams filled the car, and Alina's eyes widened in horror as long, thin fingers slid through the broken glass toward Jade. They grasped her ankle and pulled her up through the window shards, her frozen body unable to resist, her terrified eyes pleading for help.

This roused Alina, and she gritted her teeth as she tried to move. The words of the guidebook came to her. *Nightstalks prey on fear. If one can overcome the fear, one can overcome them.* Why was she afraid? This creature couldn't hurt her.

Her hand found the dart gun and trembled as she lifted it. What if she hit Jade instead? The nightstalk raked Jade across the broken glass and she screamed, her legs and arms flailing. The pain had roused her.

That was it! Pain could be stronger than fear!

Alina focused all her energy on the thought of losing Jade, then stood up, aimed her gun at the red, beady eyes, and fired. The nightstalk dropped to the ground, bringing Jade with it. At the same moment, Rex and Baylor relaxed.

"Jade!" Alina shrieked. "Are you okay?" She flung open the door and ran to her. She was moaning on the ground, blood dripping through her torn clothes.

"You're shaking so hard," Alina said.

"From fright, that's all," Jade said weakly.

Alina looked at Baylor, who switched on a light and rummaged through the first aid kit. "Bring her inside and shut the door," he ordered.

Rex helped Alina, and once inside, they grabbed the bandages and ointment from Baylor and got to work. Baylor was trembling uncontrollably.

He collapsed on the seat and released a breath that sounded like a cry. "A nightstalk," he murmured. "I've never encountered one before. I'm sorry, I was so unprepared. I always thought I could defeat one, but I was completely helpless."

"Don't worry, we all felt that way," said Rex. For once, he seemed more adept than Baylor. The sight of Jade dissolved his fear, and he began cleaning her wounds. Alina held Jade's hands as she groaned with pain.

"I felt it, too," Alina said. "It took a lot of concentration just to remember it couldn't hurt me."

"I couldn't have taken on that nightstalk," said Rex. "I love you, Jade, but it controlled me, and you would've died had you been in my care." He worked gently with her, but his jaw twitched with rage.

"Don't be hard on yourself. I don't know how anyone overcomes them," Baylor said as he worked on covering the window with heavy tape and plastic. Despite the weak shield, he assured them they would be safe if they stayed out of sight.

Jade's cuts were deep but not serious, and after Rex picked out the glass pieces and cleaned and bandaged the wounds, they settled uneasily back into their seats. Baylor administered medicine to Jade for the pain, and before long the car went quiet. Alina was again left to herself.

In the excitement she'd forgotten to tell Baylor the tires had been slashed. Would they have to walk? How far was Millflower? The idea of traveling in the open was terrifying.

The protective role she'd assumed pressed down on her. If harm happened to any of them, she would blame herself. She couldn't die, so she must protect those who could.

But so much was out of her control. She couldn't die, and that was her only strength. Nothing more.

CHAPTER 21

The remainder of the night passed without incident, though Alina kept hearing noises outside that startled her. A low growl, a pitter-patter around the car, and a strange hiss kept her on alert, and she didn't relax until the sun rose. The others slept on, exhausted from the events of the night. Alina, restless from holding still for hours, slipped outside to examine the car.

The tires were in sad shape, the metal rims sitting in shreds of rubber. Baylor mentioned when they left Stormport they had two spares, but they needed four. It was a day's travel to both Stormport and Millflower. They'd have to contact someone on the radio who could bring them new tires, or another car. Alina sighed. This would put them a day behind schedule, at least.

She walked around the car and gasped. The ground was bare. Blood stains covered the dirt where Jade and the nightstalk fell in the night, but no corpse.

She woke Baylor, and as she explained the slashed tires and missing nightstalk, he bolted upright, his eyes wide with terror.

"The nightstalk is gone?"

"Yes. And the tires—"

Baylor flung open the door and jumped outside. He didn't even look at the tires as he examined the ground.

"What is it?" Alina asked.

"We're being tracked. Do you remember how nightstalks can signal each other? It usually takes a few days for one to find the corpse and summon the others. But this indicates one has come and retrieved it. There's more of them, and they're closer than we think."

"But in the night I didn't sense another nightstalk. I didn't feel scared or—"

"They emit fear when they want to attack." Baylor rubbed his face in his hands. "They use caution when one of them is killed, then band together to confront the enemy—*us*. It's risky to walk but more dangerous to stay."

"How far away is Millflower?" Alina asked.

"About a hundred and twenty miles. We'll have to take our packs and start walking until they can meet us with a car."

Alina nodded. "I'll wake the others."

"I need to contact Lance." Baylor rummaged through his bag for the radio.

Jade looked pale and exhausted. Alina woke Rex first, and after hearing the urgency of their situation, he turned his worried eyes on Jade.

"I don't think she'll be able to walk easily, and carrying her might hurt her wounds."

"I know. I wish we could stay here until another vehicle arrives, but Baylor says it's too dangerous."

Rex leaned over and rubbed Jade's shoulder. "Wake up, Jade. We have to leave right away, and we have to walk."

Jade looked alarmed, but as Alina explained everything to her, she nodded and sat up, wincing. Jade did whatever was needed without complaint. Alina didn't like pushing her, but if it could save their lives, she would do it for a day.

Jade got out of the car and told Rex she felt fine, but Alina caught a grimace as she lifted her pack onto her back.

"Um, no!" Rex shouted. He grabbed the bag from her and heaved it above his own pack on his back. He shifted for a few moments before relaxing under the weight. Jade started to protest, but Rex's stern eyes silenced her.

With ear shields in place and guns poised, they abandoned the car and started down the road on foot. Baylor urged them to eat as they walked. He and Alina took the lead.

"Did you talk to Lance?" she asked.

He nodded. "He wants to send someone from Stormport to help us, but they're nearly as far as Millflower. It makes more sense to call Millflower since they're on our way."

"How many miles did we travel yesterday?"

"Almost a hundred."

"In all those hours of traveling? That's all?"

"Yes. Infuriating, isn't it?" Baylor balled his fists. "I can barely hit ten miles per hour on this awful road. Every time we try to refine it, Sampson unleashes something new on us. It's like he knows somehow. Then the death toll for workers gets so high we can't spare anyone to do the work, and no one is willing to risk it, anyway."

"But, look, we've traveled this far without any deaths."

"You know that's because you've killed what we could not. Plus, we've been in a car, which is much safer. Construction workers are always out in the open. Lance is building another factory for cars and machines. He's hoping to construct an aircar if he can get the materials, which would solve everything—at least until Sampson finds a way to endanger the skies as well."

The topic clearly frustrated him, so Alina changed the subject. "Have you spoken to Janet or Trinee since yesterday?"

"Yes. They have a radio, too. I spoke to them this morning, but I didn't mention our situation. It never helps for them to worry."

Alina hoped to improve his mood. "How did you meet Janet?" she asked.

He relaxed and smiled a little. "We grew up together, but she couldn't stand me for a long time." He chuckled. "Not that I blame her. I was pretty annoying. But after the awkward years passed and I became easier to look at, she decided to give me a chance. That's what I tell Trinee when my usual speech of 'looks don't matter' isn't working. I tell her to be patient, and others will notice her true beauty."

"I would've liked to hear that in Pria, but I don't know if I would've believed you."

"Well, Trinee doesn't always believe me, either."

Alina smiled and looked at him. "For different reasons, I'm interested in hearing your speech now. I worry my looks will be all others see in me."

He studied her. "Maybe, if it's all you think about. But keep showing the bravery you did last night, and people will see your true character."

"Bravery? You mean with the nightstalk?"

"Yes."

"How is it brave when I can't die?"

"Simple. You faced an awful scenario, and you fought back. Dying is a terrible prospect, but losing a loved one to death is much worse."

Alina reflected on this for a moment, then looked back at Rex and Jade. Rex hovered over her, but Jade didn't seem to mind. He kept a hand on her back as he guided her steps.

Baylor was on the lookout for anything unusual, and more than once he fired his dart gun into the grass. The brainwastes were so abundant, he constantly brushed them off his legs. Rex especially hated the creepy things and smacked them the moment they crept onto his or Jade's legs. For some reason, the brainwastes left Alina alone.

No one complained of the heat, but as the sweat rolled down their necks and faces, Alina felt guilty for being so comfortable. She kept a sharp eye on Jade, who seemed tired but didn't ask to rest. Alina wished she could carry her, but with one pack on her back already, Jade would be uncomfortable.

Rex caught up to Baylor. "I don't think Jade can continue at this pace. Can we rest? The nightstalks don't hunt in the day, anyway."

Baylor wiped his forehead with his sleeve. "They don't attack, but they travel and can still induce fear. They'll be much closer to us when the night comes if we stop."

"But the people from Millflower are on their way, right? Do you know how close they are?"

"I don't. I can't get a radio signal at the moment. If anything, we should be quickening our pace, not stopping to rest."

"But Jade—" Rex started.

"Then carry her, for crying out loud!" Baylor barked. "We're all hot, we're all tired. But we have to keep going, so *push* yourself a little! Sheesh, you immortals can be such whiners."

Alina stiffened. The statement had enough truth to bother Rex, and it did.

"I'd like to see you live hundreds of years without pain and see how you deal with mortality," Rex snapped back.

Baylor rolled his eyes. "And you've lived hundreds of years?"

Rex paused. "I was referring to Jade," he said coolly.

Alina spoke as she slipped off her backpack. "Let's keep moving. If someone can take my pack, I can carry Jade."

Baylor grabbed Alina's pack and threw it on his back. "I'll take it. I don't want to burden any pampered shoulders." He looked at Rex, who glared back at him.

"Come get on my back, Jade," Alina called to her. "It'll help us go faster, and we need to for safety."

Jade agreed, and Alina lifted her onto her back. She stiffened with pain as Alina started walking.

Baylor marched ahead, trying to hurry them along. "The nightstalks move quickly," he called back to them. "If any of you start feeling that paralyzing fear again, speak up. If there's a group of nightstalks, we should sense them from a good distance away."

Alina's heart stopped. Did his words chill her, or was something else nearby? She skipped to catch up with him.

"I'm feeling the fear again," she murmured. "It's not too strong yet."

"I feel it also," Baylor said under his breath. He turned around. "Hey, Rex, how are you doing?"

Rex scowled. "I'm fine."

Baylor chuckled. "Well, I'm glad I stirred him up a bit. Maybe his anger is overpowering any fear. If it *is* the nightstalks, then they're still far away. Let's move faster."

"Rex, can you go any faster?" Baylor called out. In a flash Rex stormed past them and took the lead, still scowling.

They followed until Rex halted and Alina ran into him. "Do you sense something?" he asked, shuddering.

"No," said Baylor casually. "I just thought I'd ease off in case my pace was too much for your delicate body."

Rex fumed a bright red. "Now, listen here. I'm capable of doing anything your middle-aged body can do." He stammered for a moment, searching for a good retort, then huffed off ahead of them. Baylor looked at Alina and smiled.

"If he mentions he feels scared through *that* anger, then we'll know the nightstalks are close."

"I doubt he's going to admit anything now, no matter how scared he gets," Jade piped up.

"We'll see. I'm feeling better, at least. How about you?" Baylor asked Alina.

She thought for a moment. "Yes, I am. Maybe it was nothing."

"Let's hope so."

Alina shifted Jade a little, who moaned with pain. Alina never felt tired, but Jade did slow her down. For the first time since leaving Pria, she felt clumsy.

The trail led them into a grove of trees. They welcomed the shade, but the stillness of the woods unnerved Alina.

She heard a soft rustle in the leaves and clasped Baylor's arm. "Did you hear that?" she asked.

They all stopped, and Baylor raised his gun. "I don't feel frightened enough for a nightstalk, especially a lot of them," he whispered. "It must be something else."

They stared for a long time. Alina's skin crawled. She felt certain they were being watched.

Baylor frowned. "Quick, let's move out of these trees."

He held the gun steady, and just as they started to move, a gruff voice broke the silence. "Take one step, Baylor, and I'll shoot."

Baylor's mouth dropped open. He froze.

"Drop. The gun. Now."

Baylor lowered his gun. Alina spun around, her eyes scanning the trees.

"Don't look so scared, pretty girl. I won't hurt him so long as you do what I say." They heard a dark chuckle. "What we *all* say."

Alina was shaking, but she straightened her back and set her jaw. "Then show yourselves."

She stepped back in alarm as the trees rustled and men dropped to the ground like heavy rocks. At least a dozen men surrounded them, each with a gun leveled at Baylor's heart.

"Do I know you?" Baylor asked the man who appeared to be the leader of the group.

The man smiled, showing stained, jagged teeth. "I knew your father. He was the one who banished me."

"*Gerard?*" Baylor seemed to lose his composure for a moment. "How have you survived this hostile wilderness for so long?"

"Oh, it's not so hostile to me. I control the wild, you might say. Makes it easy to track you. *And* your father."

Baylor tensed up. "My father was killed by a nightstalk."

Gerard gave a soft chuckle. "That's what we wanted you to think. I couldn't let Lance know I was still alive." His cold eyes narrowed. "I took pleasure in carrying out my revenge on your father, and it's a pleasure to throw it in your face now. He died slowly—I made sure of that."

"I don't believe you," said Baylor, his voice shaking.

"Oh, you don't, huh?" Gerard's nostrils flared. "Do you know how nightstalks kill? They go for the heart! When it's frozen solid with fear, they cut it out with their fingernails. And they always cut from the front so they're eye to eye with their victim. Keeps them in control, you see? But if you remember, your father's heart was cut from the back. I wanted his face in the dirt so he knew where he stood with me. The best part was, he got more of a shock outta seeing me than a nightstalk. Who thought I'd survive twenty years out here?" Gerard roared with laughter and his men joined in.

Baylor's body convulsed, his veins bulging through the muscle in his arms. He opened his mouth, released a broken gasp, and fell forward onto his knees. The laughter grew louder. Alina crouched by him with Jade on her back.

"Don't worry," Gerard scoffed. "It's the girl we want. Hand her over, and no one will get hurt. At least not by us," he added, and the men chuckled again. "I think there's a group of nightstalks heading this way, and it's unlikely you'll escape them. Act quickly and maybe you'll have a chance." He flashed his vile teeth.

Alina hesitated for a moment, then stepped forward, lowering Jade from her back. "Take me, then."

Rex went pale. "No, Alina."

"I'll be fine," she whispered. "They can't do anything to me."

"*Yes*, they can," Baylor warned, regaining his composure.

"We have no other choice," Alina said, tears coming to her eyes. She leaned in, hoping the men couldn't hear. "You go on to Millflower, and I'll find a way to meet you there. I promise."

Baylor looked around at the guns pointed at them. Beads of sweat covered his bald head. "We'll send help for you," he whispered. "Protect yourself until then."

Alina stood and faced Gerard. "I'll stand here as they leave. You must allow them to pass through, and once they're gone, you can take me."

"Are you giving orders to *me*?" Gerard laughed. "You're lucky I'm letting them go at all."

Jade's face betrayed her panic as Baylor led her away. Alina forced a smile, hoping to reassure her. Rex's eyes darted around them, as if looking for a way to save her and still escape. He dropped his head in defeat and followed Baylor.

Alina's entire body trembled, but she set her jaw, determined not to look afraid. How much did they know about her?

Gerard circled her, leering from head to toe. He stopped in front of her face. "It's a *pleasure* to finally meet you, Alina." His breath was rank.

She wanted to punch him but restrained herself. The others were not yet at a safe distance.

"Tie her up," Gerard commanded. "We have a long walk to the Blue Forest. We don't want her slipping away."

Alina started. "The Blue Forest?"

"Why yes! Heard of it?" He smirked. "Our dear friend Sampson is anxious for your return."

Alina swallowed as a man tied her wrists behind her back. "Are you from Pria?"

"No. We're the rejects of Carthem. People here have found our ideas too—how'd you call it—*radical* for their liking." He tilted his head to her ear. "I know what you are," he whispered. "We all do. Don't assume it'll give you an edge. We can't kill you, but there are plenty of other things we can do. Your strength's limited, you know." He drew a grimy finger across her cheek from her ear to her chin. Alina shuddered, her heart sinking at his words.

Gerard chuckled to himself as he walked away. He was right. Although the rope didn't hurt her wrists, it bound them tightly together. She couldn't move.

CHAPTER 22

The group traveled briskly, and Alina kept their pace, her eyes focused on the path ahead of her. The men surrounded her as they walked—ogling from every angle and taking pleasure in the discomfort this brought her. Though she wanted to cry, she lifted her chin and ignored their stares as she tried to think of a plan. They were traveling north toward the mountains. If she found a way to escape and go east, she might find the search party from Millflower.

Gerard slunk up beside her. "So, Alina," he said, his hand touching her neck under her hair, "we're feeling pretty lucky. You don't know this, but there's a hefty price on your head."

She recoiled at his touch and tried to steady her voice. "I know how valuable I am."

He chuckled. "Yes, so valuable to both sides. Poor Lance. Poor Baylor! Stolen from right under his nose."

She set her teeth. "If you hate Baylor so much, why didn't you stalk and kill him like you did his father? He travels this wilderness a lot."

He sensed her sarcasm. "You don't believe I killed his father?"

Alina didn't answer.

"I would have killed Baylor long ago, but I'm not usually in this part of Carthem. I have better places to be. But I agreed to come when Sampson asked me to fetch you for him."

"How do you communicate with Sampson?" she asked in surprise.

He grinned. "We've been a team for many years now. It's how I survived the wilderness so long. But until recently, we hadn't been on speaking terms. I cut him off for denying me what I want most."

"And what's that?"

He snickered. "I have you to thank. You've created quite a crisis for him, darling. He needs you back so desperately, he'll do about anything. So, he's called on his few allies in Carthem, promising we can enter his world and gain immortality as long as we bring you with us."

"He's a liar. Sampson will never do that," declared Alina.

"What makes you say that?"

"Well, he—" she tried to think of everything Rex told her about Sampson. "He doesn't like former mortals living in Pria because they know how much better life is in Carthem—"

Gerard threw his head back and roared with laughter. As if on cue, his men joined in. "Do you *really think*" —he emphasized the words— "I would *ever* think this mortal hell is better than Pria?"

Alina returned his glare but didn't argue. True, the carnal pleasures of Pria suited some people very well. Gerard and his group of thugs were likely candidates.

His hot breath reached her nostrils as he leaned in. "And if all the women there are as tasty as you" —he clicked his tongue— "I'll have a wild time."

Alina stepped away and shuddered. She must escape, and soon. She would not spend the night near these detestable, vulgar men.

As THE DAY WORE ON, Alina kept silent so she could catch conversations between the men, hoping to discover a weakness. Listening was a difficult task as she found their conversations repugnant.

"Any sign of Oscar?" she heard Gerard ask another man.

"No. We think he saw a mirage," the man answered.

"Why do you idiots keep falling for those—" Alina closed her eyes as Gerard let out a string of expletives.

"How should I know?" the man argued. "Shouldn't we be protected from them? He left the group to get water. Maybe he went too far—"

Gerard hushed him and glanced at Alina, who focused on three men passing gas and chortling. She didn't have to fake her disgust.

Her mind raced. They hadn't encountered any dangerous creatures in their travels. The men didn't even wear ear shields.

Sampson protects them to aid them in their mission.

Gerard dropped his voice. Alina quickened her pace to hear him. She caught fragments of his rebuke.

"Remember...find the girl. Sampson knows...best chance... someone like you to ruin it!" His voice swelled at the end.

The sun dipped low in the sky, and Alina grew anxious as the group became more unruly. Time was running out, but her bonds were tight, and several men watched her—not because they had to, but because they couldn't keep their greedy eyes off her.

The company walked for another hour before agreeing on a campsite, and the men grinned and promptly complied when Gerard ordered them to tie Alina to a tree. They glanced frequently in her direction as they cooked their food, making comments to each other and bursting into raucous laughter.

Alina was grateful she couldn't hear them, but their stares made her skin crawl. She became desperate as the sky grew darker and they consumed more whiskey. She blinked back tears, reminding herself she didn't need to be afraid. These men couldn't hurt her, at least physically. But she might prefer physical pain to what she was about to experience.

Gerard walked toward her, and she looked him straight in the eye. No matter how frightened, she wouldn't appear vulnerable.

"Well, pretty girl, you're certainly the best thing we've ever had in our company. My men are looking forward to guard duty tonight." He licked his lips. "We'll all take turns, you know."

"You won't lay a finger on me." Alina's voice shook.

Gerard chuckled as his eyes swept over her body. He stepped in close, and the smell of his sweat choked her nostrils. She turned her nose and pressed her back against the thin trunk, trying to put space between them.

"You forget you're tied up," Gerard whispered, grazing his hand up Alina's arm. Her wrists were bound behind the trunk; she couldn't escape his touch. He stroked up under her sleeve and caressed her shoulder with his palm. Alina stiffened, clamping her jaws together.

"Relax," Gerard whispered again. "Enjoy yourself. I think I'll go first tonight. I can break you in."

She glared at him, and as he lifted his finger to stroke her cheek, she snapped her teeth.

Alina hadn't meant to bite him, but he hollered in pain and lifted his hand to strike her. When the blow hit her face, he yowled harder, and Alina bit her lip to keep from laughing. She'd already provoked him more than she meant to. At times her own body surprised her. She knew so little of what she could do, and this was the boost she needed. She lifted her chin. Not one of them would lay a finger on her that night.

Gerard cursed but thrust out his chest when he faced his men, who watched him curiously. He muttered something that sent them roaring with laughter, followed by more demeaning looks in her direction. Alina curled her lip. *What a conceited liar.*

As the sky grew darker and more concealing, Alina worked on the bands around her wrists. At first she couldn't move at all, but as she pulled her wrists apart, she felt the fibers of the ropes stretch slightly. It might work, if she had enough time. Mortal skin would become raw and sore before a rope like that weakened, but it did nothing to her.

She stretched the rope as far as it would go, over and over, until her wrists no longer touched. A little more space and she could slip a hand through.

Then she heard the dreaded conversation begin.

"I vote we all retire early tonight!" yelled a greasy, potbellied man. "We want as many guard shifts as possible, don't we?" They howled with laughter.

"Who gets to be first, then?"

The men argued for a while, and as they drew lots, Alina tightened her muscles and used all her strength to pull her hands apart. She *must* catch the first one by surprise.

Not a moment too soon, she slipped her hands one by one from the rope as the first smelly man trampled through the bushes toward her. He wasted no time but put his face an inch from hers and reached for her waist.

"Hello, you pretty—"

Her hands clamped around his throat. He shoved her away, and with her ankles tied, she fell, bringing him with her. She tightened her grip as he clawed, kicked, then seized her hair, attempting to rip the strands out. When his panicked hands tried to pry hers from his neck, she leaned forward and sank her teeth hard into his fingers. His scream was lost in his closed throat.

When he went limp, Alina hastened to untie the knots at her ankles. The rope didn't budge.

The men at camp cheered and whistled at the rustling in the bushes. "You only got ten more minutes, Hank, y'hear?" Gerard called out.

Ten minutes! Alina hunted through Hank's pockets until she found a small pocketknife. She cut the rope and fled into the forest. As she picked up speed, she began to laugh. Ten minutes at this pace, and they'd never catch her.

Alina had paid careful attention as they traveled throughout the day, but the thickness of the trees and the night disoriented her. She ran in the direction she believed to be east, knowing that for now, building distance between her and Gerard's men was the safest path to take. They expected her to travel to Millflower, so she must find Rex, Jade, and Baylor before Gerard found them again. She thought of the nightstalks hunting them and quickened her pace.

Immortality felt strange—still fresh and new to her. As a child in Pria, she possessed instincts others did not. She knew falling off her bike or slamming her fingers in the door would hurt. She avoided trying new things but rarely had to since Jade didn't encourage her. She never went near a swimming pool, and after the incident with Pierce never climbed a tree again. But immortals didn't have this apprehension. They mastered everything on their first try. They didn't crash their bikes or slip from the trees they climbed—they jumped!

And now *she* was the one who succeeded without effort, whose eyes could see clearly in the darkness. She soared through the woods, dodging branches and leaping over fallen logs. The invincibility was intoxicating.

AFTER A FEW HOURS OF RUNNING, the fear hit.

Recognizing the feeling at once, she climbed a tree with heavy limbs and hid in the leaves. If the fear paralyzed her, at least she couldn't be seen.

Her body stiffened like the branches around her as she glimpsed a nightstalk creeping through the wide trunks, its beady red eyes scanning the trees, aware of her presence.

They sense fear, she reminded herself. She closed her eyes and thought of Jade, Rex, Baylor, and the people back in Stormport. She began to relax. As courage warmed her limbs, the nightstalk's eyes blinked, puzzled. It whirled around and scanned the trees, as if its prey had just escaped from under its nose.

This encouraged Alina, and as her eyes stalked the creature, she remembered how defenseless she was. Gerard had confiscated all her weapons when he took her. She had Hank's pocketknife, which didn't seem sufficient. But facing the nightstalk without weapons didn't worry her; it just required more thought.

She stood up on the branch and watched the confused creature for a moment, then hurled herself into the air. She twisted and flipped until she landed firmly on the soil, thirty feet from where it stood.

They stared at each other. She almost faltered at the nightstalk's eerie red eyes but held its glare. The moonlight shone on its sickly complexion, making it almost transparent. Purple veins throbbed under its gray skin. She did not flinch until something in its face stopped her with a gasp.

The creature bore a resemblance to the immortals of Pria: graceful, swift, and symmetrical but as hideous as they were beautiful. Its skin looked decayed and putrid, the whites around its red pupils sunken—as if everything good had been sucked out.

The nightstalk intrigued her more than it frightened her, and as she examined it with both repulsion and fascination, it lifted its head and released a bone-chilling howl. She darted behind a tree, her fear returning like ice in her veins.

In the distance several howls answered. Others were coming to its aid to destroy the enemy that killed one of their own. She panicked, until she realized they were moving away from Rex, and Jade, and Baylor, to her.

Alina set her jaw as she stepped out from the tree. *They're frightening to my eyes, but they can't hurt me.* She repeated this in her mind as the sight grew more terrifying.

Over a dozen nightstalks walked into the moonlight from the dark trees, their skin glowing with their pupils. Alina could sense the fear thick and heavy around her, but with focus, she stayed above it.

I can't die. I can't die. I can't die.

She walked forward to meet them, and they surrounded her. How quickly she could take them out with a dart gun. She pulled out Hank's pocketknife and released the short blade. Each of them raised their hands, their long fingernails shining in the moonlight, and pointed them right at her heart.

She examined each one as they approached, trying to decide which was easiest to overcome. She crouched and glared at the one drawing nearest, until it gave a blank smile and pointed to something over her shoulder.

She spun around to find a nightstalk right behind her, flooded in moonlight, creating a mirror out of its transparent body. Alina screamed at her reflection, which instead of a flawless, immortal figure showed a plain, awkward girl from Pria—with plump legs, stringy hair and blemishes spotting her face. Her hands flew to her mouth in a startled gasp and the reflection followed.

She looked down at her body but saw nothing in the darkness—she'd lost her immortal vision. Dread closed around her and filled her lungs. Had she become mortal somehow? She cowered in a fetal position as the nightstalks approached, her muscles too rigid to move.

They raised their sharp nails above their heads and plunged them at her heart, and her chest relaxed long enough to release a desperate, blood-curdling scream.

CHAPTER 23

The pain didn't come. She heard a clean rip of fabric and felt nails scratching her throat, followed by angry snarls and footsteps fleeing on soft earth. The fear released her like fingers loosening from her neck. She opened her eyes and looked around. She was alone.

She got to her feet and broke into a run, shaking with fear. Gerard would be searching for her by now, and if she was mortal—

She stopped and touched her face. Her skin was smooth. She ran her fingers through her hair and met no tangles. She could see the outline of every tree and stick on the ground, though no moonlight penetrated the woods.

If she was still immortal, what had she seen in the nightstalk's reflection? Was it a trick of the eye to weaken her?

If so, it had worked. But in the end, they couldn't harm her, and that angered them. She shook her head in disbelief. Why had she fallen for the illusion? The nightstalks were more cunning than she expected. She took off again, her graceful legs running more swiftly than before. She must find the others before it was too late.

The forest thinned and opened into thick prairie grass, and the sky to her left grew pink with the rising sun. She squealed and clapped her hands. She had come the right way! A slight breeze ruffled her clothes, and she looked down and gave a startled cry. In her haste, she'd forgotten the nightstalks had ripped her shirt. She clasped the fabric together, then pulled her arms into the sleeves, twisted the shirt around her neck, and slipped it on backward. The tear now dipped low on her back.

A rustling nearby startled her, and she dropped into the tall stalks of grass. As the sound drew closer, a dark, curly head bobbed into view. She frowned. The person wasn't Rex or Jade and didn't seem to be one of Gerard's men. She lay on her stomach and tried to disappear in the weeds.

Alina gasped as a small, wasted man came into view. His clothes hung in tatters around his bony frame, and dark circles framed his eyes. His bare chest sunk with each breath, and his skin stretched over his ribs like tissue paper. Alina had never seen such a wretched-looking being, and as pity overwhelmed her, she stood up and started toward him.

With a screechy cry, he flung himself at her, kicking her legs and punching at her face. He teetered backwards and collapsed on the ground.

"I'm sorry," Alina said. "I didn't mean to startle you—"

The man jumped to his feet and snarled. She kept her distance as he surveyed her. He seemed to be considering whether to attack again or not. With a dramatic shriek, he turned and fled into the grass.

Alina's heart raced, reminding her that while her body was invulnerable, her emotions were not. She grieved for the man and his haunting, distrustful eyes and felt certain he came from Pria. Her eyes widened as she made the connection.

Sampson tortured this man until he went mad, then sent him into Pria to search for a lost loved one. Someone out there would be heartbroken to see him so miserable. Alina swallowed and pushed the thought of Zaiden from her mind.

In the distance she heard the sound of an engine revving, and her heart leaped. The rescue party must be close by now. She scanned the horizon until she spotted a brown vehicle bouncing over the hills in the distance. She dashed toward it.

As she drew near, she noticed the vehicle had no roof. A middle-aged man sat behind the wheel, craning his neck and scanning the grass. Alina waved her arms as she ran, and when he saw her, he stopped the car and jumped out.

"You must be Alina!" he called, pulling off his hat.

"Yes!" she exclaimed.

"I'm so glad I found you! I'm from Millflower. My name's Maxwell Gardel."

Alina beamed. "How did you know to look for me?"

"Lance called me. He made contact with Baylor, who said you'd been separated from the group."

"Do you know if Baylor and the others are okay?"

"Oh, yes, they're fine. They're in Millflower, being treated for wounds, but nothing too serious."

Alina blinked back happy tears as Maxwell motioned for her to get in the car. After they settled in the front seat, he slapped his hat on his head and jerked the car into motion.

"When did they arrive in Millflower?" Alina asked.

"This morning. About midnight I received a call from Tim, another of the search crew, confirming he'd found them. He called again this morning after they arrived safely in Millflower. Lance called yesterday afternoon and told me you'd been taken. Eight of us have been searching since then. You aren't easy to find! How did you get this far out?"

"I traveled for a long time with Gerard and his men. They headed north."

At the mention of Gerard's name, Maxwell darkened. "Vile brute," he muttered under his breath. "I'd love to hear how you outwitted him. We expected a fight to get you back, after all." He gestured to a stockpile of guns and explosives in the back of the car.

He looked at her expectantly, and she realized he was waiting for the story. "Oh! Well—" she flushed. She didn't want to explain what Gerard's men almost did to her. "Once they made camp, they tied me to a tree a short distance away. While they ate dinner, I worked hard at the ropes around my wrists, and since I feel no pain, I could stretch them loose. Then I freed my ankles and ran into the woods. I'm sure they're searching for me, but I can run forever and not get tired, so the escape was pretty easy."

Maxwell threw back his head and laughed. "What idiots, thinking they could contain an immortal!"

"Are we far from Millflower?"

"Not too far. We should arrive by evening." He picked up his radio and called the others in the search party, and Alina smiled at the cheers that followed. A short time later, other vehicles appeared in the distance, all traveling parallel in the same direction.

Maxwell whistled cheerfully as they bounced through the grass, and Alina smiled. He didn't seem bothered that he'd spent over twenty-four hours looking for her. He looked tired but pleasant. His wide-brimmed hat covered the ear shields and his thin, red hair. She noticed his freckled arms and calloused hands and concluded he spent a lot of time working outdoors. Alina felt safe with him. He respected her personal space and took no notice of her beauty.

"How long have you lived in Millflower?" she asked.

"Thirteen years," he answered. "I took my family there when the wilderness got too dangerous. I have a wife and three daughters, and I didn't want them threatened by nightstalks or forced to wear ear shields every day of their lives." His friendly tone encouraged her questions.

"Millflower produces most of Carthem's food, right?"

"Yup. Carthem would starve without us. A large wall surrounds our town and farmland. Only those cleared by Lance can enter."

"But if Millflower is so important, shouldn't it have the same security as Stormport and Jaden?"

Maxwell shrugged. "Perhaps, but we're not set up for it. The town is too small—the cost to maintain that security isn't worth it. It would require more workers to move in, which would strain our resources. Besides, our isolated location provides some natural protection."

"But how do you get the food to the cities?"

"We have trucks that transport the supplies, and drivers make a trip to Jaden and Stormport monthly. This is dangerous, but the vehicle keeps them safe, and they have the best-paid job in Millflower. Those are the only cities we supply food to. People who live outside of them have to sustain themselves."

Alina chewed on her lip. "Do you think my presence will bring danger to your town?"

Maxwell reflected for a moment, then shook his head. "No. Animals can't get in, so all we have to fear are human enemies, and we're good at keeping them away. There's one trying to get in now. We're shocked he's eluded the brainwastes this long."

Alina thought of the wild man in the grass. "Who is he?"

"One of the Sad Cases." Maxwell looked at her. "That's what we call those who suffer insanity by Sampson's hands. This one's obsessed with entering Millflower to find a woman there. She's lived there for about ten years, though I don't know how long she's been in Carthem. I don't know her history. She doesn't talk much but seems sad when she hears of him. We make sure she never sees him because that could be the end of her. Fortunately, she's never tried. Some people are driven to meet their old lovers, and that usually results in miserable deaths for both."

"Do any seek them out, thinking they can cure them?" Alina asked.

"Yes, sometimes. They want to beg forgiveness or find closure. It's one of Sampson's tricks. He likes to do this when two people become attached to each other. Loyalty threatens his rule, you know. He usually expels one under false notions that he—or she—betrayed the other. Then he takes the one left behind, imprisons him until insane, and sends him into Carthem to kill. It's heart-wrenching to see."

"How do you know so much? Did you once live in Pria?"

"No. But Sampson's ways are no secret here. I'm a town official and close confidant of Lance. It's important I understand all of Sampson's tactics and the motivation behind them. Millflower has been targeted many times and is never fully safe. After the safety and well-being of my family and city, Sampson's downfall is my top priority."

Alina nodded, respecting the power in his words. "Do you know what happened to Baylor and the others? You said they were wounded."

"I don't know. Tim didn't say. I'm sure they'll fill you in once you get there. You've got a great story for them as well." He looked at her and grinned.

One by one, the other vehicles met up with them, the drivers raising their fists and cheering. They drove up close and gaped at Alina. She blushed, feeling uncomfortable in her ripped shirt.

She leaned in toward Maxwell. "Do you have an extra shirt, or a blanket or anything?"

Without turning his head, Maxwell reached into the back of the car and tossed her a large, heavy sweatshirt. She slipped it on and rolled up the sleeves.

As the men stared at her, she felt relieved Maxwell had found her. Some of them smiled or winked, while others looked away when she met their eyes. All of them glared at Maxwell. A competition appeared to be driving them as to who would find her and take her back. Maxwell ignored their jealous stares, and Alina smiled, realizing the one man who hadn't played the game had won it.

She made light conversation with Maxwell for the rest of the drive; he talked about the farm he ran and how his daughters worked the land with him. His oldest daughter was her same age. Alina knew their stay in Millflower would be short, but she hoped for a friend. She missed Trinee.

By late afternoon, the brick wall of Millflower came into sight. Maxwell called on his radio as they approached, gave a code, and the tall metal gate opened for them.

Alina surveyed the town as they drove inside. Small shops lined the main street: a bakery, a butcher's store, a deli, and a small doctor's office. Rich, green land separated the homes in the distance. On the breeze, Alina caught whiffs of manure and sweat, but she liked the town right away.

She appreciated her worn clothes and dirty face, as she hoped to blend into the modest culture. As they drove through town, a crowd lined the street to congratulate the search party. She soon realized they came to catch a glimpse of her.

Their eyes widened when they saw her, followed by loud gasps and exclamations of her beauty. Few had seen an immortal before. Alina shifted in her seat.

"You're quite a celebrity here, Alina. You could wave and smile if you like," Maxwell suggested.

Alina realized she must look snobbish, so she forced a smile and waved. Her heart sank as a group of teenage girls sneered at her, then huddled and whispered to each other. Somehow, she knew their words would sting if she heard them.

She was relieved when Maxwell turned onto a dirt road and left the crowd behind. As they approached a large house on the end of the street, Jade hurried toward them, arms flailing with excitement. Maxwell slammed on the brakes to keep Alina from leaping from the moving vehicle.

They broke into laughter when they embraced. "I'm so glad you're okay!" Jade exclaimed. "I've worried so much about you!"

"*I've* been worried about *you!*" Alina responded. "Maxwell said you were injured. Is everyone okay?"

"Oh, we had a little skirmish with the nightstalks. Don't worry; we're all fine," she added, seeing Alina's expression. "I'll tell you the story when we're with Rex. He's the hero, and he'll want to hear it again. I'm healing nicely. The nightstalks didn't hurt me the second time."

She waved to Maxwell as he drove past them. "You met Max, I see. This is his home. His sweet wife has been kind enough to house us, though there was no shortage of offers—nearly everyone in town volunteered their home to Carthem's 'chosen one,' it seems. But the mayor and some others requested no young men be living where you stay. You're such a famed beauty, maybe they didn't think it safe." Jade giggled.

Alina crossed her arms. "Why? Because I plan to seduce every boy in sight?"

Jade noticed her irritation and stopped laughing. "They meant *your* safety. I'm sure no one thinks you're a danger to the boys, or they're a danger to you. But it's good to be careful. Maxwell is trustworthy, and he has three daughters. You like him, don't you?"

Alina nodded. "Yes. I'm glad he found me. Some of the other men gave me the creeps."

Maxwell's home was so charming, Alina couldn't pull her eyes from the scene as they walked up the path. A wide porch wrapped around the brick walls, with three dormer windows extending from the roof on the second floor. A maple tree towered over the home, its broad leaves covering the lawn in deep, cool shade. Several chickens roamed through the yard, pecking at the ground and squawking at the cat that stalked them.

They climbed up the porch steps and a beautiful, fair-skinned woman came out to greet them. She smiled warmly at Alina.

"Welcome, Alina. I'm Christine. We're honored to have you stay with us."

"Thank you," Alina said. "I'm grateful your husband found me."

A young girl peeked around Christine and eyed Alina shyly. Christine smiled and put her arm around her, bringing her forward. She possessed her mother's blue-green eyes and long blonde hair.

"This is my youngest daughter, Rachel."

Alina smiled. "Hi, Rachel."

"Hi."

"How old are you?"

"Ten."

Alina paused. She wasn't good with kids. Jade stretched open her arms and Rachel ran into them. *Why can't I be more like that?*

"Rachel is an expert on the farm and will teach us our duties while we're here," Jade said as Rachel beamed. "Of course, they say we don't have to work," she spoke over Christine's protests, "but I told them nothing could stop me. I love the animals already."

"I'm sure I'll love them as well," Alina agreed.

Another girl came out, this one with Maxwell's red hair. Her eyes grew wide when she saw Alina.

"Wow! You really *are* pretty!" she exclaimed.

Christine smiled and put her arm around her other daughter. "This is Katherine. She's my thirteen-year-old."

"All my friends want to come over to see you. I hope you don't mind. Maybe you can tell us stories about Pria," Katherine jabbered without drawing breath. "Everyone is so jealous you're staying here. Well, except Nicole."

"Katherine!" Christine chided under her breath.

"Everyone will find out soon anyway, Mom. She just told me she won't come down to meet her."

Christine flushed. "Run upstairs, Kat, and make sure Alina's room is ready for her."

"It is, but Nicole won't leave."

Christine reddened further. "Just go!" she whispered. Katherine went back inside.

Christine looked at Alina. "I apologize for both Katherine and Nicole. Katherine is a chatterbox and slow to learn manners. Nicole is suffering from the jealousy I'm afraid many girls in town are suffering from. She hasn't wanted to give up her room."

"Oh! Please don't have her give it up. I don't sleep anyway."

"Yes, dear, but you need a place to go when you want to be alone. It's hard being in a strange home."

"Let me be with Jade, then," Alina said. Jade looked at Christine and nodded.

Christine sighed. "Very well. But you may be denying my girl a valuable lesson. I had hoped sacrificing something for you might change her feelings. But it's difficult for the girls here. They outnumber the boys two to one. The competition is already so fierce —you know how girls are, and since the news of your coming, the boys haven't paid much attention to them. I suppose they all want to be free in case you should choose one of them."

Alina's mouth dropped. "I won't be choosing any, thank you very much!"

"She left her heart back in Pria," Jade teased.

"That will break many hearts here, then," Christine said as she led them inside.

"Your pack is in Nicole's room," Jade told Alina as they followed Christine upstairs. "We'll grab it and take it to the guest room where I'm staying. Rex and Baylor are set up in the parlor downstairs."

Christine knocked on a door and opened it, where a cross-looking girl sat on the bed, writing furiously in a notebook. She jumped up when they entered. Her eyes found Alina and looked shocked for a moment, then narrowed.

"Nicole," Christine said, "Alina has offered to share Jade's room so you may keep yours."

Nicole fumed. "I suppose you think I'm very rude, then," she blurted.

Alina tried to sound friendly. "No, of course not. I understand why you don't want to give up your room for someone you don't know. I don't want to make you do that for me."

"You aren't making me. In fact, *have it*. I've changed my mind." She stormed out of the room.

Christine sighed, closing her eyes. "I'm sorry, Alina. You may not receive a warm welcome from her. But the rest of us are glad you're here. There are your things in the corner."

Jade grabbed her hand and pulled her out of the room. "Let's go see Rex and Baylor. I want to hear everything that happened to you, and we've got a great story too."

Alina followed her downstairs, past the dining room and kitchen to the back of the house. She caught a glimpse of Nicole in the yard, talking with a girl outside the fence. They frowned with their arms crossed. Alina bit her lip.

Jade led her to the back parlor where Rex and Baylor were recovering, and when she opened the door, Alina covered her mouth and screamed. Jade put her arm around her.

"I'm sorry, Alina, I should have prepared you. Don't worry. The doctor says they'll recover fine."

"Hi, Alina," Rex growled from his recliner. Baylor sat next to him in an identical chair, sipping a drink through a straw. A movie blared on the monitor in front of them.

The slashes on their faces made them almost unrecognizable. Thick bandages wrapped their arms and legs, covered with red and yellow splotches. A pale discharge oozed from a cut on Baylor's forehead, just above a patch on his eye. Rex's left leg was in a cast.

"What happened?" Alina exclaimed.

"The nightstalks found us," Rex replied.

"I know that part—how did you get away?"

"It wasn't easy. We escaped because there were only two of them. We don't know where the others were."

"They came after me," Alina answered.

"Hmm," Baylor said, shifting his weight in his chair. "They must have traced you as the killer of the first one."

Rex continued, "Well, that's a good thing, or we never would've survived. It was bad enough facing two! We were frozen stiff with fear." He winced and groaned, then leaned his head back and shut his eyes.

"Let me tell the story," Jade said. She lowered her voice. "I think it hurts him to talk. He's still in a lot of pain."

"How is he handling the pain so well?" Alina whispered. "I mean this is Rex we're talking about."

"They're on some pretty strong medication. Rex says it numbs the pain but makes them sleepy."

Alina sat down on a blue couch with frilly cushions. "So, you were all frozen stiff. What happened next?"

Jade cleared her throat. "The nightstalks went for Rex and Baylor first. The attack was awful to watch. Night had come, but I could see in the moonlight—claws scraping their skin and blood dripping down their bodies. Their screams horrified me, but the pain roused them from the terror, and they started to fight back. Baylor recovered first and after a lengthy struggle, finally killed one of them."

Jade took a deep breath. "But during all this, the other nightstalk saw me a few feet away, still frozen. I was an easy target it couldn't resist. It started toward me and then—" She broke off.

"What?" Alina asked.

Jade shook her head, too overcome with emotion to speak.

Rex's eyes flew open and he sat up. "Something snapped in me the moment it started for her, and my fear vanished. Let me tell you something else, though, that Jade doesn't know. Right before the nightstalk went for her, it turned and looked at me. It stood in the moonlight, and its body became a window—and I saw the nightstalk slicing out her heart. I even heard her screaming. Then it smirked at me, like I'd never be able to save her. I think it was trying to kill any courage I had. This almost worked, but as it turned toward her, the panic in her eyes did it for me.

"I jumped on that devil, and seconds later it was dead. I don't know how, but I killed it without a gun." Rex flaunted his bandaged hands. "With my bare hands."

Then he looked at Jade with hot, feverish eyes, and she held his gaze for a long time, through her tears. They stared so fiercely that Alina cleared her throat and looked away. The moment was too intimate for any eyes but their own.

She didn't know what their gaze meant but couldn't help thinking if J'koby were there to see it, he wouldn't have a hope left.

CHAPTER 24

Alina's time in Millflower passed more unpleasantly than she expected. Maxwell's home felt welcoming as long as she avoided Nicole, but if they found themselves in the same room, a sudden chill filled the air. Nicole dismissed Alina's friendly efforts, which hurt deeply coming from someone she hoped would be a friend. Max and Christine, appalled by their daughter's behavior, attempted to reason with her, but this resulted in shouting matches and slammed doors.

Nicole worked hard to look beautiful, but her genes seemed set against her. Instead of her mother's fair skin and hair, she got her father's short eyelashes, freckled skin, and strawberry blonde hair, which was too frizzy to manage. Tall for her age, she appeared bony and lank. The heavy makeup she used did little to minimize or enhance her features but caked her face like a mask.

Alina found it curious that someone so homely could be as haughty as the stunning girls of Pria, which Alina always attributed to their vanity. Nicole's confidence was so forced and false, however, that Alina pitied her more than she disliked her.

Rex and Baylor improved each day, but healing was slow, so travel plans to Jaden were put on hold. This depressed Alina's spirits, but she enjoyed caring for the animals on Maxwell's farm. Often on boring nights, she headed out before the sun rose and finished the work before the others awoke.

On one such day, when Alina completed the chores before breakfast, Jade persuaded her to walk into town.

"Maybe you'll make some new friends," she encouraged.

Alina forced a smile. "I don't think anyone wants to be my friend."

"Jealous girls don't make good friends, anyway. I was thinking of the boys."

Talking to boys intimidated Alina more than the mean girls. She felt they expected her to be without faults, as if perfection in appearance meant perfection in everything else.

"Come on, Alina, they're just people. Nothing to be afraid of."

She gave a small shrug. "All right, I'll go with you. But I'm not talking to any boys."

MILLFLOWER WAS SO SMALL, everyone called each other by their first name and knew if they were having a good day or not. Alina received warm smiles from the older women and winks from the men. Children ran up and hugged her, and some gave her hand-drawn pictures of her in a long gown with a crown on her head.

They think I'm a fairy princess like in their bedtime stories. If only they knew how ordinary I am. The older girls found out soon enough.

These girls huddled in groups and glared at her without meeting her eyes. They whispered to each other and didn't offer to include her in their activities. The boys gawked from a distance, but if she got close enough to speak to them, they stared at the ground as if it hurt to look at her. All around, she felt uncomfortable.

She clung to Jade but watched the girls in their clusters and ached for a friend like Trinee. Jade struck up a conversation with everyone they passed, and before long seemed to know every person in town, except the girls who avoided her because of Alina. By noon Alina wanted to hide, so when Jade said she was hungry, she pulled her into an empty cafe with heavy drapes at the windows.

The hostess, a girl about her same age, put her nose in the air as she led them to a table. She filled two glasses with lemon water and left without a word. Alina slumped in her seat.

"Are you okay?" Jade asked.

She shrugged, twirling the straw in her glass. "It's awkward."

"I can imagine," Jade sympathized. "I don't know what it's like to stand out so much."

Alina closed the drapes as people walked by the window. "I'll be glad when we leave. Jaden is a bigger town. Maybe they'll be more welcoming."

"Perhaps you can forgive the girls. They feel threatened by you, you know. Getting married is so important to them, and the limited selection of boys is all they have to choose from. They can't move to another town; it's too dangerous."

"So, they marry and stay here their whole lives?" Alina asked in surprise.

"That's what Christine said."

A waiter approached them with a small grin on his face. The snooty hostess glared from across the room.

"I can't believe my luck!" he exclaimed when he reached their table. "My friends told me to take the day off because the famous Alina was in town and I'd miss my chance to meet her. Wait until they hear where you showed up!" He laughed, then smiled warmly at her. "I'm Oliver, by the way. Oliver Brook. I'm sure you're tired of everyone fussing over you. Why else would you hide in here? You don't even eat, right?" His relaxed nature put her at ease.

"No, not really, but Jade does, and she's very hungry—right, Jade?"

"*Starving*," she said with a big grin.

"Then I'll take your order and bring your food as fast as I can," Oliver said, reaching into the pocket of his apron and clicking a pen.

As Jade looked over the menu, Alina stole a glance at Oliver. She found him interesting. She knew staring was rude, but he wasn't looking at her, so she continued to study him.

He was a good-looking boy, nothing to Zaiden of course, but it didn't seem fair to compare him to an immortal. Though not drop-dead gorgeous, he wasn't plain, either. Oliver was simply nice-looking. He tucked his dark, wavy hair behind his ears, showing off a handsome jawline. His sharp, blue eyes rested on Jade.

As he waited with his pen poised above a notepad, he moved his eyes without turning his head and met Alina's stare. He gave her a caught-you-in-the-act kind of smile, and Alina looked away, blushing. She listened to Jade's questions about the menu and smiled at his witty answers. He wrote down the order, and as he turned to leave, Alina risked another glance at him. Their eyes met, and he smiled softly. Something fluttered in her stomach.

After he left, Jade raised an eyebrow at her. "So, what do you think?"

Alina played dumb. "Huh? What do you mean?"

Jade giggled. "Come on, there was some chemistry between you two. I felt it."

Alina rolled her eyes. "You know I like Zaiden."

"Yes, and you know him *so* well and see him *so* often."

"Don't remind me that I left him behind. Besides, we're leaving Millflower soon anyway."

"Who knows how long it will take Rex and Baylor to recover? We could be here a while yet. You may as well have a friend."

Alina chanced another peek at Oliver across the room. He leaned over a counter as he talked to the hostess, who now seemed likable. She giggled like a chipmunk as he spoke to her.

A short while later, Oliver brought Jade's food and set it in front of her, then took off his apron. "Well, ladies, I'm off. It was nice to meet you both. Now I have to tell my buddies how I met you and make them all jealous."

"Oh! Stay and visit with us first," said Jade. "You need to give them a better story than you simply brought us food. Maybe Alina will give you a kiss on the cheek to make it really juicy."

"Jade!" Alina exclaimed, but she laughed.

"You know what's funny," said Oliver, sitting down as if Jade's invitation was exactly what he planned on, "I told some of my friends last night that you" —he looked at Alina— "are no different from the other girls in town. You just look better, that's all. They're all nervous about talking to you. I told them to pretend you're the ugliest thing they'd ever seen, and they'd do fine. 'Course now I see that's easier said than done."

"I see. So, right now you're pretending I'm ugly. *That's* why you talk so easily with me," Alina teased, not knowing whether to be flattered or offended.

He laughed. "I put my foot in my mouth, didn't I? Well, if you want to know the truth" —he leaned in toward her— "I talk easily with you because I'm not dumb. I know you're not going to fall for me. I'm a bit of a realist, you see. Reality doesn't bother me; I prefer it, actually. Give me reality over dreams any day. I can do a lot more with it." He grinned and took a sip of her drink with such self-assurance, it astonished and lightened her.

"I was drinking that, you know," she said, laughing.

He dropped his jaw and reddened. "What? I thought you don't eat or drink!"

"I don't *have* to. But I like to sometimes."

"Oh wow, I'm sorry," he said. "I've had really bad manners." He stood up. "I'd better go now, please excuse me. My mom needs my help this afternoon. But, Alina, come hang out with me anytime you get tired of those back-biting girls or tongue-tied boys. I'm over on Wheaton Drive, third house on the left. It's blue. Or come here. I'm here just as often, it seems." His eyes lingered on her for a moment before he turned and headed for the door.

Jade watched him go, then gave Alina a knowing smile. "There! You've got a friend!"

Alina beamed. She had a friend. He was fun and easy-going and made her feel normal. She didn't care if it seemed forward. She'd call on him as soon as she could.

THE NEXT MORNING Alina waited impatiently for the sun to rise. She enjoyed the night outdoors, relaxing on the back deck and completing the farm chores, but went inside at the first sign of dawn. She changed into simple clothes, hoping to downplay her beauty, but it was no use. Even jeans and a t-shirt flattered her. She never needed to brush her hair or put on makeup and wondered why so many in Pria used it. She pulled her hair into a ponytail, then looked in the mirror and sighed. She wanted to fit in but looked far from normal.

She went downstairs and found Jade in her farm clothes, eating breakfast. "Did you leave any chores for me?" Jade asked.

"Yes, the eggs. I know how much you like the chickens."

"Thanks! Where are you going?"

"To Oliver's, of course."

Jade broke into a grin. "Have a good time and don't fall in love," she teased. Alina rolled her eyes as she went out the door.

The morning was calm. Maxwell's neighbors were outside tending animals, and Alina smiled and greeted them, even the girls who pretended not to see her. The sun appeared close in the sky, and she suspected the day would be hot, though she couldn't feel it.

She found Wheaton Drive and the blue house but hesitated, rubbing the back of her neck. She looked so eager, calling this early in the morning, which likely broke some social rule. But her time in Millflower had been unbearable, and there was no more time to waste. She skipped up the porch steps and rang the bell.

After a few minutes Oliver opened the door. He was bare-chested, wearing only plaid flannel pants. His eyes widened and he shoved a hand through his tousled hair.

"Alina!" he exclaimed. "I just woke up—uh—will you give me a minute? Come in." She went pink, wishing she'd been more patient that morning. But he smiled at her as she stepped inside.

She stood in the entryway as he ran up the stairs. His shoulders flexed as he gripped the handrail, skipping two steps at a time. Alina stared after him for a moment then looked away. She didn't want to like him like that. She only wanted a friend.

After a few minutes she heard a door open and close. A pretty woman with Oliver's same dark hair stepped into the hallway from the kitchen. She smiled warmly at Alina.

"Alina, how nice to meet you!"

"Thank you," she answered. "You must be Mrs. Brook."

"You can call me Linsie. I hoped you might stay with us, but having a teenage son, it wasn't permitted. I suppose that's wise. Ollie told me he met you yesterday and you might get together. I'm glad he has someone to keep him out of trouble."

Alina smiled. "Well, I'll do my best. I'm glad to have a friend."

Linsie's face softened. "He told me how the girls have treated you. It's awful. How interesting; you are the most popular girl in town and yet no one will be your friend. Give them time and I bet they will change."

"I hope so, but I don't have much time left. There are many kind people, though. Max and Christine are wonderful."

"They are, I know. Christine and I are dear friends."

Oliver pounded down the stairs and gave his mom a kiss. "I see you met Alina."

"I did. She's charming."

Alina blushed. "Thank you."

Oliver beamed at her. In the short time upstairs, he showered, combed his hair, and changed into jeans and a snug t-shirt. *Oh no. He smells and looks really good.* Alina swallowed. *Maybe this isn't the best idea. I'm sure to do something wrong.*

"Have you eaten breakfast?" he asked.

She smiled. "No."

"Oh yeah, that's right! Have some with me anyway, will you?" He led her into the kitchen. Linsie put fruit and a tray of muffins on the table, then took her mug outside to the porch.

"Thanks, Mom. You can stay with us if you like," Oliver called. She laughed lightly as the screen door banged shut behind her.

Oliver rolled his eyes. "She thinks we want to be alone."

"Do you have any brothers or sisters?"

Oliver bit a muffin, then chewed for a moment before answering. "No. Just Mom and me. My dad died when I was ten."

"Oh—I'm sorry."

He didn't offer any more information, and an awkward pause followed. She hunted for something to say. "What's life like here? Do you go to school?"

Oliver straightened his back and swallowed his food. "Yes, but we're off for the summer and part of the fall, until the harvest is over. Everyone in town helps with that. It's not bad here—I have a lot of good friends—but we have to get creative to have fun. Millflower is a small town after all."

Oliver chatted about the things they did to stave off boredom—cow tipping, childish pranks, and sneaking into the granary to play games without getting caught. In earlier days, he and the other boys amused themselves by trapping animals and sticking the carcasses to the windows of girls' bedrooms, but he had matured since then. Or so he claimed.

Alina sat back in her chair and listened, enjoying the enthusiasm in his gestures and his animated blue eyes. It seemed everything in life, no matter how dull, became fascinating when spoken from his lips.

The hours raced by, and as lunchtime grew near, he asked if she'd like to go into town with him. She hated to leave the comfort of his kitchen, but he persisted until she agreed.

"I have to work in a couple of hours, but we could get some lunch. Or *I* could, I should say, and you can sit and watch me eat," he said.

She laughed. "I'll eat lunch with you; that would be nice. But I've taken your whole morning. Do you have chores to do?" Linsie had long since left for work.

He waved a dismissive hand. "I can do them when I get back. Today's been worth it."

"Can I help you with your work later?"

He stared at her for a moment. She realized how bold she sounded and reddened.

"Yes. I'd love for you to come over later. But I have a lot to do. You might have to stay a while." He grinned.

They walked into town, where he showed her all the places she hadn't yet seen. Whispers followed them wherever they went, and both the girls and boys smoldered with rage, except for Oliver's friends who flashed him a thumb's up when they thought Alina wasn't looking. Oliver seemed to enjoy every minute of it.

They talked for another hour over lunch, and though their conversation never reached great depths, his stories amused her. When the time came for him to go to work, she offered to walk him there. She wanted to see the small cafe again because as the spot where they first met, it was now her favorite place in town. But she'd never tell him that.

"You know, Alina," he said, putting his arm over her shoulder as they walked, "I think I've found my new best friend. You're more fun than any of my buddies, and *way* more relaxed than any of the girls." She pretended to look shocked, and he laughed. "Yes, I see you know what I mean. Who'd want to cuddle with those prickly things? But you—you're like one of the guys!"

She wasn't sure she liked his compliment but felt relieved he wanted only friendship from her. "I've had a great time too, more than you know," she responded. "Thanks for helping me feel at home for the first time since I've been here."

He licked his lips and squeezed her close to him. As he pulled away, his hand grazed her arm down to her fingertips, then grabbed them briefly. Her eyes followed him to the cafe door where he turned and flashed a tiny smile, as if he knew she noticed his touch, and he wanted it that way.

CHAPTER 25

Over the next two weeks, Alina and Oliver spent almost every minute together when he was off work, and often when he wasn't. She'd sit at the corner table of the cafe and watch him serve customers and laugh at the theatrics he'd sneak in for her amusement. He loved to make her laugh, and since his humor matched hers, he excelled at it. Her presence became such a distraction that his boss allowed her to stay long enough to eat a meal, then ordered her out. So, every day she ate a meal at the cafe to be with him.

She enjoyed their time together but didn't feel attracted to him like she did Zaiden, which relieved her. She welcomed no romantic confusion in her life. Oliver seemed content with their friendship as well, but he often found a reason to touch her—on her hands, her hair, even her face.

She further appreciated Oliver's friendship when it severed all hopes of finding it elsewhere. The girls in Millflower coolly ignored her, yet their furious glares when she was with Oliver indicated they might kill her, if only she could die.

The boys took it as a personal rejection and became aloof. Even the friendliest of them now avoided her, as if all purpose in becoming acquainted was gone. It seemed choosing Oliver meant spurning everyone else.

Nicole, who Alina thought couldn't get any worse, muttered such degrading remarks in Alina's presence that she feared going home each day. Nicole appeared to take the friendship with Oliver as a personal insult.

One afternoon, as Jade and Alina sat on the porch, Nicole slammed the front door and passed them in a huff. As she stormed out of the yard, Alina whispered to Jade about her.

"She seems to hate me more now I'm friends with Oliver—and so does everyone else in town. Did they want me to be miserable and friendless, and this ruined their plans?"

"I have a different theory," Jade said quietly. "When you first started hanging out with Oliver, Christine mentioned the girls might never warm up to you now. You've nabbed the boy they all wanted."

"I haven't nabbed him," Alina replied. "We're just friends."

"*Right.*" Jade's eyes twinkled.

"I don't like him that way. I was worried I might, but there's still Zaiden—and besides, we're leaving soon. Maybe then everyone will see there's nothing going on between us. If I do succeed in freeing Carthem, I'd only be more hated here. I guess I have to fail for anyone to like me."

Jade put her hand on Alina's back. "They aren't worthy to be your friends. Enjoy your time with Oliver. He's fun, and handsome. I'm not surprised so many girls like him. Are you sure he thinks of you as a friend, though?"

"Yes, pretty sure. And if not, we're leaving anyway." Alina traced her finger along the wicker of the porch swing. "I'll miss him, though."

They sat in silence for a few minutes until Christine poked her head out the door. "Alina, Jade—Baylor wants to speak to both of you right away."

THREE WEEKS after the nightstalk attack, Rex and Baylor were healing nicely, though the doctor expected some scarring. In spite of this, Rex looked more like his handsome self, and Baylor removed the patch from his eye.

"Hi, ladies, please sit down," Baylor said as they came in. "We have some things to discuss. I spoke with Lance this morning about our trip to Jaden."

"How soon will we go?" Alina asked. The idea of leaving Millflower unsettled her. She would be both sorry and relieved.

"As you can see, Rex and I are doing a lot better. Doc thinks we'll be recovered in another week or so. But the trip to Jaden concerns us, and we're unsure of the best way to proceed. Gerard has really thrown a snag in our plans. We never thought he was alive—much less recruiting men and acting as Sampson's puppet."

"He won't give up, will he?" Alina stated.

"No, he won't, and your escape will make him wiser and more cautious. Their number is their advantage—there's so many of them, and they must have something protecting them. We don't understand how a group that size could survive in the wild."

"Yes!" Alina remembered. "I meant to tell you—they have something from Sampson protecting them."

"How do you know?"

"I heard them discussing it when a man disappeared after leaving the group. Something about the group offering protection, and Sampson was behind it. Gerard got upset when they talked about it. He didn't want me to hear."

"Interesting," Baylor murmured. "Maybe Lance will have an idea what it is. Our best strategy might be to take it from them; then they'd be dead in a matter of hours."

"You're sure they'll try to take me again?"

"I'm sure, and with no such protection, it's useless to organize a group large enough to match them. They could simply wait for the creatures to reduce our numbers, which would surely happen."

"What if we spread out?" asked Jade.

"If we're close enough to unite to fight Gerard's gang, then we're close enough to be hunted by deadly creatures. You saw how many grimalkins came, and there were only four of us. Traveling in a large company wastes lives. Alina can't defend us all. Gerard has a huge advantage."

"What do you think is the best plan?" Rex asked.

Baylor sighed. "Lance and I discussed many ideas and kept coming back to the same thing. Our best option is to take Millflower's most reliable vehicle—which isn't much, mind you—hurry to Jaden with the four of us, and hope we don't meet Gerard along the way. It's simple, risky, and the only plan we've got."

"But we need a defense in case we *do* meet him," Alina said.

"Absolutely. Lance and I discussed that, too. We need to be as prepared as possible."

Alina pulled up her knees and hugged them against her chest. She'd told the others how she escaped from Gerard that night in the woods but had left out some important details. It was too uncomfortable to remember, much less speak of, what the men wanted to do with her. But Baylor needed to know.

"Baylor," she said, her voice trembling. "I haven't told you everything Gerard did to me last time."

Baylor turned hard eyes on her. His nostrils flared but he spoke in a gentle tone. "I worried you hadn't. I understand this might be hard to talk about." He paused. "Did his men take advantage of you?"

"No," she answered, and Baylor's chest relaxed. "But they planned to, all of them in their turn, and they came very close. I overcame the first man who tried because I stretched the rope loose. Then I escaped into the woods."

Baylor shot to his feet and paced the room. He cursed Gerard through clenched teeth.

Alina blinked back tears. "I know I can escape them, but I'm terrified of being taken again."

Rex spoke up. "Don't worry, Alina, we'll protect you better this time. We'll have a plan."

"Yes," Baylor agreed. "I'll consult Lance and see if he knows what might be protecting them."

"The way I see it, the longer we stay here, the more time Gerard has to plot against us," said Rex. "Can we set a date to leave?"

"That's a good idea," Baylor answered. "One week from today, and we go. That's enough time to prepare and complete our recovery."

A knock sounded at the door, and Christine entered. "I'm sorry to interrupt, but your wife is on the phone, Baylor. She says it's urgent."

Baylor pinned his eyebrows as he took the phone. Christine left the room, closing the door behind her.

"My love, what is it?"

Baylor's eyes widened as he listened, then he covered his face with his hands and rubbed his forehead. The others exchanged worried looks.

"Oh no," he whispered, and fell into a chair. He continued to rub his face. "Yes, tell Lance to contact me as soon as he has a moment. I understand he must be busy. I will alert everyone here...yes, of course. It will be good for Trinee to tell her." He glanced at Alina. "Please be careful, Janet." His face scrunched up. "I love you, too."

He handed the phone to Alina. "It's Trinee."

Alina snatched the phone. "Trin? Is everything okay?"

"Yes, we're fine, at least for now. But there's something I need to tell you." She paused. "Zaiden's here. In Stormport."

Alina almost dropped the phone. By the sound of Trinee's voice, this wasn't a good thing. "Zaiden?" she whispered. "Is he insane?"

"No, you can stop worrying about that," Trinee rushed.

Alina closed her eyes and placed her hand over her heart. "But how did he escape?"

"No one knows yet." Trinee cleared her throat. "He's very ill, Alina."

"Ill?"

"Yes. With a virus no one has seen before. The doctors are baffled. They suspect Sampson sent it in."

Alina covered her mouth. "Are you certain?"

"Yes. And it's spreading like crazy. There's another man who came with him from Pria, named Crome. He's infected as well."

"Crome!" Alina gasped, and Rex started at the name. Baylor was quietly sharing the news.

Trinee continued. "Any who have come in contact with them have fallen ill, and it kills fast. Already three nurses have died, and Zaiden and Crome arrived only a few hours ago. Lance is certain this is an attack from Sampson. You know how valuable Stormport is to Carthem. We've completely shut down."

"How many are sick?"

"Last we counted, twenty-nine. We can't leave our homes. Once someone is sick, there's nothing anyone can do. No one can get near them. We have to sit back and hope their bodies are strong enough to pull through." Trinee broke into sobs. "It's scary, Lina. I wish Dad was with us, but I know you need him more right now."

Tears came to Alina's eyes. "Thank you for letting him help us."

Trinee steadied her breath. "You're welcome."

"Can I ask you one more thing?"

"Of course."

"How bad is Zaiden? Has he talked to anyone?"

"Well," Trinee giggled through her tears. "It could be a rumor, but I heard he's been calling for you since he got here. He's delirious, of course, which makes his words more sincere!"

Alina's heart jumped. "I wish I was there. I could take care of him and everyone who's sick."

"There you go again, wanting to save the world," Trinee teased.

"I can't help it. Immortality does that to a person." Alina managed to laugh. "Stay safe, Trin."

"You too."

"Bye."

Alina hung up the phone. Baylor turned to her.

"Stormport is being quarantined," he said. "No one can go in; no one can leave."

"Why can't they leave? They should go before they get infected!" protested Rex.

"Like many diseases, people are contagious before they have symptoms," Baylor explained. "We can't afford to have this spread outside of Stormport. Lance is worried it will wipe out all of Carthem —in fact, he believes that's Sampson's intention. He knows there's a rebellion growing, and Lance is leading it—Sampson's been trying to kill Lance for years. Losing him would be a crushing blow." Baylor rubbed his eyebrows. "We need to get to Jaden right away. A quarantine could really complicate our plans. We must leave tomorrow."

Alina's heart dropped. Tomorrow! She wasn't prepared for this. Stormport called for her now, not Jaden! She could fly there at full speed, and if Zaiden was calling for her from his deathbed, she could save him. But it would mean abandoning the mission when so many counted on her.

"Can we talk to Lance before we go?" Jade asked.

"No, he's busy working with the medical team to find a cure," Baylor said. "We must manage without his advice for now. Rex, can you travel tomorrow, or would you rather stay here?"

"Stay here!" Rex exclaimed. "You think I'd let you go without me? I'm coming. I'll be fine."

Rex did look better. His face was scarred, but that would fade in time. His leg needed a few more weeks in the cast, but as long as they had the car, that wouldn't matter.

"Pack up tonight, then, all of you. We must get off early, while Gerard's men are sleeping. I don't know where they are, but any head start will give us an advantage."

Jade and Alina left the parlor and headed toward the stairs. As they passed the front door, they heard a knock.

Oliver grinned through the window on the door. "Oh—I forgot!" Alina said. "We planned to work at the granary this evening. Do you think I should still go?"

"Of course," Jade said. "You have all night to pack, remember?"

Alina sighed. "I don't feel like going, actually. I'll talk to him."

She opened the door. "Hey, Lina! Ready to go?" Oliver asked. His smile vanished. "What's wrong?"

She stepped outside. "We've had some bad news." She glanced up the street at Mayor Nelson and Maxwell, who were marching toward his home. "Here they come to speak to Baylor. There's an emergency in Stormport."

"What's going on?" Oliver asked. The men came inside the gate and nodded, then went into the house, their eyes heavy with worry.

"They've had an outbreak of a serious illness. Sampson smuggled a virus in. Many people are dying, so the city is under quarantine."

Oliver went pale. "How was it smuggled in?"

"Two people brought it."

"From Pria?"

"Yes."

"That's awful. You must be worried for your friends there. Are any of them sick?"

"Yes. I know both of the boys who brought in the disease. One of them was the reason I escaped Pria in the first place."

"Do you think Millflower will be quarantined?"

"Yes, most likely."

Oliver released a long breath. "Well, I'm not going to lie, I'm happy to hear that. I was dreading the day you left. I've had more fun these past two weeks than I have in my whole life."

Alina swallowed. "I need to talk to you about that." She sat down in a wicker chair. "Baylor says we can't afford to get stuck here. We must leave before a quarantine happens, here or at Jaden." She paused. "Tomorrow morning, in fact."

"Tomorrow?"

"Yes."

Oliver slumped down on the chair next to her, took off his cap, and began twisting it in his hands. "That's a real bummer."

"I know."

He hesitated, then took a deep breath. "I want to go with you. Do you think Baylor will let me?"

Alina stared at him in shock. "Go to Jaden? You're not old enough!"

"I'm seventeen! Is there an age requirement or something?"

"They need you here to help with the harvest. Your mom needs you. You have a job and school to finish next year."

Oliver's cap popped out of its spiral. "Everyone I'm close to, including my mom, knows I don't want to stay in Millflower. I've wanted to live in Stormport or Jaden as long as I can remember. But those opportunities don't come often. The road is dangerous, and yes, there's always too much work to be done here. But here's my chance! Oh, Alina, I want to go! Can't you ask Baylor?" He turned his pleading, blue eyes on her.

She sighed. "He won't let you, Ollie. We have to keep the group small. Even four is pushing it. Big groups attract the creatures, you see."

He looked so devastated, she almost agreed to beg for him but decided against it. Did she want him there? If he found out about Zaiden, he wouldn't like it, and then their friendship would change.

"How about you come to Jaden next year, after you finish school? You can choose to go then, can't you?"

"Yes. I planned to leave, even before you came along. You—well, let's just say Millflower will be unbearable with you gone. Will you be in Jaden next spring?"

"I don't know," she said. "I don't know what the plan is for ousting Sampson, or what my role is. But it keeps proving to be bigger than I think."

"Can you promise me something?"

"What's that?"

"Whatever your adventure is, will you include me? Send for me, or even better, come and get me yourself. I want to join the fight against Sampson. I want more than this small town can give me."

Alina shifted in her seat. This could get complicated. But then, maybe she was analyzing too much. Zaiden needed to get well and come to Jaden before he could complicate anything—and she and Oliver were only friends. His companionship would be a comfort to her.

"I'll do all I can, Ollie, I promise."

He smiled and put his cap back on. "Can I help you pack, then?"

"Sure," she said, and stood up. Then she remembered Zaiden's info-disc stashed in her backpack, which he would surely see.

"On second thought, I can pack later; I have all night. Let's do something fun."

"Not the granary, then, I suppose."

"Yes, let's do the granary! We said we'd be there. I want to do something for Millflower before I leave."

"Well, that's the place to be, then. Carthem depends on it."

They didn't speak as they walked past the wheat fields to the granary, the golden stalks stretching all the way to Millflower's back wall. Alina kept glancing at Oliver. He stared at the ground, frowning, but when they reached the granary, his shoulders relaxed. He met her eyes and smiled.

As they filled bags with grain, he told her they should share their deepest secrets with each other. He confessed he liked to dance and often shut the door to his room, turned on his music and let himself loose. Alina asked him to show her some moves right there, but he said he could only dance to music.

Then she broke into a song, something she'd never done before, and was surprised by how perfect she sounded. Oliver's jaw dropped as she danced along the platform, swinging her hair and belting into the wheat scooper in her hand. He grinned and jumped in, blending his voice with hers, and though his dancing wasn't as polished, they complemented each other.

The sun was setting when they left, casting a bronze glow over the wheat fields. The hard work put them in good spirits, and Oliver put his arm around Alina's shoulder like he'd done so many times before.

"You know, Lina," he said. "There are moments I love Millflower. This is one of them."

"Well, from what I hear, Millflower loves you, too. At least half the population does."

He blushed down to his shirt collar. "Actually, you're unfamiliar with the demographics of Millflower. Women outnumber men two to one."

"Oh, so two-thirds of the town loves you, *sorry*, my mistake."

"And half of *that* population is already married."

"Okay."

"And another twenty-five percent are under the age of eight. But for the last twenty-five percent, yeah, you're pretty much right."

Alina burst into laughter, and when she stopped there was an awkward silence. She decided to steer the conversation from where she'd led it.

She wasn't fast enough.

"You know," Oliver said seriously, "that percentage of the female population means nothing to a guy. All he wants is for that special, point-zero-one percent to love him."

Alina tilted her head for a moment, then furrowed her brow. "Huh?"

He cringed. "Never mind."

They walked in silence, his arm still around her. Neither of them wanted to disturb the moment with words. When Maxwell's house came into view, Alina felt tears come to her eyes. They reached the gate, where Oliver stopped and took her in his arms.

She could feel his heart racing as she pressed against him. "Thanks for the best two weeks of my life," he whispered.

She blinked back the tears. "Thanks for being such a good friend. I hope you still have some after I leave."

He laughed, and the tension loosened. Alina was afraid to pull away and look at him. After several minutes, he released her.

She couldn't meet his gaze. "Goodbye," she mumbled to the ground.

He put his hand under her chin and lifted it. The lights from the house illuminated his sharp jawline. He stared into her eyes for a moment, then glanced at her lips.

Voices from the house saved her. She turned her head and saw a group gathered in Maxwell's dining room, veiled by thin drapes.

"I need to go," she whispered. "Goodbye." She squeezed his hand as she ran off. She reached the porch steps and heard his soft reply.

"Goodbye, my timeless friend."

CHAPTER
26

Alina stepped inside Maxwell's home and found the mayor sitting at the dining table. Christine, Maxwell, Jade, and Rex huddled together with grim expressions on their faces. Baylor stood next to the window with his arms crossed.

"Uh oh," she said as she closed the door. "This can't be good." She thought of Zaiden and Baylor's family in Stormport, and a lump came to her throat. "Have you heard news?"

"Alina, sit down," Maxwell said, pulling a chair away from the table. "There have been some new developments."

Alina looked at Baylor. His jaw twitched, and he did not meet her eyes.

Panic rose in her chest. "Baylor, what's going on?"

Mayor Nelson spoke up. "I will explain. I heard the news first. Please, sit down."

Alina sat on the edge of the chair.

"I suppose your long stay here, waiting for Rex and Baylor to heal, was unwise. It's given Gerard time to collaborate with Sampson." The mayor cleared his throat. "Gerard and his mob have surrounded Millflower."

Alina blinked twice. "There's only about twelve or thirteen of them. How can they surround the town?"

"Sampson has sent aid," the mayor explained. "According to Gerard, they now number six hundred. That matches the entire population of Millflower, including our women and children."

"Six hundred!" Alina exclaimed. "And are they all protected from wilderness dangers?"

"It appears so, yes."

"Have you seen all these men?"

"I've seen enough to believe his estimate is probably accurate. And they're not all men. Many are women, and they're armed."

"That's not the worst part," Baylor cut in. "Can you think how Sampson might have readied an army so quickly?"

Alina shook her head.

Baylor dropped his voice. "They are his experiments. Their brains are programmed to follow orders from him, and now Gerard."

Alina stopped a gasp with her hand. "Prisoners from the dungeons?"

"Yes. This is a declaration of war. We've never had such an influx from Pria before. Gerard met them at the portal, and they've obeyed him blindly since."

"What are they planning to do?"

"Gerard says they're not interested in war. They want *you*. And if they don't get you, they'll attack the town."

Alina stood up and began twisting her fingers. "But how can you be sure they won't attack after they take me? Won't Sampson destroy Millflower if he can?"

The mayor rubbed his temples. "I know. We must play our cards carefully."

Maxwell spoke up. "I believe Gerard doesn't want to attack the town. The chaos would make it easy for you to escape. You've proven difficult to contain. But we can't risk it. We don't have much choice."

Alina put her face in her hands to hide her tears. Gerard and his men terrified her more than anything she could think of—except seeing her loved ones die.

She couldn't endanger Millflower. The people of Carthem would starve if it fell.

She wiped her eyes and raised her head. "How much time do we have?"

"Until midnight. Three hours. If he doesn't have you by then, they will attack."

"Should I take anything with me?"

At these words, Jade stood and left the table, holding back tears.

Baylor watched her leave. "There's hope, Alina. I have a plan that might work. At least it will keep you safe from their filthy hands. You don't need to bring anything—they'd only confiscate it anyway."

She nodded, chewing on her lip.

Baylor turned to Mayor Nelson. "I'll take Alina to Gerard. You contact Lance, and I'm sure he'll have a plan for getting her back. We'll act quickly, before they take her far." He turned back to Alina. "Don't worry, you won't be with them long."

The mayor nodded, drumming his fingers on the table as he frowned. He let out a long breath. "I guess that's our only option." He looked at Alina. "We'll do everything we can to get you back soon. I promise."

They all rose to leave, patting Alina's shoulder as they passed. Baylor embraced her.

"It'll be all right," he whispered. "You are like a daughter to me, and I will protect you as such. When will you be ready to go?"

"I'll pack my bag so it's ready for Jade to take, and then let's go."

"I'll wait here for you."

She went upstairs and found Nicole sitting on her bed with an icy glare on her face. Alina ignored her as she gathered her clothes and folded them into her pack.

"I know what's going on," Nicole hissed.

Alina didn't look at her. "Good for you."

Nicole slid off the bed and approached her with crossed arms. "I knew it was a mistake to let you come here."

Alina said nothing.

"Now you're putting all of us in danger. My only comfort is no one will let you come back after this."

Alina spun around to face her. "Why do you hate me so much?" she blurted out louder than she meant to, and Nicole shot an anxious glance at the door. "Is it because I'm beautiful, and you're not?"

Nicole's eyes flashed. "Of course not. I'm not vain like you are.

And just so you know, that boyfriend of yours is not as nice as you think."

"Well, maybe not, but he's the nicest person I've met here, so that doesn't say much about the rest of you," Alina retorted. "I would've taken friendship from *anyone* and been happy. It's not my fault the town heartthrob was the only one who reached out to me." She threw her packed bag by the door and left without looking back.

Baylor waited for her at the bottom of the stairs. "Is everything okay?" he asked, looking up the stairs over her shoulder.

"Yes." Alina fumed.

"What is it?" he asked.

"I just want to be normal," she snapped.

He smiled faintly. "Alina, your life from the start has never been normal." He opened the door for her and followed her outside.

The darkness made her anxious. Why must Gerard take her in the evening? The homes they passed revealed families watching the monitor, eating dessert and washing dishes, unaware of the danger surrounding them. She swallowed a lump in her throat, surprised by how sad she was to leave.

As they passed Wheaton Drive, she stretched her neck to see Oliver's house and caught a light from his bedroom window. He didn't mention it, but she knew he planned to see her off in the morning.

"Baylor," she said, "we have some extra time, don't we? Can we stop by Oliver's house so I can explain everything to him?"

He shook his head. "Not a good idea. You can't tell him why you're leaving. Only the town officials know of the danger we're in. We don't want to cause a panic."

"You should've held the meeting at a more private place, then. Nicole heard the whole thing. Tomorrow everyone will know."

"By then you'll have already left, and the town will be safe. You tell Oliver now, and he'll do something drastic and foolish to protect you. Boys overreact when it comes to saving their girlfriends."

"We're just friends!"

Baylor coughed. "Right."

"I won't tell him why I'm leaving," she pressed. "I'll just say goodbye."

"He'll be able to tell something is wrong. Can you keep it from him?"

She sighed. "Probably not."

"You'll see him again," Baylor said.

"He asked me if he could come with us to Jaden. He wants to join the fight against Sampson. Do you think there will be something for him?"

"I'm sure of it. We're at war now, and we'll need every able person to fight in order to win. And then—" he paused. "I hope it's enough."

They approached the front gate. Two guards stood at the entrance, peering through a slit in the door. They turned to Baylor and Alina as they arrived.

"You brought her," said one of them. "Is this what was decided?"

"Yes, it's our only option. But I have a plan I hope will keep her safe until we come for her," said Baylor in a low voice. "I must speak to Gerard. Alina will come with me."

The guard nodded. He opened the gate and led them outside, twenty feet from the wall.

"Gerard!" Baylor called out. "I'm here with Alina. I want to speak with you. Alone." Alina stiffened as a dark figure approached them from the forest.

"Thank you, Hans," Baylor whispered. "Please watch us from the gate." Hans nodded and returned to his post.

"I won't pretend I'm happy to see you, but I'm not surprised," Baylor said as the figure drew near.

Gerard chuckled darkly. "I'll always be around, whether you like to see me or not."

Baylor spoke in a steady voice. "I'll hand Alina over on one condition."

Gerard's rough features looked ghastly in the moonlight. "And what's that?" he sneered.

"You let me speak with Sampson."

Gerard threw back his head, his laugh echoing through the woods. Then he glowered at Baylor. "You've got a lotta gall, you know. Just like your father."

Baylor's nostrils flared. "Let me speak with Sampson, or I'm not handing her over. Go right ahead and attack this town. She'd have a chance to run, and you know how fast she is. The people of Millflower would gladly give their lives for her."

Alina thought of the spiteful girls and how wrong Baylor's statement was, but she squared her shoulders and looked Gerard straight in the eye.

Gerard glared at her, then turned back to Baylor. "Fine. But just you. She stays here."

"She stays with me, or she goes back inside the gate with the guard," Baylor demanded.

"Call the guard, then," Gerard snapped.

As Hans came to get her, Alina clutched Baylor's arm. "Are you sure this is a good idea?" she whispered.

"I'll be fine," he whispered back. "I know what I'm doing."

He walked into the forest with Gerard. Hans took her arm gently and led her back to the gate.

"Let's stay here," Alina begged. "I'm worried about him."

Hans drew his gun from its holster. "If anything happens, I want you to run to Jaden as fast as you can." He pointed down the dirt road leading into the forest. "But I think he's safe. You're not in Gerard's hands yet, so he won't want to hurt Baylor."

Alina relaxed a little, and after several long minutes, Baylor appeared, striding back to the gate. Gerard marched after him, cursing from behind.

Baylor's voice carried through the trees. "I'm sorry you don't like this arrangement. But you have Alina, so we expect you to be on your way and no longer threaten this town." He reached Alina and Hans, and turned to face Gerard, who flashed him a rude gesture.

"Come with me," Gerard growled at Alina. "No running this time, or this hole of a town will be flattened the second we notice you're gone." He seized her arm. She looked desperately at Baylor.

"Don't worry," he whispered. "You'll be well treated."

"Wait," she cried, reaching for him. She had questions now. How would she get away if her escape threatened Millflower? What should she do?

"NO!" Gerard screamed. "No talking!" He yanked her away with him, clenching her wrists tighter as she tried to break free.

"Go, Alina," Baylor assured her. The calm in his voice surprised her. Then he put the light to his chin and moved his lips. He repeated the name twice before she caught it.

"Stan," he mouthed.

CHAPTER 27

G erard yanked Alina into the trees, and one by one his men came out, leering at her. She scanned the group for Stan but didn't see him.

Although the men terrified her, the real fright came from the people standing in the darkness behind them. They carried lights, which cast shadows on their demonic features. Their eyes looked like dark holes and their skin shriveled on their cheekbones. Ratted hair hung from their heads, some touching the ground.

"Listen up," barked Gerard. "No one is to touch this girl or be left alone with her. Three men will guard her at all times. Under no condition is anyone to make love to her. Not even if she begs for it!" he yelled over their protests.

"She won't escape this time; stop worrying," said one of them, "but three of us can guard her; we don't mind." They roared with laughter.

"You want her all to yourself, is that it?" another jeered. Alina cringed, tears filling her eyes.

"IT. WILL. NOT. HAPPEN!" Gerard hollered, silencing them at once. "Not by me. Not by any of you. She is to tell me if any of you disobey, which I'm sure she will. You'll be thrown out of this company and dead in minutes. Do I make myself clear?"

Alina's mouth dropped, then she smirked as the men stammered their consent. Some glared at her as if this was her doing, and she glared back. *Why would I allow them to do whatever they want with me?*

"We'll walk as far as the stream and camp there," Gerard ordered. "I'll guard her first. Mick and Pete will be with me."

Gerard yanked her arms together and began tying her wrists. She rolled her eyes.

"Come on, we've been through this. You know ropes can't hold me. I agreed to come and I'm not going to run away. Let me keep my hands free." Gerard glowered at her, then put the rope back in his pack and grabbed her arm so tightly, she was grateful she couldn't feel pain.

Mick and Pete walked behind them, and the Sad Cases followed, their eyes not straying from Gerard. They stopped when he stopped and moved when he moved. They listened when he spoke, but whether or not they understood, she couldn't tell. It appeared Sampson had mastered the immortal mind. He put it through such torture that when the brain became mortal, no functioning part was left.

Gerard hissed in her ear. "No funny business this time. We won't bother going after you. We'll head straight for Millflower and kill everything that breathes."

"I know, I heard you the first time," she snapped. "But just so we're clear, if you break your side of the deal and hurt anyone from Millflower, *I'll* be gone faster than you can blink."

His lip curled. "I'm glad we understand each other."

"Yes. And I'm not complaining, but I'm curious about this sudden vow of chastity you've required from your men."

He stopped moving and yanked her arm, so she faced him. She had gone too far.

"Don't *ever* ask that again, or I might change my mind," he threatened. She suspected he was bluffing but didn't push it.

"Are we going to the Blue Forest?" she asked.

He hesitated. "Eventually, yes. You'll come along and ask no questions. You're forbidden from talking to anyone, especially the lunatics from Pria. Not that they'd understand you, anyway."

What could she learn from the Sad Cases that Gerard didn't want her to know?

She accepted the terms willingly. She'd obey, be silent, and learn a lot that way.

AFTER THREE DAYS of traveling with no hint of being rescued, Alina began to despair. She doubted if she read Baylor's lips correctly when he mouthed Stan's name because she'd seen no sign of him. Baylor heard an account of Stan from Rex, but was the description enough to recognize him?

Although the men kept their distance, their company was far from pleasant. Resentful of Gerard's decree, they harassed her with their words rather than their hands, and their comments became so explicit and personal, she felt almost as violated.

The Sad Cases were not as frightening in the daylight, but like the man from the prairie, they looked sick and malnourished. Their clothes hung in tatters, and their pasty skin was stark against the wounds and bruises on their bodies. Alina worried they were being mistreated until she saw how strictly they obeyed Gerard. They scaled large boulders and plowed through thick brambles if it was the straightest course to his orders. They'd walk off a cliff if he asked them to.

She looked for Miss Vivian among them but didn't see her. Sampson said he might never release her. The memory of Miss Vivian, locked up and hysterical, haunted Alina, but she was grateful not to see her beloved teacher in this dismal group. The way their eyes clung to Gerard chilled her. They watched and waited for his next command, all of them.

Except one.

The woman's sunken eyes disturbed Alina because they stalked *her* instead of Gerard. Whenever their eyes met, Alina shivered and look away. This woman looked as wild as the others, yet something in her face seemed lucid and terrible.

What had Sampson done to these wretched beings? Was this the result of isolation in his dungeons, or something more? So far, Sampson's experiments produced all his weapons of war—creatures, disease, and assassins. Now they produced an army.

Alina shuddered, and turned her thoughts back to their usual place—to Rex, Jade, and Oliver in Millflower, to Zaiden in Stormport, and if he was still alive.

BEFORE LONG, Alina knew every man in Gerard's company by name and face, so when the new figure appeared, she noticed at once.

He kept his head and face covered, a peculiar thing in the heat of the day, and traveled several paces from them in the woods. Alina hadn't seen him before because he kept himself hidden.

Stan.

She tried to meet his eyes, but he never looked at her. Three guards surrounded her at all times, but he never took a turn.

Gerard didn't want her to notice him.

She stared at the ground, her mind racing, then peeked at the guards around her. It wouldn't be easy, but she must speak with Stan. She had a plan. Now she needed the right moment.

THE NEXT DAY, Gerard took them straight up a mountain, and as the path became more strenuous, the group stopped frequently to rest. By the time darkness fell and they made camp, the men dropped to the ground. Alina pursed her lips to hide a smile. *Perfect.*

At night, Gerard allowed Alina's guard number to drop to two. The men complained of the double night duty, but Gerard held firm, not trusting anyone to be alone with her. Alina didn't know what

Baylor had done, but every night when the men drank and became rowdy, she thanked him.

She sat by the smoldering fire as the men settled down, weary from the day's hike. The Sad Cases waited for Gerard to lie down, then followed him as they did every night—without blankets or pillows, and wherever they happened to be standing. One lay on a thorn bush, and Alina's only comforting thought was they seemed oblivious to pain.

The first guards of the night, Roy and Mick, sat on the ground with their backs against a log. Each night Alina stared into the dying embers as her guards chatted irreverently to keep themselves awake. Tonight, however, would be different.

She'd tracked Stan all day, which wasn't easy as he disappeared into the trees and remained unseen for hours at a time. Gerard sometimes met him in the woods and handed him a small canvas bag. At dinnertime he left again, and this time Alina followed his direction as he returned.

"Wow, I'm beat," groaned Roy, stretching his arms. "I hope I can make it tomorrow. Why Gerard is taking us straight over the blasted mountain, I'll never know." He swore under his breath.

Mick mumbled agreement through a yawn.

Alina had obeyed so far, never speaking to any of them, but Gerard's snoring encouraged her. The men jumped when she spoke.

"If you want to go to sleep, go ahead. I won't tell."

They eyed her suspiciously. "Then you'll take off and Gerard will leave us to the nightstalks," Mick retorted.

She tried to sound calm. "You know I'm not going to run away. Gerard is overreacting, that's all. Take turns sleeping, if you're worried."

"No way," Roy said. "You'll frame one of us."

She chuckled. "And how would that benefit me?"

"I saw what happened to Hank. I won't be alone with you."

"Oh yes, Hank. I haven't seen him around. Did he recover?"

They said nothing, but their silence revealed enough.

"It's too risky," she heard Roy mutter, but he sank lower against the log and stared at the fire, his eyes growing heavy. Mick was already lying on the ground. She regretted saying anything—they would've fallen asleep anyway.

They fought the drowsiness for a while before giving in, and once their breathing settled, Alina got up quietly and walked into the woods where she last saw Stan. Her eyes adjusted to the dark, and as she scanned the trees, she spied him several feet away, lying still on the ground.

He woke with a start when her hand closed around his neck. She held his throat firmly, like the night Hank threatened her, and pulled the hood back from his eyes.

"Tell me everything, Stan," she demanded. "I'll let go long enough for you to speak." She let go of his neck but grabbed his hand and bent his fingers backward. Her other hand covered his mouth to stifle his scream. He tried, in vain, to pull her fingers from his mouth.

"You've forgotten how powerful immortals are," she hissed. "You're fighting against someone who can't feel pain. But you on the other hand," she seized his throat again, "are very vulnerable. What are you doing for Sampson? How are you helping Gerard?" She twisted his hand again.

Stan whimpered, "S-stop, please. I'll tell you." He waited for her to let go of his hand, but she didn't. He winced as she tightened her grip.

"I'm trying to free my lover. She's locked in Sampson's dungeons, but he promised to release her if I brought you back. I'm doing this for her. Not for Sampson, or Pria." He paused, his eyes pleading. "I have to," he whispered.

He looked so desperate. Alina almost pitied him.

"You care so much about this woman, you're willing to betray all your friends and help Sampson just to get her back?"

"My time with her is the only time I've been happy. In three hundred years."

"Did you stop to think Sampson might be using you? That he

doesn't intend to release her—and if he did, she'd be like one of these lunatics sleeping nearby?"

Tears came to his eyes. "It doesn't matter. If there's the smallest chance I can free her, I'll take it. I'd rather die without her, anyway."

"You're pathetic," Alina snapped. "The most useful puppet Sampson could find. Live for yourself and forget her."

Stan thrashed out at Alina, a sudden fire flaring inside him. She straddled his torso and pinned his arms to the ground.

"Don't you say a word about her," he ordered through clenched teeth.

"Tell me one more thing," Alina demanded.

"What?"

"What protects you and Gerard? Is it something you carry?"

Stan stared at her for a moment, then smirked. "You should think about who you're fighting against. Sampson doesn't lose." Then without warning, he hollered at the top of his lungs.

She grabbed his throat to silence him, but a rustle from camp sent her running back, worried she'd been missed.

Gerard loomed over the fire, his eyes hard as stone.

"What were you doing back there?" he demanded. The men were awake now, staring at Alina. Mick and Roy exchanged worried looks.

"N-nothing," she stammered.

"NOTHING?" he bellowed. She covered her ears as he fired a string of expletives at her. She'd never seen him so angry.

He began kicking Mick and Roy on the ground. "OUT!" he screamed. "YOU'RE DONE! GONE! Finish them off, loonies!"

At these words, Mick and Roy fled into the woods. A pack of the Sad Cases chased after them, clutching their knives and snarling.

Gerard turned to the rest of his men, his eyes flashing. "This is what happens if you let me down. NONE OF YOU WILL KEEP ME FROM GETTING INTO PRIA!"

He marched to Alina, and she coldly met his eyes. He raised his hand as if to strike her, then dropped it and stormed into the woods toward Stan. Her body trembled, but she didn't shrink.

She controlled these men. The only power they held was over the people of Millflower. But it was enough.

THE NEXT MORNING the men were on edge, obeying Gerard promptly and refraining from their usual crude banter. Alina held her head high, more confident than she'd ever felt, but as they hiked farther up the mountain, she grew worried. Baylor hadn't come for her. Should she go along with them all the way back to Pria? Was it better to risk Millflower than herself? She didn't know what to do.

After several hours of hiking, Gerard turned up a neglected trail with prickly weeds and old tire tracks. Alina wrinkled her brow. Why did they take this steep route over the mountain? From her memory of the guidebook map, it didn't lead to the Blue Forest at all. She became more puzzled when Gerard stopped to tie her wrists.

"Why are you doing this?" she demanded. "You know it can't hold me." He glared at her, nostrils flaring, and said nothing.

Up they climbed, the men panting, the Sad Cases trudging through thorns without flinching but keeping their eyes fixed on Gerard.

Alina stopped mid-stride and tilted her head. The trail ended at a rotted wooden shack built into the mountain wall. She looked around for the path to continue, and glimpsed Gerard nodding to someone behind her.

Three men snatched her and stood close, their dirty whiskers catching strands of her hair. Gerard watched her startled face with a smug grin.

"We made it, pretty girl," he sneered.

Alina's eyes darted around them. "This can't be the Blue Forest."

"Who said we're going to the Blue Forest? That's an old plan. Sampson's adaptable. He thought the situation here needed a more *aggressive* approach." Gerard flashed his yellow teeth. "There's a rebellion to crush, after all, and you're the fire behind it. You must be extinguished."

He cracked open the door of the shack, and as the men yanked Alina toward it, she screamed, digging her heels into the dirt.

"No!" she shrieked. "What do you need? I'll go to the Blue Forest, I won't struggle, I've been good so far—"

"We don't need you anymore!" Gerard yelled back. "You're a stupid girl to fight against Sampson. Stormport is almost wiped out by disease, and now it's Millflower's turn." He smiled at her stunned face. "Well, of course we planned to attack them all along! Finish them off, just like Stormport. Then Jaden is all that's left. We'll starve them for a while to weaken them, and the rest will be easy. Wipe Jaden out, and Carthem is clean. And only *then* will someone come back for you, if at all. See if you can keep your wits that long."

With one hard shove the men tossed her into the empty air and her panicked scream echoed down the long, dark shaft.

CHAPTER 28

S he fell for a long time, somersaulting through the darkness until her feet met the hard ground. She fell to her knees, sobbing, and yanked at the rope around her wrists until it snapped. She hadn't seen this coming. Nor had Baylor or anyone, or they would've tried something else. Any desperate plan would've been better than this.

She hastened to free herself, then stood up and put out her hands, walking until she met the wall. Her eyes adjusted slightly but not enough to see. She ran her fingers up the wall as high as she could reach, then all the way to the ground. The stone was smooth and slippery; years of movement up and down the shaft had polished all of its rough edges.

She followed the wall horizontally until it opened up, then yelled into the darkness. Her voice seemed to echo for miles. She took a few steps, then froze and backed up. If she fell farther, she would be lost forever.

She looked up to the distant, pinpoint light at the top of the shaft —her only hope of escape. She jumped as high as she could along the wall, searching for a ledge, but her hands slid on the smooth rock back to the ground. She crumpled to her knees.

Gerard was on his way back to Millflower. She cradled her head and screamed, the sound vibrating around her. *Oliver and Maxwell's family. Rex, Jade, and Baylor. Trinee and Zaiden in Stormport.* Her scream turned into an anguished wail.

They would all die, and she'd be left behind. Gerard and his men would become Prian citizens, and the Sad Cases would die carrying out Gerard's orders. If they did survive, they'd roam an empty

Carthem until they starved or were killed by wild creatures. Sampson would never take them back.

She felt no pain or fatigue; she couldn't die and yet could do nothing to free herself. Nature's laws held her. She screamed again, pounding the walls and biting her knuckles.

I don't know how to fight the despair. I will go mad before long.

She huddled on the ground, wishing for sleep—anything to escape the mental anguish. Maybe with enough focus she could enter a trance. But the thought frightened her. That diversion must be how immortals went insane. They stayed in a hypnotic state until their minds were so far gone, they couldn't return.

I won't run away. I'll focus on the pain, on the memories of those I love to keep my brain alive.

She reminisced on her favorite memories of Oliver—when they first met in the empty cafe; when they sang and danced in the granary, and the night they said goodbye. She ached for his presence, for the ease she felt with him. She needed him now to make her laugh, to reassure her that somehow things would turn out okay. Despite claiming to be a realist, Oliver seemed to think anything was possible.

One evening, while walking to Maxwell's home together, he accused her of flaunting her looks. He demonstrated by swinging his hips and flipping imaginary hair.

She punched his shoulder and laughed. "I do not!" she insisted. "It's how immortals are. No matter what we do, we look intriguing. It's all part of the illusion."

He stopped laughing and looked at her. "Illusion?"

"Yes," she stated. "We don't seem real, do we? We're too good to be true, like all things in Pria. Everything is so perfect, so captivating —like a mirage."

"Careful how you use that word. It has a different meaning here," Oliver warned. "Though I think the comparison is quite fitting." His eyes twinkled. "Maybe that's what you are. You're my mirage."

Alina hugged her legs in the dark, smiling at the memory.

Though his presence seemed so long ago, Oliver felt real—the first boy she'd known as a friend and not a father figure. Zaiden was her friend but in a different way.

Is Zaiden my mirage?

She hardly knew him. They'd shared two conversations and one long, intense gaze. Did that make it love?

How would he be as a mortal? Would she still be attracted to him, and would they talk and laugh easily together? Like Oliver, would he flip her ponytail and look for a reason to touch her, and would it feel natural?

Her brain was lucid now, but a thought crept in and cut her. *It's useless to examine my feelings. I'll never have the chance to choose either of them.*

The despair returned, and she allowed her mind to go numb. It was time to surrender. Sampson had won.

She put her face in her knees and started to cry. Carthem had given her the life she always wanted and not because she was immortal. Here, she had family who loved her: Jade finally open and honest, and a father and grandfather who longed to see her. Now they would never meet.

I'll never feel my father's embrace, look into his eyes, or see how he resembles me. He'll never be able to tell me about my mother. I'll never have a family of my own.

She should've killed herself and stopped Sampson when she had the chance. Before Rex rescued her in Gordian, she should've cut herself on those sharp instruments, or flung herself into the depths of the laboratories. Rex led her to believe she could go to Carthem and fulfill her mission. Now it was too late.

Sampson won't come back for me.

Why would he, when this pit was as good as his dungeon? Gerard's army would destroy Millflower and starve the rest of Carthem while Sampson maintained his control over Pria. Carthem would rebuild slowly, if at all. The survivors wouldn't know what happened to her. Eventually, they'd doubt she ever existed. She'd become a legend: the lost immortal hero of Carthem. One who could've saved the world but fell short.

And she'd live on in this dark hole. Forever.

She may as well go where she wouldn't suffer. She closed her eyes and let her mind drift—anywhere open, bright, and far from the stone walls that confined her.

"ALINA!" a voice called.

Zaiden stood in the Prian fields with a perfect, balanced six-petaled flower, handing it to her with the same smile he'd given her in the school hallway. He said her name again, but his voice echoed as if trapped in something hollow and empty.

"Alina!"

Darkness began to swallow the bright colors, shrinking him to a small circle. He stood in the center, smiling, unaware of the danger around him. Alina screamed and jumped to her feet as the darkness enclosed him. She stretched out her arms and felt the smooth, hard wall in front of her.

"Alina, is that you?" a woman's voice called.

She blinked her eyes. Someone called for her! She cupped her mouth and answered hoarsely, "I'm here! Who are you?"

She heard nothing and bit her lip. She was losing her mind.

Then she heard the voice again. "I'm lowering a rope. Watch for it."

A rope! Alina burst into tears. Was the war over? How long had she been in there? Did Sampson send this woman to fetch her? It didn't seem to matter, as long as she got out.

A distant sound occurred at regular intervals, and after many long minutes, something hit the ground next to her. Reaching out, she felt a thick rope with a frayed end below a knot. She stepped on the knot and gripped the rope.

"I have it!" Alina shouted. "Don't crank it, I can get there!"

The shaft seemed to run the height of the mountain, but she sailed up the rope, and as she neared the top, a silhouetted figure hunched in the doorway. Alina climbed higher and jumped through the wooden door, embracing the woman as the sun hit her eyes. She pulled away to view her rescuer, then slammed her hand over her mouth.

It was she—the most frightening Sad Case of all, whose sunken eyes had stalked Alina and turned her veins cold.

CHAPTER 29

Alina took a step away from her. "Who are you? Are you—?" The words stopped in her throat.

"Insane?" the woman finished. "My mind is whole, if that's what you're wondering. It hasn't been easy keeping my sanity, though."

"You're telling me you lived in Sampson's dungeon and came out with your mind intact?"

"Yes."

"For how long?"

"I don't know. As you probably realized, it's impossible to keep track of time when you're locked up. But I was imprisoned before you were born."

"But that's over seventeen years!"

"Horrible years. I can't tell you how glad I am to be out."

Alina shook her head. "I can't believe it. I could barely keep my wits in that deep pit, and I was in there for—how long was I in there?"

"Three days."

"*Three days!* That's all?"

"I would've come earlier, but I had to wait until nightfall to slip away or the others would've tattled on me. Then, I'm embarrassed to say, I got lost. I tried to pay attention when we first left this spot, but I didn't do a good job. It's a miracle I got here at all. I was about to give up and let myself die when I recognized the path with the wheel tracks."

Alina smiled gratefully. "Thank you. What's your name?"

"Mae."

"Is there time to save Millflower before they attack?"

"I don't know. I tried to overhear their plans. The men aren't careful with their words around us, but they didn't say much about Millflower. They were heading back in that direction, though, so we better move quickly."

Mae looked pale and gaunt, with bony legs protruding from her ripped dress. "When did you last eat?" Alina asked.

"This morning. I found some berries."

"Is that all you've eaten since you left the group?"

"I ate leaves off a tree yesterday. I've been doing that for days. We don't get much to eat in Gerard's company."

Alina gently took her arm and lifted her onto her back. "You've done a service for me. Let me do one for you. I'll carry you."

Mae did not object, and Alina took off at full speed. Mae spoke in her ear, her voice breaking as she bounced against Alina's back.

"We were all pretty healthy when we first entered Carthem, coming from an immortal state. But we arrived two weeks ago, and each day we've had so little to eat. Gerard gives us one small meal every other day in the evening. The rest of the time we must scavenge for ourselves. The devotion to Gerard provides some adrenaline, but their bodies are weak. We're so close to death, little is needed to overpower us."

"But you're all so frightening, *especially* you. I thought you the maddest of them all."

"I've gotten good at it. I've been feigning madness for years, hoping Sampson would set me free into Carthem."

Alina raced down the mountain slope. "Do you think there are others like you? Pretending to be mad?"

Mae groaned as she slammed against Alina's shoulder. "It's possible, of course, but I don't think so. They follow Gerard so faithfully. But if there are, they can only help us because they hate Sampson as much as we do." Alina chuckled in agreement as she jumped over a fallen tree.

"We're making great time," Mae said.

"I can travel faster, if you can handle it. Do you think we can beat them to Millflower?"

"Maybe so. It's about four days' travel from Millflower to the mine shaft."

"Mine shaft?"

"That dark pit you were in. Gerard called it that."

Alina wrinkled her forehead. "I don't get tired, so yes, I can go faster. But I want to find you some food."

"I can last until we get to Millflower. Don't stop for me."

Alina worried about Mae but also feared arriving too late. She quickened her pace, and after a few hours they reached the base of the mountain and the flat prairie grasses. Mae's grip loosened on her back. Alina sensed she was asleep.

As the sun set, Alina ran harder, desperate to reach Millflower in time to warn them. But then what? A knot formed in her stomach. Gerard's army would be hard to defeat. If Mae was right and the Sad Cases were weaker than they looked, Millflower might have a chance. The citizens might be preparing to defend themselves just in case. She hoped so.

As the light from the rising sun hit her face, Mae stirred. "Where are we?" she mumbled.

"Not far from Millflower, I think. I've been running through the prairie all night."

"I hope we're not too late."

"Did Gerard or his men speak about the protection Sampson gives them?" Alina asked.

Mae hesitated. "I think so. Gerard told his men they had to stay close to someone in their group, or they could be killed."

"Do you know who it was?"

"Yes. A man who used to travel with them, but after you came, he walked a short distance away and kept a hood over his face."

"Stan!"

"I don't know his name, but he was the one your friend spoke to the night they took you from Millflower. I spied on them from behind a tree."

"Baylor! What did you see that night?"

"Gerard led Baylor to this man, who was alone. Baylor spoke with him, then spoke to Gerard, who became so furious I thought he might kill someone. Baylor returned to the gate with Gerard screaming from behind."

"It must be Stan. But how does he protect them? Does he carry something?"

"I have no idea," Mae answered.

Alina thought for a moment. "You know, Baylor and Lance wondered why we didn't encounter more dangers when we traveled from the portal. It's the most dangerous area in Carthem. But when Stan was nearby, we never met anything. Maybe it's embedded in him—part of the spying chip or something. That's why Gerard was so protective of him. I bet if Stan died, they'd no longer be safe."

Alina jumped over a stream, and Mae paused to catch her breath before answering. "You're probably right. Gerard kept him concealed, which says he's concerned for his safety."

Alina's mind raced. "Mae," she said, "instead of going to Millflower, let's find Gerard and his men. Let's keep this battle from starting. You don't have to do anything—I know you're weak. If we sneak up on them, I'm sure I can kill Stan."

"Sounds good to me," she said. "I've been worried about Gerard noticing my absence. I don't think he would, but Sampson might've told him to keep an extra eye on me."

"Why is that?"

"A story for another time. Let's just say Sampson has good reasons not to trust me. But if we find them, I can slip back into the group unnoticed and perhaps aid you in killing him."

"Yes, that might work," Alina mused. "I suppose we'll have to see where they are when we find them. If they're a good distance from Millflower, it'll work. If they're close and about to attack, we'll have to think of a different plan. Killing Stan only works if there's time for the wilderness creatures to get them. But with a large group like that, it shouldn't take long." Alina swallowed. "I hope I have the courage to do this. I killed once but out of self-defense, and I didn't intend to. This is different."

"I understand. But think of it this way—killing him will save many others. And besides—" Mae broke off.

"Yes?"

"It's horrible to be controlled by Sampson." Her voice caught as she spoke. "Stan is a captive. You'll be setting him free."

ALINA HAD BEEN RUNNING for twenty-four hours when she glimpsed smoke twirling in the distance. Could Gerard be making camp already and preparing to attack? Was the smoke coming from the town?

A panicked cry escaped her throat, and she accelerated toward the smoke. Her body continued to surprise her, especially when confronted with danger. She felt sorry for Mae, who grunted with pain each time her body slammed against Alina's back. But she did not slow down.

As she drew nearer, Alina dropped into the grass. She spied the Sad Cases in the woods near Millflower's front gate, where Gerard took her from Baylor. She crept toward them until she reached a tree, then set Mae on the ground. "Stay here while I go listen to their plans. I'll be right back." Alina whispered.

Mae grabbed her shoulder. "No. Let me go. I can hear more because I don't have to stay hidden. I'll sneak in and act as if I've been there the whole time. We can't let him catch you again."

Alina shook her head. "You're too weak, Mae. What if he hurts you? He can't do anything to me. If he catches me, I can escape."

"Please," Mae insisted, clutching Alina's arm with renewed strength. "I can do this. It's crucial Gerard doesn't find out you escaped. He might change his plans and make things harder for us.

I'll go. I'll find out what they plan to do and come back as soon as I can."

Alina chewed her lip as she studied Mae, then nodded. "All right. But I'm going to follow you from a distance to make sure you're okay. You can't stop me."

Mae smiled weakly. "Fair enough."

Mae approached the Sad Cases on her hands and knees, and Alina inched behind her in the tall grass. When their backs were turned, Mae stood up and strolled casually toward them.

A scraggy woman with long, tangled hair caught sight of her. "Hey! Where've ya been?" she yelled.

Mae drew back her shoulders. "I took a bathroom break in the weeds."

"Nah, ya didn't," the woman charged. "I hadn't seen you for a few days now."

"I've been here," Mae insisted, planting her feet apart.

The woman sneered. "Gerard's been looking for ya. He noticed you'd gone missin' and told us to bring ya to him if ya ever came back."

Alina clapped a hand over her mouth, but Mae didn't falter. "Bring me to him, then," she said calmly.

The deranged woman grabbed Mae's arm and started pulling her, but Mae yanked herself free. "I can walk myself, thank you."

Alina scrambled through the grass on her hands and knees, following them into the grove. *No, no, no, no, no!*

Alina reached the grove and stood up behind a trunk, then darted between trees as she tried to keep Mae in sight. When she spied Gerard and his men, she dropped onto her stomach and scooted over the rocks and limbs until she came within hearing distance, then stood up behind another tree.

"Where the hell have you been?" Gerard yelled.

Alina peeked around the trunk. Gerard stood in the middle of about fifteen men, scowling at Mae, who knelt before them with her head bowed.

Alina caught only fragments of Mae's quiet answer. "Sorry, master Gerard," she pleaded. "I...separated...lost. I came...you'd be."

Gerard glared for a moment, cracking his knuckles, then hurled his pointed boot into Mae's belly. She cried out in pain and collapsed on the ground. Alina gasped and shoved her knuckle into her mouth.

"Get some food," Gerard ordered. "You have extra work to do now. I won't let you out of my sight again."

Mae scrambled to a pot next to the fire, grabbed a bowl, and scooped up the sludge with shaky hands. She began consuming the food without utensils.

One of the men turned to Gerard and dropped his voice. Alina stretched forward to hear him. "Do...suspect she...?" he murmured.

Gerard laughed darkly, then spoke as if he wanted Mae to hear. "Do you think that nutcase has the brain capacity for anything clever like that?" He nodded toward Mae as she licked the bowl like an animal, porridge dripping off her chin. The men broke into laughter.

Gerard dropped his voice. "But I'll still teach her a lesson. Jed, tie her to a tree when she's done eating. You can have your way with her tonight."

Jed wrinkled his nose in disgust. "I might pass. We'll be in Pria soon enough."

"Speaking of that," Gerard said smugly, "Sampson's offered a generous bonus if we capture Jade and Rex before we destroy the town."

"What's the bonus?" several men asked at once.

"Mansions in Pria. Top social status. He'll introduce us as brave heroes from Carthem, and we'll have plenty of beautiful women whenever we want them. Even Stan will get his little pet back."

The men howled with laughter. Stan crossed his arms and glowered at them.

"What does Sampson want with Rex and Jade?" Jed asked.

Gerard smirked. "Sampson wants the names of every resistance member in Pria. The more names we get, the better the reward. We're free to use any method that works. Rex is a pampered cupcake.

He'll be spewing names the second I press my boot on his coin purse. Jade is worthless, but Sampson wants her to suffer anyway. Sounds like he has plans for J'koby, too."

Alina's teeth were leaving marks on her knuckles. *I must get Mae out of there and into Millflower. I need to warn them!*

"It won't be easy luring Rex and Jade out," another man said.

"Yes, it will," Gerard crowed. "I've got good leverage here." He walked to a bag on the ground near the fire and rummaged inside, then pulled out a round orb, the size of a small melon. A wicked grin spread across his face as he lifted it for his men to see. Alina narrowed her eyes, trying to identify what the round thing was.

"What is it?" someone called.

Gerard dropped his voice and pointed to the top of the object. Alina leaned forward, straining her ears.

"...light it here. About one minute later—" Gerard stretched out his arms. "BOOM! I have three of these explosives—with catapults. Sampson sent them in with the loonies!"

"But won't they throw them back over the wall?"

Gerard shook his head. "No! These babies will be on fire!"

"But they're so small! How big is the explosion?" another man pressed.

"Trust me, if we launch all three at once, the town will be flattened. If one explodes near the wall, their puny army will be wiped out. Now all we need—" Gerard motioned for the men to move in. Alina pressed her back against the tree, bouncing her fist against her mouth. *How do I stop this?*

Gerard pointed to three different areas of the wall. He curled his fingers into claws, thrust his hands away from his chest and released another boom. The men guffawed and bounced on their toes, rubbing their hands together. "What are we waiting for, then? They know we're here."

Mae finished her food and slunk back toward the trees with her head down.

"Where do you think you're going?" Gerard hollered after her.

"Come back here! You're our personal slave tonight. Jed, I told you to tie her to that tree!"

Jed flashed Gerard a dark look as he walked toward Mae. He snatched her arm and dragged her to the tree, then shoved her to the ground. He grimaced as he tied her ankles together and her hands behind the trunk, as if he hated touching her.

"Let's head to the gate," Gerard called. "I'll tell them it's Jade and Rex, or *else*." He lifted the small ball. The men cheered, some of them punching the air.

Gerard stuck his fingers in his mouth and gave a loud, shrill whistle. The Sad Cases converged into a dense mass and hastened toward Gerard, shoving each other to be the first to heed their master's command.

"Listen up, loonies!" Gerard jeered, and some of the men snickered. "Me and my men are heading to the gate for some important business. Stay here until we return." He pointed a thick finger at Mae, who cowered against the tree.

"Keep an eye on that tramp—that deserter," he spat. "If she tries to escape again, kill her. Break every bone in her body and rip her to pieces." Gerard turned back to his men and grinned. "And they will, too."

The men roared with laughter as they lifted their packs and followed Gerard through the trees, moving like a dark cloud toward Millflower's front gate.

The Sad Cases turned their crazed eyes on Mae. Several approached her, sneering and pounding their fists against their palms. The woman who took her to Gerard planted her skinny legs directly in front of her. "You betrayed Master Gerard," she hissed. "I'm going to kill you and tell him you tried to escape."

"We'll do it together!" another one protested. "You can't have all the glory!"

Alina stepped out from behind the tree. "OVER. MY. DEAD. BODY!"

Every Sad Case snapped their eyes to Alina. She barreled toward them with flared nostrils, unleashing a muted but ferocious battle cry.

Dozens of Sad Cases pounced on her, punching, kicking, and scratching her skin with all the feeble energy they could muster. Others hoisted heavy rocks and hurled them at her, but they fell short. If the scene wasn't so pitiable, Alina might've laughed. These humans possessed nothing but obedient adrenaline: explosive, volatile, and fleeting.

Alina plowed through them and dropped to the ground next to Mae, her fingers working frantically to loosen the knots. The Sad Cases pelted her with small rocks that bounced off her like rubber balls. A few grabbed her arms to keep her from untying the knots, and another attempted to strangle her around the neck. Alina sprung to her feet and whipped around, flattening a row of them with one swipe of her arm. "BACK OFF!" she screamed.

The startled creatures retreated, and the nasty woman clenched her fists. "I'm telling Gerard!" She tripped over the bony knees of someone on the ground, then popped up and scuttled toward the gate.

"Be my guest," Alina muttered as she wrenched the rope away from Mae's ankles. "I'll see him at the gate soon, anyway." She lifted Mae onto her back, stepped over the Sad Cases on the ground, and broke into a run. They gaped after her with a dazed look in their eyes.

She backtracked through the prairie and within minutes reached Millflower's back wall. "Mae, I need you to hold tightly around my neck; I can't carry you. I'm going to climb the wall."

"Okay."

Mae held on as Alina dug her fingernails into the mortar, but her fingers could not grasp the wall, and her feet slid on the rough stone. The town wisely made the wall unclimbable. *Should I face Gerard at the front gate? What about Mae?*

No—I'll jump. With enough momentum, I can make it.

She backed up into the grass. At full speed with Mae clinging to her, she soared through the air and hit the top of the wall with a thud. Mae went rigid for a moment, gasping for air.

"Sorry, Mae," Alina said as she swung her legs over the wall and dropped into the parapet, then jumped down into the sunflowers of the back field.

"Don't be," Mae said. "That was—brilliant."

Alina ran through the field, and as she reached the first street, she froze. The town was deserted and quiet.

She ran to the nearest house and hammered on the door. When no one answered, she rattled the doorknob, then kicked a window and slid through the broken glass, taking care not to cut Mae. She stood up in the front room.

A whistle rang out and she spread out her arms, dropping Mae to the ground behind her. The dart bounced off her shoulder and dropped to the floor with a plink.

"Who's there?" she called. "It's Alina!" She realized, too late, it might be unwise to reveal herself.

"Alina?" A timid voice peeped. A young girl stepped out of a closet, trembling. Her face was pale.

"Is everything all right?" Alina asked.

The girl began to cry. "Daddy left me here. He didn't want to, but he had to go fight the bad men. He said not to open the door and told me to shoot anyone who came in."

Alina bent down and hugged the girl. "I'm sorry I scared you. Your house was the first one I came to. What's your name?"

"Isabel."

Alina smiled at her. "You're very brave, Isabel. Can you help me?"

She nodded.

"See this woman here?" Alina lifted Mae and settled her on the couch. "She's sick, and I need you to wrap her in blankets and give her milk to drink while I help your dad fight the bad men. You keep that gun close to you and shoot them through the window if you see them coming."

Isabel nodded and beamed at Alina, who then slipped through the window and took off running down the street.

This explained the empty streets. Anyone not fighting was hiding inside. They must have been prepared for the attack—a good sign, and since the town was quiet, maybe Gerard hadn't acted yet.

She raced through the streets to the front gate, where she found the wall stocked with men and women. They lined the top with guns poised over the edge. Alina gulped as she recognized Baylor, Maxwell, and Oliver crouched above the gate. Jade and Rex were nowhere in sight.

She approached the wall and heard Mayor Nelson shouting from the top.

"You won't have either of them!" he screamed. "You swore to leave us alone when you took Alina! Why should we believe you now?"

Gerard yelled back. "Because we can wipe out your town! Hand over Rex and Jade, and we won't kill you today!"

"It won't happen! We'll kill your army one by one before you can enter!"

Gerard gave a chilling, confident laugh. "You leave me no choice, then! We'll blow up your sad army and destroy your wall! Then we'll walk in and get them ourselves!"

Nelson lifted a tight fist. "Not if we kill you first!"

A cluster of darts whistled from the wall. "Aim for the trees!" Nelson screamed. "They're hiding in the trees!"

A loud cracking noise split the air, followed by a tense, silent pause. The townspeople ducked and shrieked as three fiery balls hurled over the wall, each heading to a different place in Millflower.

Alina dug her nails into her cheeks. *One minute! They will explode in sixty seconds!*

The nearest one sailed high above her, approaching a tree. She broke into a sprint and tore up the knobby trunk, snapping limbs as she rushed to the highest branch. With a grunt she leaped and collided with the bomb in mid-air, clutching the fiery mass against her chest.

She met the ground with a somersault and rolled to her feet, racing on without pause, the burning ball tucked in the crook of her elbow. A small group gathered around a home down the street, staring up at a window on the second floor. Smoke billowed from a hole in the rooftop as flames licked its walls.

The trees and homes along the street blurred as Alina kicked her legs to increase her speed. As she approached, a woman's scream met her ears. "Sammy! Push the screen and jump out! We'll catch you!"

Frantic cries came from the window, drowning out the woman's voice.

"Sammy, listen to me for once!" the woman shrieked, wringing her hands. She bolted around the corner of the home and flung open the door, disappearing inside.

"No!" Alina hollered as she reached the yard and tore up the porch after her.

Flames consumed the ceiling above Alina. The woman was climbing the stairs, each step buckling under her weight. She reached the second floor and collapsed under the dark smoke, coughing.

"Stop!" Alina called as she bounded up the stairway, skipping nimbly over the broken steps. "Get out, right now—I'll get him!"

The woman shook her head. "You'll be killed! I'll die for him, I'm his mother!" She gasped at the fiery bomb in Alina's arms.

"The fire doesn't hurt me!" Alina insisted.

Recognition dawned on the mother's face. "Alina—you're here!"

"Get out!" Alina screamed. "Meet me outside the window!"

The woman struggled down the crumbling stairs and Alina followed the sound of the boy coughing and croaking. The smoke had stifled his cries.

The bomb sat outside his door, with flames engulfing the floor around it. Alina launched into the air, hollering as the floor collapsed beneath her, and swept up the explosive just before it fell. She tucked it in her arm with the other one, then snatched the child with her free arm and burst through the window. He wailed in pain and terror as they soared through the air and Alina planted her feet on the ground. His mother staggered into the yard, still coughing.

"I burned him—I'm so sorry!" Alina thrust him into the arms of his dazed mother, then spun around, her eyes searching for the last plume of smoke.

She found it burning above the gate, on the ledge next to the parapet—right where the army had been standing. She darted in that direction, shifting a bomb into the other arm to balance herself. Slowly, they began to tick.

She clenched her teeth. She was quick, but too many seconds had passed. The fire was spreading from her shirt down to her pant legs.

The people had left the wall, except for a young man scrambling across the ledge towards the bomb with a shovel in his hands. *No!*

He wanted to be a hero. But he'd never be able to get it far enough from the wall. Alina lifted her knees and stretched her legs, swinging her arms harder. She had to beat him!

Too many people crowded her path. She'd have to jump.

"CLEAR THE WAY, PLEASE!" Alina screamed as she vaulted over the group, her clothes fully ablaze. She landed right above the bomb, where for a brief moment she met Oliver's eyes. They widened as he dropped the shovel.

His lips parted, but she grabbed the bomb and leaped off the wall before he could speak.

"Alina!" he called after her.

She entered the forest as all three balls in her hands began to tick rapidly. *Not yet!* Gerard and his men were far ahead in the trees, running and whooping triumphantly.

Alina didn't doubt whether she could run fast enough. Up until now, her body had moved as swiftly as she needed it to. With each step, she pushed harder off the ground until the trees became a solid blur around her. The men drew nearer. She could see the buckles on their packs and the gray hairs on their heads.

"This is far enough," Gerard called out. "Time to enjoy our victory!"

Stan turned around with his hood piled carelessly on his

shoulders. His startled eyes looked from Alina's face to the flames consuming her clothes.

The men froze in place with open mouths, and Alina halted as the bombs gave a final, slow tick. In a split second of deadly silence, she met Gerard's eyes and smiled.

A deafening thud shook the ground—a shock wave tearing through flesh, bone, trees and earth. The heat consumed all around her, tingling over her body as the force of the blast flung her through crimson flames and black smoke. She fanned out and flipped gracefully, her heart thundering as a triumphant cheer rang from her throat.

CHAPTER 30

Alina landed hard on her feet and gasped at her naked, soot-covered body. If no shred of clothing survived the blast, no mortal could either. She raced back to assess the damage. A gaping hole smoldered in the ground, simmering with debris. She found no sign of Gerard or his men. She closed her eyes and covered her face with a trembling hand.

It's done.

She started back toward Millflower, through the charred remains of the grove, and a lump formed in her throat. Of the Sad Cases, only bloody, dismembered parts littered the ground. The deranged men and women, too far from the blast to be pulverized, were ripped to pieces. She saw a face intact: blank gray eyes staring at her, sunken deep in yellow skin. She fell to her knees and sobbed, her tears leaving a clean trail on her blackened cheeks.

Sampson did this to them—he stole what little freedom they owned and tortured the one thing they *could* control—their minds. Sent into Carthem—unaware they served the same man who stole this from them. How unjust for them to suffer the same fate as their guilty master.

Then she heard Mae's voice in her head. "They are captives, controlled by Sampson. You have set them free."

Alina lifted her eyes and glimpsed a white flower growing from the ground, its ragged petals marked with soot. She wiped the tears from her face.

Some things survive and endure, no matter what destruction surrounds them, she thought.

She searched through the carnage, avoiding the victims' remains, but found no survivors. She opened her mouth and let the tears come again. With a laden heart, she walked toward Millflower's gate.

She glanced at her body. The black soot disguised her well enough, but she couldn't walk through the gate without clothes. She dashed between trees, hiding, until someone from the gate spied her.

"Alina?" she heard Oliver call out, and she flushed.

"I need some clothes!" she yelled back, and as the crowd burst into laughter, she relaxed enough to laugh with them.

After a few minutes, a young girl came out and gave her a robe. Alina slipped it on and walked through the gate.

The town erupted into cheers.

She found herself in Oliver's arms first, then those of Baylor, Maxwell, and Mayor Nelson. The crowd enclosed around her, some crying and laughing as they rubbed the soot from her arms and face. Others squeezed her and joked about her politeness while running with a ticking bomb in her hands.

Alina hugged all of them, even the mean girls, who now smiled through their tears. Jade watched proudly from the side with a soft smile on her face. Alina cut through the throng of people to be with her.

"That's the best use of immortality I've seen," Jade said.

"I'll try not to get big-headed over it," Alina answered. They giggled as they embraced, and the crowd respectfully backed away.

Alina's face went serious. "How are things in Stormport?"

"Oh—" Jade's face fell. "Not good. Zaiden is alive, but Crome died yesterday, and now Janet is infected."

Alina grabbed Jade's arm. "Baylor's Janet?"

"Yes."

"Oh no," Alina's heart sank. "Don't you think I could go back to help them, just for a little while? I want to be with Trinee and—"

"Zaiden?"

Alina nodded, her eyes on the ground.

Jade shook her head. "Rex and I discussed this with Baylor. We urged him to go back to his family, but he said that would reward Sampson, who wants our progress stalled. We need to get to Jaden as soon as possible. If we delay the mission, more people will die." She blinked back tears. "He's willing to give up seeing his wife for the last time to fight for Carthem."

Alina wiped her eyes. "Then I need to do the same with Zaiden. I just thought if I went to him, he'd pull through." She blushed at how presumptuous she sounded.

Jade squeezed her hand. "He's survived several days now, and he's the longest one. He's a fighter."

Alina smiled softly and nodded. She pulled on Jade's hand. "Come with me. There's someone I want you to meet. She's the real hero, because without her, I'd still be trapped in a mine shaft."

"*What?*" Jade exclaimed.

"Gerard tried to dispose of me, and she was my rescuer. As soon as she's well enough, I'll introduce her as the savior of Carthem. She's one of the Sad Cases in Gerard's army but isn't insane; she only pretended to be. Her name is Mae."

Jade seized Alina's arm. "Did you say her name was Mae?"

"Yes."

Jade's hands flew to her mouth and tears sprang to her eyes. "Oh!" she erupted and broke into a run. "Hurry, Alina, where is she?"

They ran to the house at the end of the street, where Jade pounded on the door. Isabel peeked through the window and let them in. Mae sat at the table, sipping from a mug. Her hair had been brushed and her wounds bandaged.

"Mae!" Jade shrieked.

Mae screamed and reached out to Jade, knocking over her cup. They embraced, tears streaming down their cheeks.

Two DAYS LATER, all of Millflower came to the town square to celebrate the victory over Gerard and his army. They set up a long table filled with steak and roasted pork, buttered vegetables, cornbread and biscuits, and fresh berry pies. Guitars twanged as people danced in the streets, grateful their homes and land had been spared, but even more—they were alive and with their loved ones.

Sammy's mother held Alina for a long time, tears running down her cheeks, and little Sammy embraced her with his bandaged arms. His burns were not as serious as Alina had feared.

Even Nicole kept smiling at Alina with apologetic eyes, and Alina smiled back. She happily exchanged the bitter feelings for friendship. She hated one and longed so much for the other.

She danced with every boy in town and never stumbled, though she didn't know the steps. Jade danced in her bare feet, clapping with the children and encouraging the reluctant dancers to join in. Rex watched her from the sidelines, eyes twinkling, his leg propped up on a chair.

At last Oliver cut in to be with Alina, and they glided on the beat, his turns complementing her twirls as the crowd clapped and whistled from the side. Then the music slowed, and he paused to catch his breath.

He met her eyes and held them for a moment. He reached for her waist and drew her in close, his blue eyes glinting, his hand pressed against the small of her back.

She blushed under his gaze. When she averted her eyes they rested on Maxwell, who was separated from Christine, Nicole, and the rest of his family. He stood under a black walnut tree motioning for her to join him, his eyes heavy with worry.

She stepped on Oliver's foot. "Ouch!" he exclaimed. "Hey, are you so smitten with me you've forgotten how to dance?"

His flirtations had become bolder—each more daring than the one before. A strange tingle swept through her body as he held her close, but the urgency on Maxwell's face sobered her.

"Sorry, Ollie," she stopped, stepping out of his arms. "Max needs to talk to me. It looks serious."

"Uh—okay," he stammered.

"I'll be right back," she assured him as she hurried off.

Her stomach twisted with fear as she ran to him. "What is it?" she asked. "Have you heard from Stormport?"

He shook his head. "No. It's something else. Come with me for a moment." He took her arm and led her away from the celebration. Oliver watched them, frowning.

"The cleanup crew found something in the woods."

Alina felt sick at his words. "Please, I don't want to hear it. Those poor Sad Cases—"

"I don't think this came from them," he cut in.

"What do you mean?"

"It's a surveillance chip."

Alina dropped her jaw in shock. "Stan's?"

"Possibly. It should have been destroyed. But we found it on the ground right in the heart of the blast, glistening in the sun—so bright it almost blinded us."

"What did you do with it? Does it still work?"

"We're not sure. We sent the chip with the freight crew that left yesterday morning for Jaden, so Camden could examine it. I just received word that when they entered the city, it didn't set off the alarm like it should have."

Alina stared at him. "Baylor worried about that. He believed Stan was testing the boundaries around Stormport."

"And he wasn't stunned, yes," Maxwell said. "But his chip *did* set off the alarm. It should've in Jaden too."

"What does this mean?"

He took a deep breath. "It means Sampson has figured out how to penetrate our security. His spies could enter Stormport or Jaden, and we'd have no way of knowing." He paused. "Which means no one is safe."

ACKNOWLEDGMENTS

First, to all my readers—thank you! You're the reason I keep writing. I love you!

I wouldn't be here without the support and encouragement of my wonderful husband, Derek. He is my rock and my best friend. I'm thankful for my children: Elise, Isaac, Dayton, Spencer, and Jared, who teach me about character differences and help me become a better person.

I'm grateful for friends and family who read early drafts and provided encouragement and/or constructive feedback—Kristi Thom, Kristen Hogan, Lorinda Turley, Sophia McCutchen, Annette Mortensen, Jenny Mackay, Rebecca Erickson, and my first young fans: Aimee and Amber Cooper. A BIG thank you to my fellow Inklettes: Cori Cooper and Jackee Alston, who for years have given me helpful suggestions and honest critiques over the most delicious english muffins. And a special thank you to Cameron and Shayna Hansen for sacrificing their time to fully edit my story, paving the way for this dream to come true. I wouldn't have made it without you!

I'm grateful for my supportive extended family: Dad and Margie, Tammy and Mike, Jeff, Kristen and Wade, Becky and Spencer, Lynette, Bryce and Robyn, Kevin, Darren, Ron and Marie, Jason and Amanda, Bret and Shelby and all their kids who read the book and encouraged me along the way. A special heartfelt thank you to my dear mother who passed away when I was writing draft one. I have felt her cheering me on all the way from heaven. Thanks, Mom.

Many thanks to the fantastic team at Immortal Works—Crystal Liechty who first read and believed in my story, for Holli Anderson and the acquisitions team, and to Ashley Literski and the creative team for capturing my vision with the book cover. A big shout-out to my awesome editor Audrey Hammer who pushed me to stretch my writing muscles and discover more about my characters and world, making the story infinitely better. I must also thank my fellow authors at Immortal Works and those I've met on social media. You are the best supportive group out there and I'm honored to know you!

Above all, I thank my Father in Heaven, who prompted me to write this story and gave me the creative skills to complete it. I couldn't have done it alone. I thank Him for always being there.

ABOUT THE AUTHOR

 MELISSA HANSEN is the wife of a hammock guru and the mother of five exceptional kids. When she's not reading and writing, she enjoys being outdoors, making friends, playing board games with her family and eating Thai food. Melissa lives with her family in Southern Utah. You can follow her on Facebook, Instagram, Twitter, and her blog, https://melissaohansen.com.

This has been an
Immortal Production

CPSIA information can be obtained
at www.ICGtesting.com
Printed in the USA
LVHW090958180920
666470LV00002B/415